THAT
MISTLETOE
MOMENT

THAT
MISTLETOE
MOMENT

CAT JOHNSON
KATE ANGELL
ALLYSON CHARLES

KENSINGTON PUBLISHING CORP.
http://www.kensingtonbooks.com

KENSINGTON BOOKS are published by

Kensington Publishing Corp.
119 West 40th Street
New York, NY 10018

Compilation copyright © 2016 by Kensington Publishing Corp.
"A Boyfriend by Christmas" © 2016 by Cat Johnson
"All I Want for Christmas Is . . ." © 2016 by Kate Angell
"Her Favorite Present" © 2016 by Allyson Charles

All Kensington titles, imprints, and distributed lines are available at special quantity discounts for bulk purchases for sales promotion, premiums, fund-raising, educational, or institutional use.

Special book excerpts or customized printings can also be created to fit specific needs. For details, write or phone the office of the Kensington Sales Manager: Kensington Publishing Corp., 119 West 40th Street, New York, NY 10018. Attn. Sales Department. Phone: 1-800-221-2647.

Kensington and the K logo Reg. U.S. Pat. & TM Off.

ISBN-13: 978-1-4967-0558-7
ISBN-10: 1-4967-0558-0
First Kensington Trade Paperback Edition: October 2016
First Kensington Mass Market Edition: October 2017

eISBN-13: 978-1-4967-0559-4
eISBN-10: 1-4967-0559-9
First Kensington Electronic Edition: October 2016

10 9 8 7 6 5 4 3 2

Printed in the United States of America

Contents

A Boyfriend
by
Christmas

Cat Johnson

CHAPTER I

To the accompaniment of the pounding drum-beat of marching band music, a three-story-high, inflatable, cartoon-shaped balloon floated across the screen of the living room television.

Across the apartment in the kitchen, Noelle kept one eye on the cranberries bubbling in the pot on the stove while also watching the progress of the Thanksgiving Day Parade on TV.

The homemade cranberry sauce was Noelle's signature dish. The secret ingredient—bourbon—melded with the flavors of the candied orange peel and cinnamon sticks to add the perfect zing to what was normally boring old cranberry sauce.

Her boyfriend, George, loved it.

George had been the boy next door—literally. His parents lived next to her parents and they grew up next to each other, but they'd never been high school sweethearts.

Actually, he'd never paid any attention to her

when they'd been younger. That had changed the summer they'd both been home from college between junior and senior year. They'd been dating ever since.

That his parents and hers were neighbors had made holidays simple over the five years they'd been together. Today they'd have dinner with George's parents and two brothers, and then walk next door for dessert with her family.

Noelle had offered to make her cranberries for dinner at George's house. It was an impressive recipe, but deceivingly simple to make, so she had no problem cooking while watching the parade.

Sometimes having a small apartment had its perks. Not many, but today, being able to see the living room TV from the kitchen area across the room was definitely one of them.

She never missed watching the parade. It put her in the holiday spirit.

Just the anticipation of all the hustle and bustle that started this weekend and raced full speed ahead until Christmas had Noelle singing along with the festive song on the television.

It was a busy, frenzied, crazy time of year—and she loved every minute of it. The shopping. The wrapping. The decorating. The baking.

George didn't love Christmas with quite the intensity that she did, but he'd agreed to go with her to pick out her tree tomorrow. He'd inevitably try to talk her into a smaller one, like he did last year, but Noelle was sticking to her guns. This year, she wanted a huge tree, no matter what he said.

The ringing of her cell phone broke into Noelle's thoughts.

Where had she left it? She'd had it last night . . .

and it had been almost dead, so she'd plugged it in.

After remembering that, she followed the sound to the cluttered area on the counter that she used as a desk. She tracked the cord from the wall outlet down and finally reeled in the cell, dislodging a few store flyers that she'd tossed on top. One fluttered to the floor as she hit the button to answer the call and pressed it to her ear.

"Happy Thanksgiving!"

"Aren't we chipper today?" Her sister Nikki's reply was less cheery than Noelle's greeting had been.

"What's not to be chipper about?"

"Besides my crappy part-time job and living in Mom and Dad's house until I finish my dissertation? Um, I don't know. Global warming? The war in the Middle East? The—"

"Okay, okay. Party pooper. Did you watch the parade?"

"Yes, I'm watching the parade. Mom has it on, on every TV in the house, so she won't miss any of it while she runs around getting ready for today. I can't believe you get out of having dinner here."

"I'm not getting out of it. We're spending half the day with George's family and half with mine. You know that."

"But you don't have to watch Great-Grandpa spit his food across the table every time he talks with his mouth full. And you don't have to listen to Aunt Anna hint for hours that I should be married by now."

Eating dinner at George's had some definite perks. "Don't worry. I'll get to enjoy all of that fun over dessert."

"No, you won't. You have George to dangle in front of them as a potential husband."

She did, didn't she? Noelle grinned as Nikki continued. "And by the time you get here, Great-Grandpa will be snoring in the recliner, so smart planning on your part, Noelle."

"Thank you. It was, wasn't it?"

"Brat." Nikki laughed. "I'll forgive you if you drop off some of your cranberry sauce on your way to the Higginses' for dinner. I'm going to need the bourbon you put in there."

"I told you all the alcohol content burns away."

"And I told you I don't believe that, so bring some over."

"Okay. Fine." It was the least she could do, considering Nikki really was bearing the full burden of the family this holiday, while Noelle had shaved her time down considerably. "Let me go. See you later."

"Okay. Don't be too late," Nikki warned.

"I won't." As she disconnected the call, Noelle considered that her sister was correct about Aunt Anna being obsessed with seeing them both married. Maybe Noelle would soon have news in that department, since this year things felt different between her and George.

The way he had taken her shopping with him to look at furniture for his new place. And the way he'd rented not the one-bedroom the Realtor had first shown him, but instead the more expensive two-bedroom, as if next year there could be two people living there.

A man didn't invest almost five years in a relationship unless he had plans to spend a lifetime with the woman. Noelle was ready to settle down and start that life.

The timing was right. He was finished with grad school and was well on the way to building the career he'd always dreamed of. And Noelle's lease was up the first of the year, but she'd been dragging her feet about signing a new one.

The truth was, she hadn't renewed the lease yet because maybe, just maybe, she wouldn't need her own apartment next year. Perhaps there would be a diamond ring under the tree for her from George this year.

Her mother had gotten married at twenty-five. Noelle was turning twenty-five the day after Christmas.

Her mother always joked that Noelle was meant to be a December twenty-fifth baby, but in true Noelle fashion, she'd been late. Her tardiness drove the always-punctual George crazy, but differences between people was what made life interesting. She truly believed that.

Nikki might not agree with Noelle's "opposites attract" theory, but what did she know? She was single and Noelle had been dating the same man since college. It was clear which was the more knowledgeable sister when it came to relationships.

And this time next year, Noelle could be preparing for her own guests for Thanksgiving dinner in her and George's place.

Noelle dipped a spoon into the cranberries, blew on the steaming mixture, and then brought it to her lips for a taste.

Perfection. Even better than usual.

She had tweaked the proportions a tad this year. This might be her best batch yet.

If this cranberry sauce was any indication, her holiday season was off to a stellar start. George's mother—possibly Noelle's future mother-in-law—would be so impressed.

On the television, the parade was coming to a close as Santa Claus appeared on the screen, his elves skipping along the avenue on either side of the sleigh.

Noelle drew in a deep breath and let it out with a sigh. Another year's parade had come to a successful conclusion and now it was time for her to get moving. She had to shower, do her hair, and then pick the perfect outfit.

She should probably put the cranberries in the serving dish first so that would be done. Then she could soak the pot while she was getting herself ready.

The cranberry sauce was still hot, but it would cool soon enough. It would probably cool even faster in the dish rather than in the hot pan. She moved to the cabinet and opened the door, surveying the choices.

She'd started collecting antiques in college. It seemed a person couldn't drive two miles in New England without passing an antique shop.

One stop on a sunny fall day at a little place along the side of the road had led to another and another.

Soon Noelle and her roommate were going antiquing every Sunday. She became addicted to the hunt. To the thrill of finding a gem amid the junk.

It was exhilarating and meant that when she'd gotten her own apartment, she had a great collection. Hot chocolate pots, teacups and saucers, and

Depression-era glass were her collection's main focus.

The rich deep garnet color caught her eye and she spied a ruby-red glass bowl.

George usually rolled his eyes when he opened her cabinets and saw the precarious stacks of mismatched pieces on the shelves, but even he was going to have to admit that her cranberry sauce would look perfect in this bowl on the Thanksgiving table.

Feeling justified that her love of collecting was going to be proven very useful today, she stretched and took down the whole stack of vintage dishes. She set them on the counter and gingerly extracted the bowl she wanted from under the dishes piled on top.

She ran the prized bowl under the faucet to rinse off any dust and then set it on the counter next to the stovetop just as her cell phone rang again. She saw George's name appear on the readout and jumped to answer it.

"Happy Thanksgiving!"

"Uh, yeah. You too. Are you meeting me at my parents', or do I have to come over there and pick you up?" he asked.

"Um, I can meet you there, I guess."

"Okay. Good. Mom says to be there at two o'clock."

"I will. And I have my special cranberry sauce." As she cradled the phone on one shoulder, Noelle lifted the pot off the burner and began to pour the piping-hot mixture into the bowl. It wasn't even half full when she heard the crack.

Horrified, she sucked in a loud breath.

"What's wrong?" George asked.

"Oh my God. I think I just broke one of my fa-vorite antique serving dishes."

The berries must have been too hot. Unlike modern glassware, Depression-era glass must not be able to withstand much heat. Or maybe there had been a hairline crack or an invisible flaw in the glass itself.

"You shouldn't be using those things for food anyway. They're probably full of lead and who knows what other poisons."

It was silly to be so attached to an object, but she really had loved that little ruby-red bowl.

Fighting tears, she drew in a breath. "I guess."

She put the pot and its remaining contents back on the burner. She'd have to throw away what was in the broken bowl, which meant she'd barely have enough left in the pot to take to George's parents' house for dinner. Never mind dropping off any extra for her sister.

Was it too late to run out to the store for the in-gredients to make more?

What time did stores close on Thanksgiving? And even if the store was open, would they have fresh cranberries left?

"I gotta go and shower. I'll see you at Mom and Dad's." George's voice on the phone dragged Noelle out of her thoughts.

Head still spinning about her cranberry mess, she gathered herself and drew in a breath. "Okay. Love you."

"Yeah, you too. 'Bye." The *click* signaled he'd hung up.

Noelle lowered the cell and sighed as she eyed

the bloodred juice oozing out of the crack in the bowl and all over her counter.

Just a little bump in the road. Even as she tossed the beloved bowl and the ruined cranberry sauce into the trash can, she wasn't giving up on this holiday season.

Fueled with determination, Noelle threw on clothes that wouldn't embarrass her, grabbed her purse and jacket, and ran out the door.

She drove directly to the big megastore, where she'd most likely be able to find the cranberries.

After parking in the first spot she saw in the lot, Noelle ran to the entrance and breathed in relief when the automatic doors slid smoothly open. At least they were open.

One worry down. One more to go. She made a beeline for the produce and stalked up one side of the aisle and then down the other searching for whole bagged cranberries.

If she'd needed Brussels sprouts she'd have been fine, but the cranberries were eluding her.

Just when her hopes were beginning to wane, she spotted a tall, dark-haired man in front of her. He was so broad and muscular she would have noticed him anyway. But the fact that he had not one but two bags of cranberries in his hand had her running toward him.

"Oh, thank God." She realized she'd said it aloud when he turned to level golden-brown eyes on her as he cocked one dark brow up. "Sorry. I just really need cranberries and I was afraid they'd be out."

He cringed. "They are out now. These are the last two bags."

She looked at the shelf and saw the empty place where the cranberries used to be, right between a big display of oranges on one side and a row of boxed figs on the other.

Sure. Figs they had plenty of, but except for the two bags the hulking hottie held captive in his hands, there were no more cranberries.

It was irrational, she knew, but Noelle suddenly felt close to tears as she said, "Oh. Okay."

She'd turned to go when he said, "Wait."

Spinning back, she watched him draw in a deep breath, expanding his broad chest to even greater proportions beneath his U.S. Navy sweatshirt. "Take one."

She resisted the urge to grab the bag out of his hand. "Are you sure?"

"Yeah. Mom always makes much too much cranberry sauce anyway. She'll be fine with just the one. It'll save my poor dad from eating it on everything for the next month. To be perfectly honest, her cranberry sauce is not very good."

"Oh no. I'm sorry."

He dismissed her concern with a wave of one hand. "It's all right. We humor her and pretend we like it."

Noelle considered for barely a second before she said, "You know what? I have a really good recipe for cranberry sauce. It's got orange and bourbon and brown sugar. Would you like me to send it to you?"

"Yes! Definitely."

She laughed. "That was enthusiastic."

He smiled until it crinkled his eyes in the corners. "You had me at bourbon."

"Yeah, that part usually wins over the men." She laughed as she punched the ingredients and quick instructions into a new text in her cell phone. "Here. Put your cell number in there and hit Send. That will text you my recipe."

"Great. And I'll thank you in advance on behalf of my father and all of the others attending today's dinner who won't be subjected to my mother's cranberry sauce." He punched in the numbers and handed the cell back.

She took the phone. "It's the least I can do, considering you're giving me one of your bags."

"It's my pleasure . . ." He extended his hand and frowned. "I'm sorry, I don't even know your name."

"Noelle." She juggled the bag to her left hand so she could grasp his right one.

"I'm Nathan."

"Nathan," she repeated as she felt how strong and warm his grip was. "Um, well, I'd better get going. Got to cook these berries. Thank you again. And Happy Thanksgiving."

He finally released his hold on her hand. "Happy Thanksgiving to you, too."

After one final glance at her, he tossed his bag of berries in the cart and steered it down the aisle in the opposite direction.

Noelle pulled herself out of the daze the encounter had put her in. She didn't have any time to waste.

She headed for the cash register with what might be the last bag of cranberries in all of Connecticut. All thanks to the generosity of one kind stranger.

CHAPTER 2

"Nice of you to come." Nikki's sarcasm was clear in her tone and her expression.

Noelle scowled at her sister. "We couldn't run out the moment we finished eating dinner. That would have been rude."

Besides, she'd enjoyed spending time with George's parents and two brothers.

"Sure. First no cranberry sauce, and now you slide in right before dessert."

"I texted you about what happened with the cranberries."

"I know. I got the text. Doesn't mean I was happy about it."

Noelle blew out a short breath. "I was pretty upset about it myself. Believe me."

"So, how was it over there? Are Glen and Gordy still idiots?"

Noelle cocked a brow at Nikki. "Be nice. They're George's brothers."

"Doesn't mean they can't be idiots." Finally Nikki sighed beneath the weight of Noelle's stare. "Fine. I'll be nice. Now, hang up your coat and come inside. I've borne the burden of our crazy relatives alone long enough."

Noelle slipped her peacoat off her arms and hung it on one of the hooks just inside the back door as Nikki frowned.

"Where is George anyway?"

"He'll be here in a minute. He just wanted to say good-bye to his brothers."

"All right, good. That means we can drink. I'll pour you one."

"What are you talking about? I could still drink if he was around. He wouldn't stop me."

"Oh, he wouldn't stop you, but those passive-aggressive comments and glances of his are enough to make me want to guzzle straight out of the bottle. I swear, that man acts like he's an eighty-year-old woman sometimes."

"Stop."

"I'm serious. Aunt Anna is cooler than George." Nikki kept her voice low, but Noelle still glanced at the doorway of the kitchen to make sure their aunt hadn't overheard.

"Don't fill up my glass." Noelle held up one hand as Nikki upended the bottle over a wineglass.

"Why not?"

"I have my own car. I met George here."

Nikki cocked a brow. "Why didn't he pick you up?"

"Don't know." Noelle lifted one shoulder and figured it was safest to change the subject. "So, how's it been here? Anything exciting happen?"

"Oh, Aunt Anna is in rare form today." Nikki

nodded toward her now-empty glass on the kitchen island. "I've had three glasses so far and it's only five o'clock."

"Wow." Noelle raised a brow and eyed the line-up of bottles on the counter. Two were empty, and one was well on the way to being so as Nikki moved to refill her glass.

Shaking her head, Nikki finally put down the bottle of red wine. "I swear to you, for Christmas I'm making up a fake boyfriend, just to get them all off my back."

"How are you going to make up a fake boyfriend?"

"That's the beauty of modern technology. I don't even have to. There's an app for that."

Noelle widened her eyes. "Really?"

"I kid you not. The Build-A-Boyfriend app. I read about it online. One more comment from Aunt Anna and I'm signing up tomorrow. Or tonight if I'm not too drunk." Nikki handed Noelle one glass and pressed the other to her lips. After swallowing a big sip of wine, she blew out a quick breath. "Okay, I'm ready. Let's go."

After downing a bracing swallow herself, Noelle followed her sister down the hallway toward the living room. The acoustics of the old house meant she heard the soft buzz of conversation in the hallway long before she entered the room.

"Noelle." Her mother jumped up from her seat and came forward. "When did you get here?"

"I found her sneaking in the kitchen door while I was getting some wine." Nikki sat and shot Noelle a glare as she answered their mother's question.

"I didn't sneak. It was just easier to come in the back door. Happy Thanksgiving." Noelle kissed her mother's cheek and then moved to do the same to her father. "Dad."

"Good to see you. Where's George?" Her father knelt by the fireplace to poke at the log inside, sending sparks flittering up the chimney, before he closed the screen and stood again.

"Where *is* George? Isn't he coming?" Aunt Anna asked as Noelle moved to her.

"He's coming. He's next door. He'll be right here." She bent low to kiss the older woman's cheek. "Nice to see you again, Aunt Anna."

The scene was exactly as Nikki had predicted. Their great-grandfather was snoring softly in the easy chair in the corner of the room nearest the fireplace. And Great-Aunt Anna, their grand-mother's sister, was as nosy as ever.

Nothing changed. Their father was spending his day completely absorbed in tending a fire that was burning just fine on its own, and their mother was spending the day trying to feed them more food than any human could eat.

"No ring yet?" Aunt Anna's stare settled on Noelle's bare left hand.

She smiled at her aunt as she perched on the edge of a chair and wondered if there was more wine stashed somewhere. "No, not yet."

Aunt Anna scowled. "How long have you been dating?"

"Five years next May."

The older woman let out a *humph* that spoke volumes.

The sound was ripe enough with meaning that Noelle felt the need to defend her boyfriend and their relationship. "Actually, he's doing really well in his job and he just moved into a great two-bedroom place, so I'm thinking it might be soon. Maybe even for Christmas or my birthday."

Their aunt's penciled-on brows rose. "Really. Well then, I'll look forward to seeing you again at Christmas. Maybe there will be a wedding to plan."

"Maybe. We'll see." Noelle smiled even though she'd already envisioned her dream wedding with George and no nosy old relative was going to muck up her plans.

The sound of a masculine clearing of a throat had her spinning in her seat.

"Um, hello, everyone." George stood in the doorway looking a little paler than usual.

"George." Back to tending the fire, her father nodded in his direction before leaning over to grab another log.

"George, how is your family? Did you all have a nice Thanksgiving?" her mother asked.

"Everyone is well, thank you." He was taller than Noelle and leaner than his two brothers. But like his siblings, he had blue eyes and sandy-colored hair, a few shades paler than Noelle's own brown.

With Noelle's green eyes and George's blue ones, she figured their children had a good chance of inheriting one or the other color. They'd have gorgeous babies. She knew it.

Noelle stood and walked over to George where he hovered in the doorway.

"Hi." She leaned in to give him a kiss on the lips, but he turned his head and her mouth landed on his cheek. "Do you want some wine?"

He frowned down at the glass in her hand. "No, thank you."

"Okay." Noelle took a sip from her own glass.

George followed her motion before he glanced around the room. "So, I didn't miss dessert, did I?"

Her mother jumped up. "No. I was just about to get the pies on the table. Girls, do you want to help me?"

"Sure, Mom." Nikki walked close and grabbed Noelle's arm. "Come on."

"I'm coming." Noelle asked once they were in the kitchen, "What is wrong with you?"

"Me? What's wrong with him? It's Thanksgiving. Would it kill him to smile? And what was that face when you offered him wine?"

"Stop. His face is perfectly fine." Scowling, Noelle was not going to let Nikki get her upset.

It was a holiday. There were homemade pies. She was spending the weekend with her boyfriend. Nothing was going to bring Noelle down, especially not her bitter sister.

She knew her optimism was well-founded when George rested his hand on hers at the dining room table and whispered, "I'm going to follow you to your place. I have something I want to talk to you about."

Noelle nearly choked as she swallowed the remnants of the bite of pumpkin pie in her mouth. She nodded. "Okay."

Her simple response belied what she felt on the inside as her heart thundered.

He wanted to speak to her in private. That could only mean one thing. She wouldn't have to wait until Christmas. Her ring was coming sooner than she'd expected.

Usually she wouldn't have minded hanging out to help her mother and sister do the dishes and clean up, but today she couldn't stand the wait. She had to know what George wanted to talk about, but she had to get home first.

She watched, and the moment she saw him put his dessert fork down, she asked, "Ready to go?"

He glanced up. "Um, sure."

Pushing her chair back, Noelle gathered up her glass, and her pie plate and his. She carried it all into the kitchen, coming back out with her coat in her hand. "We're going to get going."

Her sister frowned. "So soon?"

"Yeah. It's been a long day." Noelle would call later with the news. Then her sister would understand her rush. The whole family would and they'd be thrilled, she was sure.

Seeing her with her coat and purse, George stood and turned to address her parents. "Thanks for dessert."

"You're always welcome. I'll see you at our Christmas party, right?" Noelle's mother asked.

George nodded. "Yes, you will. My parents were talking about the party today. Mom's making her stuffed mushrooms."

Her mother smiled. "Perfect."

As the good-byes were said, Noelle nearly bubbled over with joy. In all her excitement she had almost forgotten about her family's annual Christmas Eve party. The entire neighborhood came, George's family included. It would be the perfect time to show off the ring.

Maybe that had been George's plan for proposing tonight instead of on Christmas. He always had been a detailed planner. It was one of the things she appreciated most about him. She wasn't so great in the advanced planning department.

Noelle was shaking by the time she pulled into the parking space in front of her apartment. George pulled in behind her. She was so flustered over what she'd built up in her mind as a definite—the most important moment of her life—that she forgot to turn off her headlights.

Walking over to her car, George said when she opened the driver's door, "Lights."

"What?"

"You left your headlights on. You'll end up with a dead battery."

"Oh. Yeah. I forgot." She reached in and flipped the button, grateful one more time for his attention to detail. "Just distracted tonight, I guess."

"Tonight?" He blew out a breath. "You're forgetful every day."

She pursed her lips. "No. Not always."

If she was distracted, it was usually for good reason. Her being forgetful was just a sign of an active mind. But she wasn't going to let George's comment put a damper on her perfect evening.

After grabbing her purse, she slammed the door and hit the key fob to lock the doors. "Okay, let's go."

"All right." He looked serious as they walked.

That wasn't a surprise, she supposed. If what she thought was going to happen was really happening, George had every right to be nervous and serious.

She unlocked the apartment door and flipped on the lights in the living room. "Come on in."

Tomorrow night, that switch would also turn on her Christmas tree lights.

Tomorrow morning, she might be an engaged

woman shopping for a tree with her fiancé. The thought sent a thrill through her.

Closing the door behind him, she asked, "Do you want something to drink? I have wine and beer. Or rum. I bought eggnog to go with it."

She'd been thinking of having an eggnog herself.

They'd need something to toast with. Since this had come as such a surprise, she didn't have champagne, but eggnog would do.

"No. I have to drive."

She drew her brows low. "I thought you'd just spend the night."

It wasn't as if he hadn't slept over before. Besides, she wanted to hit the tree lot early in the morning, before the crowds. So she wouldn't miss the best trees.

Most importantly, if he did propose, wouldn't he want to stay so they could celebrate?

"Um, yeah. No. Not tonight." He shook his head.

"Oh. Okay." She stood there, at a loss as to why he was being so weird.

"Can we sit?" He glanced at the sofa.

"Sure." She moved to the sofa and sat.

He sat next to her, reached out, and took her hand in his. "So . . . when I walked in tonight, I heard you talking to your family. About getting married."

Her heart thundered. She hadn't meant for him to hear that. Her comments had been in response to her aunt's provoking, but if it led to him proposing early, she'd give Aunt Anna a big hug and a kiss when she saw her at Christmas.

"Well, when Aunt Anna asked about us . . ." Noelle let the sentence trail off.

A crease furrowed his brow. "Is that what you want?"

Wait? Was that a proposal? "What do you mean?"

"You see us getting married?" he asked, the surprised tone of his voice not at all encouraging.

This wasn't going quite as she'd envisioned it. "Yes. Don't you?"

He let out a short burst of a laugh that did not instill confidence in her plan to be engaged by Christmas. "I don't know. I never really thought about it."

How could they have been on such different pages when it came to their relationship? Starting to get a little annoyed, she said, "Well, think about it now."

"Honestly?" he asked.

"No, I want you to lie to me." Noelle rolled her eyes. She regretted her sarcastic comment the moment it was out of her mouth and he drew back at her words. She softened her tone. "Of course, honestly. I want the truth."

"Fine, but there's no need to be a bitch about it."

Had he seriously just called her that? This conversation had disintegrated—fast. She drew in a breath that had her nostrils flaring as she considered.

Noelle had two choices to make here. She could start a fight over his "bitch" comment, or she could focus on the bigger issue. Their relationship and its future.

She chose the latter. "George, do you see us ever getting married or not?"

"Not really." He shook his head.

Her eyes widened. "Why not?"

"We're very different." He shrugged.

That was true. They were different. She'd always thought that's what they both liked about the relationship. "Then why are you with me—why have you stayed with me—for five years?"

"Habit, I guess." He shrugged again. The move made her want to hit him with one of her prized antique bookends. The fact he'd called them "expensive dust collectors" didn't help squelch that urge any.

Habit? What the hell kind of a reason was that to stay with someone? "So, what are you saying? That I was convenient? That it was too much work to find a new girlfriend?"

"I don't know. Look, can we just go to bed and sleep on it?" He stood and extended one hand to her where she sat on the sofa glaring up at him.

"Go to bed here? You're staying the night now? I thought you didn't want to."

"I think in light of everything, it might be best if I slept here. We'll kiss and make up. You'll wake up in a better mood, and we'll start fresh in the morning getting that tree of yours."

The way he said the words "kiss and make up" were ripe with suggestion, as was his smile. He thought he could drop the bomb that he'd never seen them spending their lives together and then she'd jump into bed with him?

"Oh no. You really think I'll just forget—"

"Noelle, just relax." He tipped his head. "Hey, I just thought of something. Is it coming up on your time of the month? Is that why you're acting so crazy?"

"Oh my God. This is not about me or my *time of the month*. This is all about you."

"I think you need some time to calm down." He'd kept his voice low. His treating her like a child made it all worse.

She lifted her brows high. Time? He thought that was going to calm her down? Make her forget what an ass he was?

"No. No, no, no. You've gotten all the time from me you're going to get. We're done."

His sandy brows rose. "Excuse me?"

"Yup. I'm sorry to inconvenience you, especially right before your office Christmas party, which I know you already RSVP'd to for two people, but we're finished. I'm done being a stand-in girlfriend until a woman you can picture yourself marrying comes along."

"So you're saying that if I don't promise you right now, tonight, that we're going to get married, we're done?"

"Yes." The finality of that answer had her stomach twisting.

Was that what she was saying? When he phrased it that way, it sounded illogical and irrational.

"If that's how you really feel." He waited, watching her.

"It is." She sounded more confident than she felt.

"Okay." He nodded and stood.

Noelle watched in a daze as he let himself out, without even a backward glance.

She expected him to come back. To knock on the door and tell her he hadn't realized how much she meant to him until he'd lost her.

But the minutes ticked by and no knock came.

That's when the doubt and second thoughts and regret began to hit hard.

She'd gone from thinking they'd be engaged before another day passed to realizing she was alone.

George was gone. Really gone. No longer her boyfriend, and it was all her own fault because she'd given him an ultimatum.

In one moment her whole life—or at least the life she'd lived for the past five years—was completely altered, and she'd done it to herself.

Aunt Anna. Her sister. Her parents. They'd all sat there and listened as she'd told them how great everything was and how she expected a proposal any day . . . and now this.

What had she done?

CHAPTER 3

"Noelle, you can *not* hide away from everyone in your apartment forever." Nikki's censure came through the cell phone as clearly as if she were in the room.

"Nope. You're wrong. I definitely can." Hiding had worked pretty well so far. In fact, except for restaurant deliverymen, she hadn't seen another human being in close to two weeks.

"You're eventually going to have to go to work," Nikki pointed out.

"I'll worry about that when the time comes." Luckily for Noelle, she had four weeks of paid vacation time stored up that she had to use before the end of the year or lose it.

Months ago she'd put in to take off the weeks between Thanksgiving and New Year's so she could enjoy the holidays—the shopping, decorating, wrapping, watching holiday movies. All the stuff she usually loved.

Little did she know then that she'd need the

time to hibernate in her pajamas and lick her wounds because of her breakup with George.

Thank goodness even the food store and the liquor store had a delivery service. She was going to need much more ice cream and booze to get through this.

"I'm coming over." Nikki's declaration had Noelle scrambling for a reason why her sister couldn't come over.

"Um, I'm not home." To avoid Nikki's visit, and the inevitable lecture that would come with it, Noelle crafted what she thought was a pretty good lie.

"Liar."

"I'm not lying. I, uh, had to run out for more . . . sugar."

"More sugar for what?"

"To bake Christmas cookies." Noelle drew in a breath, wishing it was true, because she could really go for some snickerdoodles right now. Or the peanut butter ones with the chocolate kiss in the middle.

"That's interesting, because I just walked past your car parked in front of your apartment."

Crap. Her sneaky sister was already here.

"I, uh, walked to the store. And I have lots more errands to do . . . on foot, so don't wait around. You might as well go home."

"See, that's interesting too, since I'm right outside your door and I can hear you talking inside."

Dammit.

"Fine." With a huff of annoyance, Noelle disconnected the call and hoisted herself off the sofa. She tossed the phone onto the kitchen island and stomped to the door—as much as she could stomp in socks. She yanked it open and scowled. "When did you become so devious?"

"About the same time you became a hermit." Looking her up and down, Nikki wrinkled her nose. "Jeez. When was the last time you showered?" She pushed past Noelle and the stack of pizza boxes by the door and glanced around the apartment. "Or picked up around here? And where's your tree? You always have it up by now."

"Tree?" Noelle's jaw dropped. "Are you nuts? My life is falling apart around me, and you're worried about a Christmas tree?"

"Someone is nuts in this room, but it's not me." Nikki glared at her from beneath raised brows. "Now, close the door."

Noelle realized she was standing in the open doorway. She swung the door shut so her neighbors wouldn't walk by and see her grungy pajamas and unwashed hair.

"Come sit down. We're getting you over this funk and taking your life back."

"Oh, sure. Just like that." Noelle snapped her fingers.

"Yup. Just like that. I have a plan." Nikki remained standing as her glance took in Noelle from the top of her messy head to the toes of her dingy socks. "On second thought, go shower and change first. I'm sure you can't think clearly while you look like that. I know I certainly can't think just looking at you."

"You're quite the dictator today, aren't you?" Noelle folded her arms.

"You've given me no choice. You've avoided my calls and ignored my texts for weeks. All because you broke up with George?"

"We dated for almost five years. Of course breaking up after all that time is traumatic."

Nikki let out a rude noise. "*Pfft.* He was never right for you anyway, and you knew it. You just wouldn't admit it. It's a blessing you finally came to your senses. It was long overdue."

"I'm sorry I even told you what happened," Noelle mumbled.

"Well, you did, so too late." Nikki came forward and, grabbing her sister's shoulders, spun her around. "Now, go. Shower. Change. And don't forget to wash your hair. You look scary and you smell."

"Oh, lovely. Thanks. With a sister like you, who needs enemies?" Noelle grumbled all the way to the bathroom.

"Complain all you want. I'm not leaving until you look, smell, and act normal again. I'm making tea."

"Fine. Do whatever you want. You will anyway." Noelle slammed the bathroom door hard to reinforce her opinion regarding everything her sister had said.

It didn't matter what Nikki did in the kitchen, because Noelle was going to take as long as possible in the bathroom. She'd stay in there until her skin shriveled. Until the hot water ran out. And then, she'd take even more time getting dressed.

That would teach her nosy sister.

Noelle stoked her rage for most of her shower. Through the shampoo, rinse, and repeat. Even through the application of her instant conditioner.

It was about the time she gave her hair and body one final rinse that she realized—in her distraction—she'd forgotten to shave her legs, and that made her realize that it didn't matter.

There was no more George in her life to comment if she had stubbly legs. No one to care if she became a hairy beast. No one to care about her . . .

That realization had the hot tears filling Noelle's eyes as she swiped the razor blindly over her legs. The blade nicked her skin, sending a streak of bright red sluicing down her shin, over her foot, and across the white of the tub toward the drain. The sight fed her self-pity and had her tears falling faster.

Noelle braced her hands on the shower wall and drew in a deep breath.

"Get yourself together." She spoke the words aloud, hoping to will herself into following her own advice.

Drawing in and letting out another breath, she felt a little calmer, even though the blood was still flowing.

Maybe it was watching the life's blood literally seep out of her that knocked Noelle into action. Grabbing the washcloth from the towel rack in the shower stall, she pressed it against her knee.

Sometimes even the smallest cuts bled a lot. The truth of that thought struck Noelle. Like this tiny razor scrape in her skin that bled a disproportionate amount in relation to its size, perhaps cutting George loose hadn't been as huge an amputation from her life as it seemed.

Or maybe she was just as crazy as she felt.

With a sigh, Noelle flipped off the water. Her cut would never clot under the pounding spray of the shower, and she'd had enough of being wet.

Time to get out, dry off, dress, and deal with her uninvited guest.

Only after she'd bandaged her knee and then

pulled on fluffy socks and a clean sweat suit did Noelle brave the kitchen and her sister.

At least Nikki had made tea as she'd promised. The steaming mug on the counter drew Noelle forward. So did the plate of cookies next to it.

"Mom's peanut butter cookies?"

"Yes. Do you forgive me for bothering you now?" Nikki asked.

"Maybe." The gift of cookies certainly didn't hurt.

As the first sip of hot tea warmed Noelle from the inside, a mouthful of chocolate and peanut butter did much to melt her icy feelings toward her sister.

Nikki sat perched on one of the bar stools at the kitchen island, focusing on her cell phone. "So, I downloaded this app. . . ."

"Mmm-hmm." Noelle sat too, reached for a second cookie, and took a good-sized bite out of it.

"I signed you up."

Her sister was always doing stuff like that. Signing her up for mailing lists and websites without her permission. Noelle pulled her mouth to one side. "Great. Now I'll get a bunch of e-mails because they have my address. What's it for, some store?"

"Uh, no, not a store." Nikki put her own cell down just as Noelle's phone vibrated with a text alert. Nikki eyed the phone on the countertop, where Noelle had tossed it. "You gonna check that?"

Suspicious, Noelle put down her mug and picked up the phone. There was a new text from a number she didn't recognize, but it was from her local area code. She frowned at the screen as she hit the button to read it.

Hello, beautiful! Reply to this number to start chatting with your new boyfriend.

"What is this? What did you do?" Noelle glared at her sister.

Nikki's face lit up with a grin. "I got you a boyfriend."

"A what?" Noelle's voice rose high.

"Not a real one. Relax. It's the Build-A-Boyfriend app." Nikki held up her phone as if that would explain it all. "Remember, I told you about it at Thanksgiving?"

Noelle grabbed her sister's phone and glanced at the screen. "But I don't understand. Who is this text from?"

"Actually, I'm not really sure. That's kind of proprietary information. I read an article about the app in the *Wall Street Journal* before I signed you up, and the owners of the company were pretty secretive about how they actually generate the texts."

"Oh, well, that's comforting." Noelle rolled her eyes.

Ignoring the sarcasm, Nikki continued. "The exact process and technology is kept under wraps, but there's speculation it might be a combination of computer technology and real-life human interaction."

"So basically the nicest compliment I've gotten in recent memory is from either a computer or someone being paid to text me." Noelle twisted her mouth unhappily.

"Yes. But that's the beauty of it. You get to pretend you have the perfect boyfriend for the family at Christmas without dealing with any of the problems of a real man."

"None of the problems but also none of the fun," Noelle reminded her overly jubilant sister.

Nikki dismissed that complaint with one flick of a wrist. "Oh, seriously. When was the last time you had fun with George? I mean real fun, where he didn't criticize you or act like a stick in the mud?"

It was a knee-jerk reaction to defend George to Nikki, but just the mention of his name raised a horrible realization that had Noelle gasping. "George's parents will be at the Christmas party."

Nikki nodded. "I'm sure they will. And I think you'd better prepare yourself that George could very well come, too."

Noelle widened her eyes. "You think he would?"

How could she face him? And what if he came with a date? He wouldn't have the nerve—would he? She had the bad feeling he might.

"Yes, I do. And I think you need to be ready. Which is why we're setting you up with a new boyfriend."

"I don't think a couple of possibly computer-generated texts are going to convince anyone I have a boyfriend."

"The app does more than just text. You can get e-mails. Even a real handwritten letter. And you can set up for flower and gift deliveries, too, but that's an extra charge."

All of that sounded expensive. "How much is this thing going to cost me?"

"Nothing. There's a free trial. For the basic membership during the trial period you get a limited number of texts, and we can design a complete boyfriend. We name him. Give him an occupation. We can even download photos from their database." When Noelle continued to look skeptical, Nikki continued. "I'm telling you, this will work. We post a couple of status updates and pictures online, and you'll have what looks like a completely convincing relationship."

"No. I'm not posting pictures of a made-up boyfriend. That's too much. Then what happens when I meet a real guy and there are these pictures of my fake boyfriend all over the web?"

"Fine. No guy pics right away, but we're going to revisit that idea before the party. Okay?"

Noelle sighed, too beaten down to fight her sister. "Okay."

"Even without pictures of a guy, we can fabricate a complete relationship online starting right away."

"How in the world are you going to do that?"

"Easy. A close-up shot of two glasses of champagne with a status update that reads something like, *Enjoying some bubbly at Sunday brunch with my new man.* A pic of a Christmas tree lot with the post, *Good thing my boyfriend is strong since I chose the biggest tree here.* A few posts like that and George and the relatives will think you have the most active social life of anyone we know."

Shocked, and admittedly a bit impressed, Noelle stared at her sister. "You do realize that if you put this much creativity and effort into your dissertation and building a career, you'd be making enough money to move out of Mom and Dad's place, right?"

"Ugh. Work and school are no fun. *This* is fun. I can't wait to create all sorts of dates for you and— wait—what are we calling him?" Nikki picked up her phone again. "There's a place for all that info in the dashboard of the app. So, what do you want to call your new fake boyfriend?"

"First of all, can we stop referring to him as my 'fake boyfriend'?" Noelle sighed with self-pity. "Other than that, I don't know what to call him."

"Just choose a guy's name. Make it something strong and sexy." Nikki waited, phone in hand, as Noelle glanced around the room, looking for inspiration and not finding much that would work for a good name.

"Strong and sexy . . . Hmm. Ooh, wait. I got it." She smiled in triumph as an idea struck. "Type in that his name is Nathan."

"Nathan. Okay. Sounds good to me." Nikki typed in a few things. "Where'd you get that name from?"

"He was this guy I met at the store when I ran out to buy more cranberries on Thanksgiving." Back when she'd been happy and hopeful for a future with George. Apparently, also back when she'd been delusional that she and he were in the same place in their relationship. "Anyway, there were only two bags left and he was going to buy them both but he gave one to me."

"That was nice of him."

"Yeah. It was. I gave him my cranberry recipe as a thank-you."

Nikki sucked in a breath. "You gave it to him and you won't even give it to me?"

"Fine. I'll text it to you." Noelle scrolled to the outgoing text with the recipe and sent a copy to her sister. Nikki's phone chimed a few seconds later and Noelle said, "There. You have it now. Happy?"

"Yes. Thank you." Nikki continued to tap away on her phone before raising her eyes to Noelle. "Okay. I've put everything in your app dashboard. You're all set up, or rather *he's* all set up. Remember to save that Build-A-Boyfriend number into your contacts under *Nathan*. It will be good proof."

"Proof for whom? Who's going to see the texts on my phone?"

"Everyone you show them to at the Christmas party when you're telling them about how great your new boyfriend, Nathan, is and reading them what sweet things he is going to text to you."

Picking up her phone again, Noelle sighed deeply. She spotted the number with the local area code and hit the button to create a new contact. She narrated her actions aloud for her bossy sister. "Create new contact. *N-A-T-H-A-N*. Save. Anything else, boss?"

"Well, you're going to have to text him back so he can respond. That's how it works."

"Stop saying '*him*' likes it's a real guy." Noelle tried not to think that at best her texts would be from some bored Build-A-Boyfriend employee, and at worst from a computer.

"If you don't start acting like he's real, how do you expect anyone else to believe it?" Nikki cocked a brow and ignored Noelle's pout. "Now, go put on something cute and festive. We need to go out and start faking some dates."

Noelle wasn't sure she had the ability to be cute or festive right now. "Why?"

"For the pictures. We'll take some of you getting your Christmas tree. Oh, and bring an extra sweater and a scarf or hat with you so we can fake a few different dates to post all throughout the week." Nikki stopped her planning long enough to shoot Noelle a glare. "What are you waiting for? Go."

"Fine." Rolling her eyes, Noelle slid off the stool and turned toward the hall.

"And put on some makeup. You look like death."

"Thanks." She shot her sister a glare over her shoulder.

Nikki responded with a broad grin. "You're welcome. Ooh and mistletoe. We definitely have to buy some mistletoe. We can take a picture of it hanging up. It'll be perfect."

Nikki continued talking as Noelle walked away. Her only concession was to raise her voice louder.

In her bedroom, Noelle shook her head at this whole thing. Faking a relationship was a lot of work. It might be easier just to find a real man.

CHAPTER 4

Naked, Nathan fell backward onto the mattress. His limbs were so wobbly he'd been happy to remain upright in the shower long enough to wash off the sweat.

Reaching down, he tugged at the damp towel he'd wrapped around his waist. When he finally wrested it loose, he tossed it to the floor. He wasn't normally a messy person, but he'd be damned if he had the energy to walk even as far as the laundry basket.

What the hell? He was in good shape. He had to be. It was his job to keep his body in top condition, but damn his CO had worked the team into the ground today. Or maybe he was just getting old.

Old at thirty-two. He snorted out a laugh and felt his exhausted abdominal muscles protest at even that small action.

Maybe command was pushing them so hard because they'd all come back from leave soft. Admittedly, traveling home and visiting his parents for

Thanksgiving had thrown off his workout schedule.

Hell, it had more than thrown his routine off. It had put a grinding halt to his PT. With all the food and beer and wine, he'd gained five pounds in not even as many days. He'd weighed in this morning, and the Thanksgiving weight was gone but not the memories.

Turkey, stuffing, candied sweet and mashed white potatoes, not to mention that crazy-good bourbon cranberry sauce he'd taken to eating right off the spoon.

Then there were the leftovers. Hot open-faced turkey and gravy sandwiches. Cold turkey sandwiches. Turkey potpie.

Just thinking of it had him feeling stuffed all over again.

He tried not to remember how many times he'd had to unbutton his jeans after eating during that visit. That was so far from his usual behavior it was like he'd left the base in Virginia and become a different person when he crossed the Connecticut state line.

Luckily he'd left to drive back to base at the crack of dawn Sunday morning, so the culinary debauchery had only lasted for three days.

But how was he going to do it all again next week when he went home for Christmas?

Nathan chastised himself for even thinking that. There were too many years he'd been deployed over the holidays. He should appreciate every day he could spend with family and not in some hellhole on the other side of the world.

That's what he should do. What he did do was

stare up at the ceiling and wish he'd remembered to turn down the bed before lying in it.

With a sigh he rallied his energy and sat up. Getting there hurt like hell, but once he was vertical he was fine. He was behaving like a pussy over a few sore muscles. He shook his head at himself and bent to grab the towel on the floor. After tossing it into the laundry basket, he pulled a pair of boxer shorts out of the drawer and tugged them up his legs.

He was just deciding if he wanted to grab something to eat for dinner or just skip it and rack out for the night, when a text came through his phone. He eyed the cell on the dresser with more than a little suspicion.

Would command have the nerve to call them in for night training after the day they'd had? Or worse, was the team being recalled for a mission?

Crap.

There was only one way to find out. He moved toward the dresser, rallying his optimism in the few strides it took him to cross his bedroom in the barracks.

Maybe it wasn't anything as bad as what his imagination conjured and his weary body feared.

It could be just his mother saying hello. After he'd convinced her to learn how to text during his past visit, she might finally be embracing the technology.

Sure. That could be it.

Happy with that guess, he grabbed the cell, but it wasn't command or his mother. On the readout Nathan saw a number with no name, but what really caught his attention was that the area code was from his hometown in Connecticut. The same area code of his own cell, since he'd never changed his number after joining the Navy, not even when he'd gotten stationed in Virginia.

Frowning, he hit to read the text.

Hey, Nathan. My parents are having a big party on Christmas Eve. I hope you can make it. Noelle.

Nathan read the text twice, pondering its meaning.

He knew exactly whom it was from. Noelle of the bourbon berry recipe. Noelle, who got an adorable little wrinkle between her brows when she typed on her cell phone. Noelle, with the really nice curves he'd had to try hard not to stare at in the store that day.

Besides her being pretty memorable, he'd saved her text with the recipe in it, so it was right there on his screen above this new text, leaving no doubt it was definitely from her.

So that left the question of, why now? Why, weeks after that five-minute chance meeting in the produce section in his hometown, did she decide to text him out of the blue?

He glanced at the words again and figured he was overthinking it. The reason for the text was clear. Her parents' party.

Maybe this invite was a further thank-you for his handing over that bag of cranberries. Best thing he'd ever done. Besides it being the decent thing to do, and his getting her kick-ass cranberry sauce recipe, he was going to get to see Noelle again.

Christmas Eve would be perfect, actually. It fell on a Saturday this year, and he'd already put in for official leave starting a few days before Christmas.

Barring any issues, he'd be in town before his

parents went to bed Wednesday night. His parents did the family dinner on Christmas Day, but the night before he was free as a bird. Free to flutter over to Noelle's parents' party.

And where exactly was that? He typed in the text to find out.

I'd love to come. Time? Address?

She responded almost immediately with the time and the address. It was in the town next to his, which made sense since they had been shopping at the same store on Thanksgiving.

Her being local would be handy if he ended up hitting it off with this woman. What would be even better would be if he wasn't currently stationed in another state. Even thinking that was really jumping the gun. But that didn't squash his curiosity about Noelle and her mysterious surprise text.

After considering it for barely a minute, he punched in another text.

Glad you texted. I didn't think I'd hear from you.

Her reply came through fast, which was a good sign, right? Nathan sighed. What did he know? Dating didn't exactly fit in his life right now. That was painfully obvious from his lack of any female companionship in recent memory.

Pushing aside his self-pity, he read what she'd written.

I know. I'm sorry. It took me a while to wrap my head around this and get up my nerve.

Hmm. Interesting that she'd been nervous about texting him. He guessed it was just as nerve-racking for a woman to text a man as vice versa. While walking to the kitchenette to grab some leftovers out of the fridge, he typed in a reply.

Nothing to be nervous about. I'm just an average guy.

Her reply came in while the microwave chugged along, heating the piece of steak he hadn't finished from last night's dinner.

Good to know. I was a little worried about that part.

He smiled, choosing to take that as a compliment. He could be a little intimating.

Two hundred and fifty pounds of muscle on a six-foot-two-inch frame could intimidate some people. Petite brunettes, in particular.

Nathan was just cutting into his steak, the phone on the table next to his plate, when she texted again.

So what are you up to?

Well, well, well. It seemed his new friend was a talker. He could handle that. He put down his fork and replied.

Eating dinner. Leftover steak. You?

As he put down the phone again and grabbed his bottle of water, she responded.

Watching my favorite Christmas movie.

He rarely had time to watch TV, but he had a television set and he could certainly use a little Christmas spirit. He typed in his question, the answer to which would tell him a lot about her.

Which movie?

If she came back with *Christmas Vacation,* he'd know she was probably the kind of woman he could kick back with and enjoy a beer and some hot wings. If she came back with *It's a Wonderful Life,* he'd know she was the serious type. Though he really wouldn't mind either.

Elf.

Her answer threw him since he'd never seen it. He told her that.

Never saw it.

Her reply came so fast and with so many exclamation points, he had to laugh.

OMG! Turn it on right now! Ch 60!

She thought he was in Connecticut and was giving him the local channel. Getting up, he grabbed the remote, turned on the channel guide, and scrolled until he found the movie. By that time, she'd texted again.

Did you turn it on? Oh wait. Are you at work?

He smiled at her persistence and enthusiasm.

Not at work. Watching now.

Good!! Best part coming up.

Laughing at her excitement, Nathan grabbed his dinner and sat on the sofa. He punched in a quick reply.

Looking forward to it.

He suspected he'd get another text shortly, so after hitting Send he tossed the cell onto the cushion next to him and settled in for a night with *Elf* and the very surprising Noelle.

CHAPTER 5

The clock ticked closer to lunch than breakfast, but Noelle was still in her pajamas, trying to wake up with her second cup of coffee.

In her defense, this was her vacation.

A knock on the door had her frowning. She wasn't expecting anyone. Besides, who on earth would be dropping by unannounced so early in the morning?

Noelle glanced at the clock and realized it wasn't all that early after all. Her butt was dragging today because she'd stayed up too late watching movies on TV last night.

The knock repeated.

Oh well. Whoever had the audacity to stop by without calling first deserved to see her in her red flannel, Santa-print pj's.

It was probably just Nikki anyway, here to force her into another fake date so they could post about it online.

At least all the orchestrated events Nikki had

made Noelle go on so far had prepared her for Christmas.

Noelle now had a tree, and wrapped presents, and all sorts of fancy bottles of wine and champagne that she would supposedly share with her fake boyfriend, Nathan.

Not to mention the cookies she and Nikki had baked just for the photo op. Noelle had enjoyed eating those, at least.

It all made for a convincingly fabulous life—if no one looked too far past the social media posts. Still, there was a sadness shadowing the victory.

The fact that she'd spent a good amount of last night texting the Build-A-Boyfriend employee assigned to her—and she'd enjoyed it—proved how pitiful her life was.

With a sigh, Noelle flipped the lock and yanked open the door. The moment she saw who stood there, she realized she should have remembered to use the peephole before opening the door.

"George. What are you doing here?"

"I just wanted to check and see how you were doing."

"Oh, really. You're concerned about me?" She folded her arms and leaned against the door frame, blocking his entrance.

Interesting that he didn't stop by or call or text for those two weeks after the night they'd broken up. That it was only after Nikki had implemented the Build-A-Boyfriend plan that George suddenly darkened Noelle's doorway.

"Yes, of course I'm concerned about you. We were together for four and a half years." His gaze swept over her, going from her unwashed hair to the faded flannel.

"Yes, we were."

Long, wasted years she could have been dating other guys, or not dating at all and just having fun living her own life rather than trying to please George.

And for what?

What did she end up with for all that effort? A man who had no plans to spend the future with her, that's what. And a Christmas spent single.

She also couldn't forget the other result of her breakup—her fake boyfriend. Though if last night was any indication, having a Build-A-Boyfriend wasn't too bad. She really had enjoyed watching television while texting him. Probably enjoyed it too much, considering . . .

Noelle would deal with her feelings regarding her surreal relationship with the Build-A-Boyfriend dude later. At the moment she had something more pressing to deal with. Namely one hundred and fifty pounds of entitled, opinionated hot air darkening her door.

Funny how she'd never noticed what a pompous fool he was while they'd been dating.

Now she was tuned in to every passive-aggressive comment he made. Every judgmental glance he directed at her and at her apartment. He looked over her shoulder and surveyed the remnants of her late-night movie session, right down to the popcorn she'd dropped on the carpet and hadn't gotten around to picking up yet.

"Anything else? I really need to get moving. I have plans for the day." Bristling at his silent but obvious censure, she had no problem delivering the lie.

Heck, it could be true. She did expect her sister to come up with some excursion to further their ruse.

"Um, no. I guess not. I just didn't want your parents' party to be the first time we saw each other since—you know."

Since she'd broken up with him?

Noelle was trying not to feel any guilt now that George seemed to actually be acting like a decent human being by checking on her. She squelched the feeling as quickly as it had arisen, remembering that she'd only broken up with him because he'd never seen a future with her.

Putting on a bravado she didn't feel, Noelle waved away his concern with the flick of one wrist. "Oh, don't worry about it. We were friends before we dated. We'll be friends after." She forced a smile. "So, you're coming to the party then?"

"Yes. I was planning on it. My brothers are going. And my parents."

"Oh good. I'll look forward to seeing them." She pushed off the door frame. "So, not to rush you, but I really do have to shower and get dressed."

"All right." He hesitated. "Will I get to meet Nathan at the party?"

That question froze Noelle in place. George had seen the posts and now was expecting to see Nathan in the flesh.

She and Nikki hadn't really worked out that part of the farce. What would they say when people asked where Nathan was during the party?

Lying on the fly wasn't exactly in Noelle's skill set, but she had no choice except to wing it. "He's going to try his best to be there. You know, prior commitment and all."

"Oh?" George sounded too interested in the information that Nathan might not be at the party.

"He had plans for Christmas Eve already when we met." The lies were getting deeper. Before Noelle knew it, she'd be drowning in them.

George's brows rose. "And how did you meet?"

She had to get him out of here. This was too much pressure. She couldn't handle it, and this was only George. What would she do at the party when faced with a house full of people asking questions?

That settled it. The moment she closed and locked the door behind George, she was calling her sister and they were going to work out every last detail. She couldn't go into Christmas Eve unprepared the way she was now.

That resolution wouldn't help her now. She needed an answer to his question.

"How did we meet?" Her brain spun for a believable scenario. After Thanksgiving she'd been a hermit, but he didn't know that. An idea struck. "Shopping."

"Shopping?"

"Yup. Shopping." Something she loved to do and George loathed, so it was perfect. "You know, 'tis the season and all. Lots of shopping to do for Christmas. So I was out, you know, shopping and there he was. And the rest is history."

Ready to pass out from her pulse pounding so hard, Noelle made a show of glancing behind her at the clock on the microwave.

"Wow. I didn't realize it was so late. I really do have to go. But I'll see you Christmas Eve." Before he could force any more falsehoods out of her, she took a step back and swung the door closed.

Not until the lock and the dead bolt and chain were secured did she breathe freely again. That's when Noelle sprang into action. She ran for her cell and punched the button to dial her sister.

Nikki answered on the second ring. "Hello."

"George was just here." Paranoid that he might still be hovering outside, Noelle moved farther from the door and cupped her hand around the phone as she whispered.

"What? Why? What was he doing there?" Her sister, having the benefit of being far away, did not keep her voice down. Nikki's shocked questions boomed through the earpiece of the phone and into Noelle's ear.

"He was asking a whole lot of questions I didn't have answers to," Noelle hissed.

"About what?"

"About my fake boyfriend."

"He saw the posts? And he believed that Nathan's real?" Nikki's jubilant *whoop* sliced through Noelle's eardrum.

"This is nothing to celebrate."

"Sure it is. We created a fake boyfriend and your ex-boyfriend believed it. That's pretty amazing."

"What's not so amazing were my weak lies about why Nathan might not be at the party and where we met."

"What did you tell him?"

"That we met while shopping, but Nathan has a prior commitment that might keep him from coming to the party."

"Perfect."

Things were far from perfect in Noelle's mind.

"Nikki, there are so many things people could ask, and I won't have answers."

"Like what?"

"You know Aunt Anna is going to want to know what he does for a living." Probably what his annual income was, too. And his parents' tax bracket, as well.

"Yeah, you're probably right."

Noelle drew in a breath and let it out on a sigh. "The whole thing makes me want to just walk in and tell everyone that I'm single and proud of it."

"You should have thought of that before we made up Nathan."

"Me? It was you driving this train. I was just a passenger." Noelle scowled.

"Whatever. It's too late now."

Nikki was right. Noelle was invested in the lie. It was too late to turn back now.

"By the way, with the party this weekend, we have to ramp up the Build-A-Boyfriend stuff. Set up a delivery of flowers. Choose a Christmas gift. And you really need to go through the app's database and choose a photo for Nathan."

Noelle groaned. "Do I have to?"

Nikki let out an audible breath. "I guess not, but it's going to start to look suspicious that there are no pictures of him. Like he's a vampire or something. Have you at least texted the app number yet?"

"I did. Last night."

"And? What were the replies like?" That information turned up the volume of Nikki's excited questions.

"Better than I expected, actually." Noelle's cheeks

heated with embarrassment at how much fun she'd had texting with an app.

"Could you tell if it was a computer responding?"

"I don't think it was. His responses seemed too . . . human." His responses? Hers? Its? Noelle didn't know what to say.

"Artificial intelligence has gotten pretty sophisticated."

This had to be the most surreal experience and conversation Noelle had ever had. Even so, she didn't want to think Nikki was right and that her Build-A-Boyfriend could be just a computer.

"No, I really don't think it was. We texted for hours last night."

Until he'd said he had an early morning and had to go to bed. Then they'd said good night.

"Be careful. You only have a limited number of texts with the free trial. Don't use them all up. You'll want to get a text or two during the party in front of George."

Noelle's eyes widened. "How many texts do I have?"

Had she used up all her texts? Was that why he'd said good night?

"I'll have to look it up again. I forget exactly. Ten, maybe?"

"Ten!" Noelle's brain exploded with panic. They had to have texted back and forth close to twenty times last night. Maybe the app only counted his replies to her. Even so, she might have used up all ten last night. "So what do I do if I used up all the texts? Can I buy more?"

Noelle panicked at the thought of never talking

to Nathan again, even if he was being paid to text her.

"I don't know. We'll have to look into it. It might have been that the free trial had ten texts, but the paid version had a hundred. I didn't pay that much attention since I didn't think you were going to go and use them all up in one night. But seriously, Noelle, don't worry. We'll figure it out."

"I am worrying."

"Well, stop it. We can straighten out the text stuff while we arrange for the flowers and gifts to be delivered. Maybe something should arrive for you at Mom and Dad's place during the party so you can open it in front of George."

The image of opening a gift from her new boyfriend in front of her old one was enough of a distraction for Noelle to pocket her panic over the texting issue for a little while. "Oh, that's a good idea. It can be like a 'Sorry I couldn't make the party. Here's a dozen red roses to make up for it.'"

"Perfect." Nikki sighed. "Darn it. I'm sorry that I don't have time to do all of this today. There's a bunch of stuff I still need to get done—"

"So let me do some of it." Noelle could handle some of the details while sitting at home stressing about a fake boyfriend's texts. She was an excellent multitasker.

"You'll have to download the app onto your phone and then log in to the dashboard. Then navigate to the settings area and enter the delivery address—"

"Okay. Never mind. That's too much work. I'll wait until you have time to do it."

Nikki laughed. "I figured you'd say that. Things

should free up for me after today. Then I can handle the app stuff, and one night this week I'll come over, we'll pour something to drink, and we'll figure out the backstory for you and Nathan so you're ready. Okay?"

"All right. Talk to you soon."

"Okay. 'Bye."

"'Bye." Noelle disconnected the call with her sister and tried to calm herself.

At least they had some sort of a plan.

Still, what if Noelle had exhausted all of her allotted texts in one night? Then she wouldn't be able to talk to Nathan again until Nikki had time to fix it.

Worried, she navigated to her messages on her cell. Holding her breath, she typed in a new text to Nathan.

Good morning.

It was closer to noon than morning. He should be at work. Unless, of course, he worked the night shift.

She didn't know how the Build-A-Boyfriend management scheduled the employees. Maybe they were on call all the time. This company provided a hell of a service, considering she was on a free trial.

Phone in hand, she sat waiting for his reply. The minutes ticked by, and as she sat, obsessing, another horrible thought hit. What if whatever employee was on duty at the time answered the texts as they came in? Her next message might not be from the Nathan of last night at all. It could be a completely different person.

Panic hit, as did the fear she'd never talk to *that* Nathan again.

This was crazy. She was going insane. This was an app . . . but it felt like so much more. No app should cause such emotions.

Sadly, she realized no response had come through. She must have used up the free texts.

That was okay. She'd upgrade. Get more texts.

Maybe there was an unlimited plan. That would be good. Then, when she did finally get a reply, she'd be able to talk long enough to determine whether it was the same person responding. She was confident she'd be able to figure that out. There had been such a connection between them last night. She had no doubt she'd be able to tell.

Having talked herself off the ledge, Noelle carried her phone with her into the bathroom to shower so she could get ready for the day. One unexpected visitor stopping by to find her in her pajamas was enough.

CHAPTER 6

Muscles protesting, Nathan forced himself to cool down after the workout when he'd rather collapse flat on his back on the cold ground. Though that might not be too bad. He could always stretch while he was down there.

"Two days in a row." His teammate Stone shook his head as if he didn't believe it.

"I know." Nathan wiped the sweat off his face with the edge of his T-shirt.

"I mean, what the hell? It's Christmas and the commander is trying to kill us."

Nathan laughed. "Not kill us. Just make us wish we were dead."

"Well, I'll tell you what, it's working." Stone huffed out a breath. "You ready to go on in?"

"Yeah." Nathan had cooled down as much as he was going to. Soaked as he was in sweat, it would do more harm than good to stay outside in the late December chill.

Stone swiveled his head to glance at Nathan as

he held open the door of the building for him. "Y'all going home for Christmas?"

"Yup. Put in for leave starting noon tomorrow. If no shit hits the fan and we don't get recalled, I'll be home for almost a full week."

"Lucky." Stone scowled. "I didn't remember to put in for extra days."

Luck had nothing to do with it. Nathan was organized. Stone was not. Nathan didn't mention that and instead waved off Stone's comment. "You know they'll cut you loose early Friday anyway. They never make us stick around for a full week leading up to a holiday."

"Yeah. And my parents' place is only a couple hours' drive. I can be home in no time."

"Two hours is a hell of a lot better than my drive home." Nathan wasn't looking forward to making that trip again. Especially not after having just done it a few weeks before for Thanksgiving.

Then again, he was very much looking forward to seeing Noelle.

And speaking of Noelle . . . Nathan grabbed his cell phone out of his locker and saw he'd missed a text from her.

Smiling wide, he read the message wishing him a good morning. He probably should be upset about his reaction to the simple text, for a number of reasons.

She was in Connecticut, he was in Virginia, and there was one long-ass drive between them.

He could be called out on a mission on a moment's notice, or be deployed for the next six months.

None of that made for a real good start to a relationship, but if the uncontrollable grin on his face was any indication, he didn't care about any of the problems. The possibilities, on the other hand, seemed pretty enticing.

Nathan shoved his phone into his duffel. He didn't want to start a conversation now. He'd text back later when he was home and free to devote the attention to her she deserved. Knowing Noelle—and he felt like he really did know her after last night—she'd text him back immediately and often.

He smiled at that thought as he headed to the shower.

"What's put that shit-eating grin on your face?" Stone asked in his usual colorful Southern drawl as he slammed his locker.

"Remember that woman I told you I met over the bag of cranberries when I was home?"

Stone's eyes widened. "The hottie who gave you the recipe for the bourbon sauce you let me taste?"

He had described her as that, hadn't he? "That's the one. Noelle."

"Yup. I remember. I'm getting my mamaw to make me those cranberries when I get home. I already bought the bottle of bourbon for it."

Nathan shook his head at Stone's one-track mind when it came to food. And booze, for that matter. "Well, she texted me to invite me to a party over Christmas."

Stone lifted his brow high. "So, you're going to see her again. I approve."

Nathan laughed. "How can you approve? You don't know anything about her."

"Don't have to." Stone shook his head. "Any woman who came up with putting bourbon in cranberry sauce is all right in my book."

Nathan couldn't argue with that.

It was all he could do to get through the end of the day and wait to be dismissed before he could run home and text Noelle.

Good thing being in the Navy had trained him how to wait. Though sometimes he was more patient than others. With Noelle's text sitting on his phone waiting for a reply, today was one of his less patient days.

When he was finally inside his barracks room, Nathan dumped his duffel on the table and fished out his cell. He'd been thinking about it for the past couple of hours but still hadn't settled on a suitable response.

He gave up trying to be clever.

Hey. Sorry I couldn't get right back to you. Work.

Her reply came back fast, which really wasn't a surprise. The girl must keep her cell in her hand at all times.

Oh good! I was worried I'd used up all my texts with you. How many more before I reach the limit?

He laughed at her little joke. She was a funny one. He'd give her that. Smiling, he punched in a reply.

For you? No limit.

Really?

Really.

After he responded to her, he went to his bedroom to change into sweats. He might as well get comfortable while he texted. He'd just pulled a sweatshirt over his head when he saw the new text from her.

So what are your plans for Christmas?

Other than your party, you mean?

He hit Send and held the phone in his hand, knowing she'd be sending him a response any second.

LOL. Yes, besides that.

I was hoping to see more of you, if you wanted.

I'd like that.

When her reply came through, he picked up the phone and hit to dial her number. Enough back-and-forth. He was tired of texting. He wanted to hear her voice.

"Hello?"

He smiled at how shocked she sounded that he'd called. "Hey. It's Nathan."

"Hi. Um, are you allowed to call?"

Odd question. She must think he was at work and could get in trouble. "Sure. I'm off work now, so yeah. I can talk."

"Oh, okay. Don't worry. I won't tell."

He laughed at her continued joking. "Thanks. So, I'm going to be in town by tomorrow night and I was hoping we could get together some day before the party."

"Get together for real?" she asked, once again the surprise evident in her tone.

"Yeah, for real. Maybe for coffee. Or drinks. Or, hell, I don't know, hot chocolate. Whatever you'd like. I probably won't get there until like eight or later tomorrow night so—"

"That's okay. I'll be awake."

He'd been about to say they'd have to put off seeing each other until the next day, but hell, sooner was better than later for him. "You sure that won't be too late?"

"It's fine. I'm off this week, so I've been staying up until like midnight every night."

He remembered their texts last night. "Watching Christmas movies?"

"Yes." She sounded adorably shy.

He smiled, enjoying how he knew her so well already.

Okay. Moving on. He had to plan this date.

It finally hit him that he actually had a no-shit, bona-fide date.

How long had it been since he'd had one of those?

Far too long, was the answer to that question. His parents could just wait to see him until they woke up the following day.

"So should I come right to your place and we can decide when I get there?" he suggested.

Fingers crossed there'd be no traffic or bad weather to keep him from getting there. Hell, he might even consider sneaking out early if he didn't think the commander would notice.

"Yeah, come here. I'll text you my address. You can see my Christmas tree."

"That sounds great. I'd love to see it," he said, and amazingly enough he actually meant it.

Not too many years ago his only reason for going to a woman's apartment would have been the hope of getting into her pants, and here he was excited by the prospect of Christmas trees and hot cocoa.

Was that a sign of maturity or just an indication of how much he liked this girl already? Honestly, he didn't care which it was, as long as he got to see her again.

CHAPTER 7

She glanced at the clock on her phone and her heart sped. In probably less than half an hour, Noelle's Build-A-Boyfriend Nathan, or whatever his real name was, would be here.

One of her first orders of business when he walked through the door would be to find out his real name.

Her boyfriend and the relationship might have started out as fake, but now both were very real and she was really going to meet him.

Last night, after one final confirmation of what time to expect him, Noelle had hung up on the surreal phone conversation and typed in her address.

She'd hesitated barely a second before sending him the text. She couldn't tell Nikki that. No way, no how.

Her sister would only throw cold water on her excitement. Nikki would say he was a stranger. That Noelle should meet him in a nice, safe public place and not at her apartment. Heck, Nikki would probably tell Noelle not to meet him at all.

But he wasn't really a stranger. They'd texted. They'd talked on the phone.

Call her crazy, but she trusted him.

Sure, they'd met under rather unconventional circumstances. But hey, people met online all the time. What did it matter if the connection was made on a matchmaking site or the Build-A-Boyfriend app?

That was her theory and she was sticking to it.

No. Noelle would not let doubt creep in. That's why she'd avoided talking to her sister for the past twenty-four hours. Nikki would have sensed something was up.

Noelle realized that their meeting wasn't without risk for Nathan, either. It had to be against the Build-A-Boyfriend employee code of conduct, but he was doing it anyway.

He felt the chemistry between them, too. A spark. A connection so strong she'd never had anything close to it with George.

She remembered how George had described their relationship. The words that had angered her so and prompted her to break it off with him.

Being with someone shouldn't be based on "habit" or "convenience." A relationship should be exciting. It should make your heart pound and your hands shake with anticipation, the way she felt now waiting for Nathan.

The sound of a loud knock had her eyes widening as she whipped around to stare at the door.

Could it be Nathan?

If so, he was early.

Thank God she'd been so nervous that she had

gotten ready hours ago, right down to her lipstick—which was probably worn away by now.

She didn't have time to remedy that as she ran to the door.

Unlike yesterday, when George had snuck up on her, Noelle was not going to be surprised again. This time she peeked through the peephole.

The man she saw looked vaguely familiar, in spite of the way the peephole distorted his features.

In all the excitement it took her a second, but finally she focused enough to realize why she recognized him.

Frowning, Noelle quickly unlocked the door. She pulled it open to reveal all six-foot-plus of her Thanksgiving cranberry savior.

After that brief encounter in the store, and that single text with her recipe, she'd never thought she'd see or hear from him again—unless for some reason they ran into each other in the fruit and vegetable aisle again.

The pieces of a puzzle she knew she should have the answer to began to shift in her brain.

This guy's name was Nathan. His number was in her phone.

Holy shit. She must have texted him instead of the Build-A-Boyfriend number.

Even as the blood drained from her face as she realized her mistake, he smiled wide. "Hey. Sorry. I know I'm early. There wasn't much traffic, so I might have sped a little bit during the drive."

"Nathan. Um, hi. Uh, come on in." Shaking, she took a step back.

"I stopped and picked up some hot chocolate. It should still be hot. I figured we could drink it in front of your tree while we decide what to do."

For the first time she noticed he held two cups in his hands. "Um, sure. That would be great."

Now that the shock was starting to wane, reality set in, and what a reality it was. The guy she'd been texting, the one she'd connected with so strongly, wasn't a Build-A-Boyfriend employee at all. He was real and he was here, not to mention gorgeous.

She knocked herself out of her spinning thoughts and realized he was standing just inside the doorway, coat on, cups in hand, waiting for her to do or say something.

"Um, take off your coat and come sit down." She gestured in the general direction of the sofa and the Christmas tree, plainly visible from where they stood by the door.

"Okay. Thanks." He put the cups down on the kitchen counter and pulled off a thick dark blue jacket that said NAVY on it in yellow.

Noelle's focus moved from the insignia on his jacket to his face, realizing she didn't know all that much about this guy. "Are you in the Navy?"

"Yes, ma'am. For over twelve years now." He grinned and glanced around him, his jacket in one hand.

"Oh, let me hang that up for you." She stepped forward.

When he handed the jacket to her, she felt how it was warm from his body. That realization did something to her, making her want him to warm her the way he had the lucky jacket.

She hung it on the hook by the door on top of her own and turned back. "Are you at the submarine base in New London?"

"No. I'm stationed down in Virginia, but I grew up here and my parents still live in Connecticut."

"Which is why you were here for Thanksgiving and now for Christmas."

"Exactly. I come home for holidays when I can. I lucked out this year to get two in a row." He grinned.

She'd been the one to luck out this year.

Holy moly, what luck she'd had. Running into Mr. Hunky and Handsome at the store and then accidentally texting him.

Wow. It was all so much to take in she was happy to lead him to the sofa and be able to sit down herself.

He glanced at the evergreen that took up the whole corner of the room. "I like your tree."

She looked at the tree herself and cringed, remembering how she and Nikki had had to squash the living room furniture together to make it all fit. "I know it's too big for the apartment, but it was so pretty."

"I've been living in the barracks for over a decade, so I've never had a tree of my own. Besides, no Christmas tree can ever be too big, in my opinion. Well, unless it's taller than the ceiling, but then a few strokes of a saw can fix that problem." Nathan grinned.

"I agree." Her heart fluttered as his gaze settled upon her. Feeling self-conscious, she raised the paper cup to her lips and took a sip of the hot cocoa. Rich, chocolaty goodness filled her mouth. "This is really good. Where'd you get it?"

"There's a little shop on the outskirts of town. I was lucky it wasn't closed for the night, but I guess since it's almost Christmas, they stay open late. Anyway, it's the strangest place. They sell everything from antiques to gifts to chicken feed to homemade pies. They make the cocoa themselves from scratch. Real milk and chocolate. None of the powdered stuff."

"I know that store. I went in and looked around once." She'd wanted to check out the antiques. George had been with her so she'd rushed through and didn't get to see everything. "I can't believe I never knew they sold hot chocolate."

"Only during the holidays. I always make sure to go in when I'm lucky enough to be home."

"Thank you for sharing it with me."

"My pleasure. Thank you for sharing your tree with me." His eyes met and held hers.

"You're welcome." Noelle felt overwhelmed and broke the eye contact, instead glancing at the tree, rather than into the soulful eyes of the man sitting at the opposite end of the sofa.

"I have to tell you, I was pretty surprised when I got your first text. I mean, I knew you had my number because of the recipe—which was great, by the way—but after a couple of weeks had passed, getting your text was a surprise. A good one, but unexpected."

Guilt overwhelmed her. She liked him too much not to tell him the truth. "Nathan, I have to confess something."

She raised her gaze in time to see him lift his brows as he said, "Okay."

"I, um . . ." She blew out a breath. "Wow, this is really hard."

A frown creased his brow. He put his cup down on the coffee table. "Just say it, Noelle. I'm a big boy. I can handle anything you have to say. I like you, but believe me, I'd rather know now if you're not interested, before I get in any deeper."

Her emotions were like a roller coaster as she soared at his words, and then dropped low as she tried to make her own confession.

She'd never wanted him to think she wasn't interested. Quite the opposite. Her interest in him was the one thing she was completely sure of in this whole mess.

"No, Nathan, I am interested." Noelle sighed. "It's not that. I just don't know how to tell you the reason I texted. . . ."

Usually she could babble with the best of them, but right now her words failed her—and at the worst possible time.

He reached out and took the cup out of her hand. After placing it on the table next to his, he held both of her hands. His were warm and slightly rough as he held her in a firm grasp. "Just take your time."

She nodded. "Okay. But it's a long story."

One corner of his mouth tipped up in a crooked smile. "That's okay. I've got all night."

Noelle swallowed hard. "Okay. It all started on Thanksgiving. The day I first met you . . ."

CHAPTER 8

Nathan remained quiet as he sat and listened to Noelle's odd tale. The cast of characters was vast enough that he had to pay extra attention just to keep them all straight. There were George and Aunt Anna and a sister named Nikki, her parents, her ex's parents, and some assorted brothers thrown in.

Then came the part about the fake boyfriend phone app and the story took a turn for the surreal.

Even so, he held her hand and let her talk as she explained how she'd set up a contact in her phone for the app so she could pretend to get texts from this Build-A-Boyfriend in front of her ex at her parents' party.

"So when Nikki told me I had to pick a name for my fake boyfriend and create a contact in my phone, I somehow set it up using your phone number instead of the app phone number. So when I sent that first text to *Nathan* in my contact list, it was supposed to go to the Build-A-Boyfriend app, but it went to you instead."

At that point he held up one hand to stop her. "Wait. Hang on a second."

Drawing in a breath, she nodded. "Yes?"

"I got lost at the part about how the app contact got saved under my name."

She pursed her lips together. Her gaze dropped before she brought it up to meet his. "I named him Nathan."

His eyes widened. "You named your Build-A-Boyfriend after me?"

Noelle cringed. "Yes. That's weird, right? I'm sorry. Nikki was pressuring me and I couldn't think of any other name." Her cheeks flooded with color.

She couldn't think of any other man's name except for his? That had to be a good sign. He'd made an impression. At least enough that his name had been on her mind.

He couldn't help his smile. "Noelle, don't apologize. I'm flattered."

"You are?"

"Hell yeah, I am." He couldn't be happier, but still, why did this woman have to fake a boyfriend? He shook his head. "But seriously, Noelle, why in the world would you think you needed to hire some rent-a-boyfriend service? Guys must be knocking down your door."

"Um, no. Not so much. Of course, that could be because I spent the past five years off the market in a dead-end relationship."

The fact remained, what the hell was wrong with the men in this town that they'd let a girl like Noelle slip by now that she was available?

Their loss was his gain. It didn't matter how or

why she'd come to text him that night. What mattered was what had happened afterward.

All those texts where they'd laughed together while watching the same movie meant something, even if they had been a thousand miles apart. And then the phone conversation the following day—that had been all him and her. No app involved.

He squeezed her hands, happy to be here with her now. "I'm not going to complain. I'm glad you signed up for that app since it led you to me. And I'm glad the men around here are idiots and didn't scoop you up the minute you dumped George because that left the path clear for me." He narrowed his eyes. "It is clear, right? No feelings left for your ex?"

Not that he'd let that stand in his way. He just needed to know what sort of battle was in front of him.

"For George? Oh, no. None." She shook her head, looking adamant. "We might be able to be friends again. That would be easiest since our parents are friends. But as far as me and him? No. That was never right. I guess I just wanted it to be, so I couldn't see that it actually wasn't."

He watched her face for a moment, evaluating whether she was being completely honest with herself. When it came to love and life, people would sometimes lie to themselves, maybe even more often than they lied to others.

Finally, he asked, "And this, between us. Does this feel right?"

"Yes." She hesitated before going on.

Compelled to get her to elaborate, he prompted, "But?"

"I'm afraid to trust my feelings after the last time. How could I be so colossally wrong about me and George for so long, but still rely on my instincts now?"

"I'm not afraid of instincts. In fact, I live by mine. They've saved my life more than a few times. I've learned to trust them. To depend on them."

"And what are your instincts telling you now?" She watched him, waiting.

He didn't make her wait long for his answer. He knew exactly how he felt about the two of them. The only question was, did she feel the same?

Nathan leaned in a couple of inches. "They're telling me I should risk getting slapped and kiss you."

She drew in a breath and met his gaze. "Your instincts are wrong."

He lifted a brow. "They are?"

"Yes, because I'm not going to slap you if you kiss me."

Nathan smiled. "Good to know."

He abandoned holding her hands in favor of cradling her face in his palms.

As he closed the small distance between them, he had to think that fate worked in strange ways, but who was he to question it?

Little did he know all those weeks ago that doing his mother the favor of running out for cranberries when he'd always hated homemade cranberry sauce would lead to this moment.

He made contact with her soft, yielding lips and there was no way in hell he was going to complain about whatever force larger than himself had brought them together.

Moving one hand to her back, he brought her in tighter against him while he tangled the fingers of his other hand in her hair.

Tilting his head, he kissed her deeper. Harder. He'd been working a lot, which meant he'd also denied himself pleasures such as kissing a woman.

That was as good an excuse as any for why he took their first kiss from casual to explosive in thirty seconds or less.

Before he knew what had happened, he had the fabric of her sweater in a death grip in his fist and his tongue was engaged in an erotic tango with hers that had him breathless.

Noelle made a small sound and he realized he'd fisted her hair, as well, and was tugging her head back as her body bowed beneath the force of his kiss.

Nathan pulled back and, smothering a curse at his own behavior, dropped his hold on her.

For over a decade he'd given his all to the military at the expense of himself. Normally that wasn't a problem. Tonight, it had him ready to devour Noelle like a starving man did a juicy steak.

He drew in a breath and let it out. "I'm sorry. I don't know what got into me."

That wasn't exactly true. He knew. Very bad, but oh, so beautiful thoughts about him and her together were what had gotten into him, invading his brain until the fantasy had melded with reality.

He'd spun a bit out of control for a moment, but he was back on an even keel now. Both feet were on the ground and his hands were safely planted on his thighs as he sat with a safe distance between them.

"Don't be sorry."

Before he could respond to her, she was on the move. The next thing he knew, Noelle was sitting astride his lap facing him.

While she straddled him and he tried to absorb what had just happened, he realized he had his hands braced on each of her hips. He wasn't sure whether he'd put them there to keep her away or close. Either way, it was obvious she had plans of her own, regardless of his.

She ran both of her palms up his chest. Green eyes narrowed, she followed the path of her hands as they roamed over the shirt that covered him.

He couldn't fault her for focusing on his chest when he was doing the same with hers.

Her deep breaths had her breasts rising and falling beneath the white sweater that was made of the softest material he'd ever laid his hands on. It was all he could do not to lean in, lift that sweater, and take her into his mouth.

He was breathing pretty heavily himself as his body, in a very obvious way, expressed his appreciation of how good it felt to have her pressed against him. There was no fighting or hiding his reaction to her, so he figured he might as well roll with it and enjoy the moment.

As she leaned in, he tipped his head back to accept her kiss. It was a whole lot more civil than his had been, but no less needy. He felt the desire inside her, held in check by more willpower than he'd shown.

Since she most likely hadn't spent this summer and fall deployed and celibate, he decided to give himself a break for getting too enthusiastic.

With her lips pressed to his, memories of that hellish deployment were fading fast. With his hands on her hips as she pressed tighter against him, all those months spent training foreign fighters to defeat terrorism disappeared.

Noelle working his mouth with lips and tongue alone would have been enough to have his pulse pounding, but when she set her hips in motion and began making small circles against his cock, his blood rushed fast enough to make him light-headed.

Cupping his face in her hands, she broke away from the kiss. She asked, "Is this bad?"

"No. This is very good." He kept his hands firmly on her hips, torn between holding her tighter against him and fearing he'd embarrass himself by coming in his pants if he did.

She smiled. "I mean because we hardly know each other."

"Not true. I've known you for almost a whole month. We've even exchanged recipes. That has to count for something, right?"

"That's right. You know, I'd never given that recipe out to anyone else before that day. Not even my sister."

He lifted a brow, feeling extra guilty he'd only been in possession of her secret recipe for a few weeks and he'd already shared it with his mother and one of his teammates. "Really? I'm honored. Thank you."

Nathan rested his head against the back cushion and waited, very happily enjoying her weight on him.

The next move was hers. She could call a halt to this unexpected make-out session. That would suck, but he'd be fine with whatever she decided.

Noelle let out a breath and looked torn by indecision. "I just don't want you to think I make a habit of doing this."

"Noelle, I don't think that at all."

"Really?" she asked.

She'd spent five years with one guy and he could tell just from what he knew of her that she hadn't been running around while she'd been with him. He had no problem reassuring her of that.

"Really."

She bit her lip. "Can we stay here?"

Stay in her apartment, where she was sitting in his lap? Or go out and be surrounded by strangers while they sat in separate chairs? Yeah, no choice to be made there.

"Sure." He nodded. "I'm happy to stay in."

"I meant here on the sofa." She looked embarrassed at the request.

He liked this woman and he'd happily take any time he could get with her and be grateful for it. If that time wasn't in the bedroom, that was fine.

Nathan ran a hand over her cheek, brushing away a stray piece of hair. "Okay."

When she reached for the bottom of her sweater and pulled it over and off, he paused, thoroughly confused now that she was straddling him while wearing nothing but a bra and jeans.

"Oh no. Why are you frowning?" She pressed her sweater toward her chest, looking horrified and making him fear she was going to put it back on.

Nathan shook his head to alleviate her concern. "No. I'm fine. This is most definitely fine. I just thought when you asked if we could stay here on the sofa, that was because you wanted our clothes to stay on. But believe me, I am perfectly on board with this plan, too."

She dropped her gaze away from his. She was obviously holding something in.

They had a chance for a good thing between them, and not just tonight but for the long term. He was not going to let shyness or insecurity or whatever this breakup had done to her mess this up.

Nathan ran his hands up and down her bare arms. "Noelle. Talk."

"It's just that I really love Christmas and I've always wanted to—you know—in front of the tree." She glanced at the glowing tree in the corner and then back to him. "But some people have said that I was crazy for that."

He controlled his smile. "I really love Christmas, too. And I don't think it's crazy at all. In fact, I would have no problem with that."

Hell, he'd do it under the tree while dressed in a Santa suit and singing Christmas carols if it made her happy. It would definitely make him happy, that was for sure.

"There's something else."

After all the twists and turns this night had already taken, Nathan couldn't even imagine what was coming next. He was well trained in controlling his expressions when necessary, though. He employed his training now as he wondered what other surprises this woman held.

"All right."

"Before, when you first kissed me and you got kind of forceful—"

He interrupted her. "I know. I'm sorry. It won't happen again."

"No. I mean, I liked it. George was always kind of . . . passive."

There was no schooling his expression now as

surprise turned quickly into raw, heart-pounding need.

That was all she needed to say. Grabbing and holding her tight, Nathan stood, lifting Noelle with him. She squealed in surprise.

"Floor or couch?" he asked.

"What?" She squeaked out the question while clutching her arms around his neck.

"In your Christmas tree sex fantasies, are you on the floor or the couch?"

"It's during a snowstorm on a bearskin rug in front of a roaring fireplace with the tree next to us."

He knew without glancing around them that that exact scenario was not an option. He cocked a brow. "Got any alternate versions of this fantasy we can fulfill without driving to a ski lodge in Vermont?"

She smiled. "The sofa is fine."

He spun back toward the sofa, laid her down, and stood to start undressing. "Good choice. I'd rather the two of us didn't have bruises and rug burns the first time I meet your parents. You're going to appreciate having the cushions under you for this, because I can assure you, I'm anything but passive."

Her eyes widened at his declaration, until he dropped his pants. Then her gaze followed the action and she looked far more interested in what was beneath them.

Passive George was probably the type to keep the lights off and his socks on. Nathan made sure to do the opposite and was shortly standing in front of her lit by the glow of the Christmas tree and as naked as the day he was born.

There were still too many clothes between them, though, and they were all hers.

Not a problem. He was both determined and capable. He had her stripped of her jeans, bra, and panties in no time.

He was about to lower himself over her when a realization hit. He let out a curse. "I didn't bring anything with me."

His lack of protection wasn't going to ruin tonight, but it would sure put a halt to the pending main event for a while. He would have to get dressed, drive to a store, buy some condoms, and then get back here, all while this very hot, naked woman waited for him.

"There are condoms in the drawer of the nightstand by my bed."

His attention whipped to Noelle. "They were your ex's?"

"Yes." She bit her lip and made him want to bite it, too. "Is that a problem?"

He considered it for barely a second before deciding. "Nope. No problem at all. Be right back."

Yeah, she was probably laughing at the pale skin of his naked ass as he sprinted for the bedroom, but he didn't care. He had no shame. Fate had given him both Noelle and condoms when he needed them, and he was a happy man.

CHAPTER 9

Noelle loved the feel of being crushed between the weight of Nathan's hard, muscle-bound body and the sofa. But that satisfaction was nothing compared to the feeling as he plunged his length into her with one hard stroke.

She gasped, drawing in a breath with a hiss.

"You all right?" he asked, breathless above her.

"Yes." She was so much more than just all right. She grabbed his ass with both hands and pulled him in deeper. "Don't stop."

"Believe me. I have no intention of stopping."

Every stroke sent sparks through her. The need she'd ignored for so long burned uncontrolled inside her, stoked by Nathan's desire, which mirrored her own.

They were perfectly matched. She took all he could give and vice versa.

She wondered if the apartment walls were thin enough that the neighbors could hear. She'd never considered that before tonight. This was the first time there'd been anything happening in this apartment that warranted her crying out loudly enough for the neighbors to hear.

He was sweating and she was breathless by the time she felt him stiffen over her. He plunged deep and held her close as he shuddered.

That unlocked something inside her. An orgasm hit that had her clutching him close. Her body clenched his with pulses that continued long after his climax was done. She was panting and weak by the time her body relaxed and the aftershocks ceased.

They stayed just like that, him over her, holding her, for what felt like a long time, but she had no desire for either of them to move.

Finally, Nathan lifted up on one elbow. "Wow. That was . . ."

She nodded. "Yeah. It was."

Indescribable was what it was.

He rolled off her and flung his forearm over his face. "I'm hoping that was just a fluke. Because if this is what it's like every time between us, there's no way I can go back to Virginia and concentrate on my job."

As Nathan blew out a breath and looked miserable because the sex between them had been so good, Noelle considered his words. "I guess we can do it again and see. Maybe it *was* a fluke." She lifted one shoulder.

He dropped his arm and leveled a look at her. "Can you give me maybe five minutes first?"

She smiled. "I'll give you ten. I want to drink my cocoa anyway."

He let out a laugh. "Can you grab mine, too?"

"Sure." She reached for his cup, loving how he

liked the same things she did. And really loving how he was anything but passive.

After handing off his cup, she reached for her own, holding it in both hands. It had cooled off, but she wasn't sure she had the strength to walk to the microwave.

Eh, it would be worth it.

She swung her legs over the edge of the sofa and stood. "Give me. I'll reheat them."

His eyes widened. "You will? You really are the girl of my dreams."

She rolled her eyes. "Oh, hush or no whipped cream for you."

Nathan's brows rose high. "Whipped cream? Well, hey now. You never mentioned whipped cream. That could be interesting."

She shook her head as she walked to the kitchen naked and strangely not feeling all that self-conscious.

A month ago, she would have scrambled for the throw to wrap around herself.

Who was she kidding? A month ago, there was no way she would have been naked in the kitchen or having sex on the sofa.

Reaching up, she grabbed two mugs from the cabinet. After pouring the cocoa into each, she popped them into the microwave and set it for two minutes.

When she turned, Nathan stood directly behind her.

"How did you sneak up on me without my hearing you?"

"I'm stealthy." He grinned while wrapping those big, warm hands around her waist.

"Yes, you are."

Nathan leaned low and nuzzled her neck before moving to her ear. "I like that you cook naked."

She enjoyed his groan as she slipped her hands around him to grab his very firm butt. "I don't. This is the first time. George would have never approved of nudity near food."

He pulled back to shoot her a look. "George is an idiot. You do realize that some men might not like it that you talk about your ex when they're about to kiss you, right?"

"I'm sorry."

"No. Don't apologize. I don't mind it at all. The more you tell me about him, the more I'm convinced you two were completely and totally wrong for each other. Besides, I enjoy knowing what things he wouldn't approve of so I can make sure we go ahead and do them. For instance, I bet he really wouldn't have liked this."

Nathan tightened his grip on her waist and lifted and Noelle found herself sitting on the counter.

Her naked ass on the same surface where she prepared food? George would have flipped out and then gotten the bleach to sanitize the area.

"No. He wouldn't have."

The microwave dinged, drawing Nathan's attention. He pulled open the door and took out one of the mugs. Dipping in his finger, he swirled it through the warm cocoa and then rubbed the chocolate mixture over one of her nipples. Leaning down toward her breast, Nathan glanced up. "And this?"

As he latched his mouth over her peaked, chocolate-coated nipple, Noelle hissed in a breath. "Nope. He would have never done that."

Nathan pulled back. "And I bet he'd really hate me doing this."

He pushed her thighs wide and lowered his head. When his tongue connected with her core, she gasped. "Yeah. He didn't believe in doing this at all, not even in a bed."

Nathan lifted his head, brows up. "Then you had better grab on to something and hang on tight."

Minutes later Noelle was writhing beneath his mouth, riding out possibly the most intense orgasm she'd ever felt and in real danger of falling off the counter if his firm grip hadn't held her in place.

It only proved to her that Nathan had been right about everything.

She should have held on to something—and George was, indeed, an idiot.

CHAPTER 10

"So I don't think that first time was a fluke."
Noelle made that announcement while sitting opposite Nathan on the sofa.

She looked very tempting wrapped in a blanket and cradling the mug of hot cocoa they'd had to microwave a second time after they'd finished christening the kitchen.

Nathan downed a swallow from his own mug and then drew in a deep breath. "Yeah. I'm starting to accept that."

"How long before you have to go back to Virginia?"

She must be thinking the same thing he was—how much his leaving was going to suck. She didn't even realize his going back to Virginia was the least of their concerns. There was a good chance he'd end up shipped off to the other side of the world by Valentine's Day.

"Next week. I'm leaving Monday. I have to be back on base Tuesday by noon."

"Oh."

She sounded so unhappy, he reached out and pulled her gently to him. "Don't worry. We can talk on the phone, and text, and video-chat."

"I know. It's not that. It's just that Monday is my birthday."

"It is?" He pulled back to look down at her.

"Yeah. The day after Christmas. That's why my parents named me Noelle."

"Do you have plans?" His mind was already spinning as he tried to decide whether he should leave Connecticut early Tuesday morning instead so he could spend her birthday with her.

It was a risk. He'd be taking a chance on no bad weather or traffic that would prevent him from making it back to the base by noon.

She lifted one shoulder. "I'll probably just go to my parents' house for dinner."

"What if I didn't leave until Tuesday morning?"

"That would be nice." She wasn't quite as excited as he'd thought she'd be. Finally, she continued. "Any chance you're coming back home for New Year's Eve?"

The reason for her sadness became evident with that question.

Driving to Virginia only to turn around and come back four days later would be a lot of damn time spent on the road, so he hadn't been planning on it. Especially not for a holiday he'd always thought was just a lot of hype and expectations that failed to be met.

Then again, he'd made the decision not to be in Connecticut for New Year's Eve before Noelle.

Everything felt different now, but it wasn't as simple as just his wanting to be here with her for that midnight kiss. Even if he put in a request to extend his official leave, and command did approve it, there was still a chance he could get recalled for a mission.

He hugged her tighter with the one arm he had around her shoulders. "I can't make any promises, but I'll see what I can manage."

"Okay." She turned in his arms. "I don't mean to sound greedy. I'm just happy you're here now and for Christmas."

She was so sweet, it made him want to hold her tight and never let go. Except to maybe punch anyone who'd ever made her feel bad.

"You go ahead and be greedy." When it came to her and the limited time they had together, he sure as hell intended to be.

He took her mug and put it with his on the coffee table before snaking both of his hands beneath the blanket wrapped around her.

A buzzing invaded Nathan's concentration. He halted in his path to kiss her, poised just short of her lips. "It sounds like you're getting a call."

Her lids hooded her eyes as they met his gaze. "They can leave a message."

"All right." He closed the distance and finally claimed her lips, kissing her thoroughly until the buzzing started again. He pulled back. "You wanna get that?"

His lips twitched with a smile when he saw Noelle scowl deeply as she said, "No."

"It might be important. I think you should check."

"Fine." She let out a huff and then frowned as she looked around her.

"What's wrong?" he asked.

"I don't know where my phone is."

He'd been in plenty of situations where his ears were his best asset, so he figured he should be able to track down one cell phone set on vibrate in a two-room apartment.

Stilling, he listened and determined which direction the noise was coming from. It was close but muffled, which was deceiving. It made the sound seem to come from a greater distance away.

Taking a chance on a hunch, he shoved his hand between the sofa's arm and seat cushion. He emerged victorious with the cell phone in his hand. It had already stopped vibrating but at least it was located.

He held it up for Noelle to see. "Yours, I'll assume."

"Yes. I don't know how it got down there, though."

"I have some idea." He smiled.

There had been some pretty energetic activity taking place on that sofa. It was no wonder things had gotten a little tossed around.

She looked embarrassed as she reached out. "I guess. Thank you for finding it."

"My pleasure." He'd happily do all sorts of things for this woman. Open jars. Take out the garbage. Scrub her back in the shower.

Really, the list of things he'd love to do for her was endless. If only their time together was, as well.

He was going to call command tomorrow and request that extra leave. Time was one thing that was too precious to waste.

While Nathan was making that decision, Noelle had been checking her missed calls.

"Everything all right?" he asked.

A part of him wanted to make sure it wasn't good old George trying to reunite with her.

If it was, George was going to be sorely disappointed, because Nathan didn't give up easily on anything. Certainly not on a woman like Noelle.

A woman who, by all indications, was meant to be with him. They'd already learned they liked so many of the same things. He looked forward to learning even more—and George was not getting in his way.

She glanced up from the cell. "It's just my sister."

"Twice in a row. You sure nothing is wrong?"

"I doubt it. She would have left a message if it was important, but she didn't. I've just been dodging her calls the past day—or two."

"Why?"

She avoided meeting his gaze. "You."

"Me?" He widened his eyes. "Why?"

"Because I didn't think she'd approve of my meeting you."

"Why not?" He was a likeable guy. People loved him. Not usually the enemy, but everyone else.

"It's not you in particular. It's because until tonight I thought you were—"

"Your Build-A-Boyfriend gone rogue?" he guessed.

"Exactly."

Their getting together certainly had been unconventional on all counts. "Well, now that you know I'm not, are you going to tell your sister? I mean, I'm assuming I'll meet her at the party."

"Yes, I'll tell her."

"When?" He cocked a brow.

"Eventually."

Nathan crossed his arms and leveled a gaze on

her. "You really should call her now. She's probably worried about you."

"Fine. I'll call. If I don't, she might drive over and just show up."

"Good idea." Nathan was guessing that her sister probably had a key so she could walk right in and find them naked, or worse, in the middle of doing something no sister ever wanted to see.

Noelle looked so adorable, naked and pouting because he was making her call her sister, he couldn't resist wrapping his arms around her and the blanket still draped over her.

He pulled her close with one arm and reached for his mug with the other since he might as well enjoy his cocoa while he waited.

"Hey. You called?" Noelle pulled the phone away from her ear and he heard why. Her sister was reading her the riot act loudly enough he could hear it sitting next to her. "Nikki, I'm sorry. I won't not answer and not call you back again. Okay?"

He took a sip from the mug as Noelle listened to the response from her sister. Nikki was talking at a much lower volume, so he had to assume she was calming down.

"Can I call you back in the morning and we'll talk about it then?" Noelle's eyes cut to him. "Yes, I promise I'll call you. Good night."

He waited for her to put the phone down. "Talk about what in the morning? Me?"

"Yes. Kind of." She grabbed his cocoa out of his hand and drank the remainder before putting the empty mug on the table.

He had every intention of drinking hers, since she'd finished his, but first he wanted her to explain. "And? Go on."

She drew in a breath. "We had plans to make up a story about how I met my Build-A-Boyfriend so I'd be prepared for any questions at the party."

He smiled, happy there'd be no need for a fake story because they had a real one. "See. Now you don't have to lie."

"Not about you, but I'd rather not tell anyone I texted you by accident, thinking you were the fake boyfriend app Nikki had signed me up for to deceive my ex and our relatives."

He dipped his head. "Yeah, okay. I'll agree to leaving that part out."

It wasn't the most flattering thing for him that she'd had his phone number all those weeks and had only texted it by mistake.

That raised a good question. "Hey, let me ask you something. Why didn't you text me? On purpose, I mean. You had the number."

"Why didn't you text me?" she countered.

"Because I was sure you were already taken, and might I remind you that you *were* taken at the time. And don't avoid the question. Why didn't you text me after you broke up with George?"

She shrugged. "I wasn't exactly feeling all that great about myself after the breakup. And look at you. You're like Adonis or something. Who'd have thought you were single?"

Adonis, huh? He smiled at the compliment but had to set the record straight. Little did she know he had been single for as long as she'd been tethered to the unimaginative George. "Well, I was single, so you could have texted. But now that you finally did, I'm happy to attend the party as your real boyfriend so you don't need a cyber one."

She bit her lip. "And when we're not at the party?"

"Will I still be your boyfriend, you mean?"

Noelle swallowed hard. "Yes."

"I hope so."

"I hope so, too."

He blew out a breath. "Good. I'm glad that's settled."

"You might not be once you meet my family. Aunt Anna can be quite a tyrant. And George's brothers are probably going to put you through the wringer."

Nathan snorted. He'd been fighting actual tyrants and men out to kill him for over a decade as part of an elite, highly trained team. He could handle Aunt Anna and George's brothers. "I think I'll be all right. Now come here and let's talk."

He moved to pull her closer, but she resisted. "What are we talking about?"

The suspiciousness in her tone had him laughing. "Everything. What you do for a living. How old you'll be for your birthday on Monday. What your parents are like. Do you have any other brothers and sisters besides Nikki? How many other exes have you got?"

She looked at him like he was nuts. "You really want to know all of that? Now?"

"Yup." He nodded.

An adorable wrinkle appeared between her brows. "But why?"

"Because I take my position as your boyfriend very seriously. That's why."

Giving in, she lifted a shoulder. "Okay."

As she drew in a breath before launching into her answers to his many questions, he leaned forward. He grabbed her mug off the table and took a sip, smiling when she narrowed her eyes at him for stealing her drink.

Nathan lowered the mug. "How about we go shopping tomorrow and get more cocoa?"

"Can we really?" Her whole expression lit at the suggestion.

He laughed. "Of course. We can do whatever you want."

They'd only just started really getting to know each other, but still, he was certain he could spend a whole life making this woman happy, just to be the reason for that expression of pure joy on her face.

CHAPTER II

"Noelle Christina Chambers, spill. Why have you been avoiding my calls and acting so weird these past few days?"

Nikki only used that tone and Noelle's full name when she was serious about something.

"Are you sitting down?" Noelle asked.

"Now you have me even more concerned. Why do I have to sit down? What's going on?" Nikki's voice rose higher.

"Nathan is real."

"What do you mean, real? What did you do?"

"Nothing." Noelle rethought that answer. "Okay, maybe I did do something, but it was a good thing."

"You'd better stop with the riddles and start talking or I'm coming over there."

Since Nathan wasn't there any longer, it wouldn't be horrible if Nikki showed up, but Noelle was expecting him later that morning. He'd promised to be back for their shopping trip as soon as he'd spent some time with his parents.

A man who loved his parents and liked to shop—where had he been her whole life? He was perfect. But before she could get back to being with him, she had to defuse her sister.

"Stop interrupting and I'll tell you everything."

Nikki let out an audible breath. "Okay, fine. Talk."

"So remember that guy from Thanksgiving who gave me his cranberries? The original Nathan whom I named my Build-A-Boyfriend after?"

"Yes."

"Well, his number was in my phone because I'd texted him the recipe. And the Build-A-Boyfriend number was in my phone, too, from that first text from the app. I guess I mixed them up and—" Noelle stopped at her sister's gasp.

"You've been texting the real Nathan instead of the app?"

"Yes." The silence on the other end of the phone prompted Noelle to say, "Nik? You still there?"

"Yeah. Just trying to absorb it all. What's going to happen with the real Nathan? Are you going to meet up? Did you tell him about the app?" Nikki might have been momentarily speechless, but it didn't last long as she followed up with a barrage of questions, some of which Noelle was less than keen to answer.

She didn't know where to start so she just dove right in and braced for the backlash. "He knows. I told him last night when he was here."

"What? He was there in your apartment?" Nikki's

exclamation had Noelle pulling the cell farther from her ear.

"Yeah. And we're kind of—well, more than kind of—dating. He's coming to Mom and Dad's party. And we're going out Christmas shopping together today."

"Oh my God. I can't believe you."

"I know. You have every right to be upset. I took a chance inviting him over, but it all worked out." Noelle braced for her sister's lecture.

"I'm upset because only you could sign up for a fake boyfriend and end up with a real one. You have everything. Job. Apartment. Boyfriend. Meanwhile, I'm still single, still in school, still working in a crappy, dead-end job, and still living with Mom and Dad."

Noelle couldn't help her smile. Her life was pretty amazing. She tried to temper her glee. "I'm sorry, Nik."

Nikki let out a deep sigh. "It's okay. I'll forgive you. It'll be worth it to see George's face when you walk into the party with the hottie from the store."

She laughed. Yeah, though it was bitchy and she shouldn't, Noelle had a feeling she was going to enjoy that moment herself. Christmas Eve was certainly going to be interesting.

That thought had Noelle drawing in a gasp. "I need to get Nathan a Christmas gift."

"What are you going to get him?"

"I have no idea." She sighed.

Getting gifts for George had been easy. She pretty much bought him a new tie or some gloves.

Practical. Useful. Boring. All the things he liked best.

But Nathan—what could she get a man like him? A man who took what he wanted and gave back even more than he took. She thought back to their time spent together last night and felt her cheeks warm at the memories.

She was going to have to think about this and decide—fast. There wasn't much time left. Maybe she'd be inspired while they were together today.

The sound of a knock had her spinning toward the door. "I gotta go. I think he's here."

"Call me as soon as you get back. And take pictures while you're out to post online."

Noelle rolled her eyes. She didn't need to post pictures anymore to fake having a boyfriend, because she had a real one. But it would be nice to have the photos for herself when Nathan went back to Virginia.

"Okay. Now I really gotta go. I'll call you later." Noelle hung up without waiting for Nikki's good-bye and tossed the phone onto the counter. She trotted to the door and yanked it open. One look at Nathan standing in the hall had her smiling. "Hey."

"Good morning." His low, husky greeting was followed by a warm embrace and a kiss that took her breath away. He backed them both up into the apartment and pushed the door shut without breaking their lip-lock. She was pressed up against the door, lost in a kiss she wished would go on forever, when he pulled back and smiled. "Ready to go shopping?"

She had been, before, but not now after that welcome. They wouldn't be going anywhere anytime soon if he kissed her like that one more time.

Noelle blew out a breath and tried to get a grip on herself. "Yeah. We can go."

"Good." His smile broadened into a wide grin that was infectious.

"You're in a good mood."

"You can't even imagine. It's been a good morning so far."

She laughed at his enthusiasm. "Are you going to tell me why?"

The day had barely begun, so she couldn't imagine what had happened already to put him in such good spirits.

"Nope." He pressed his lips firmly together.

"No?" She drew back in surprise.

"Not yet. You have to wait. It's a surprise."

"A surprise for me?"

"Maybe." He grabbed her hand and squeezed. "Now, put on your coat and let's go."

She held firm, shaking her head when he tried to hand her the coat hung by the door. "I want to know now."

All he did was smile at her declaration. "Ah, so you're one of *those* people."

"What people?" She pulled her hand out of his to fold her arms over her chest.

"The kind who shake their gifts to try to figure out what's in the box. The kind who can't stand not knowing something even if it ruins the surprise." He lifted a brow. "Am I wrong?"

She scowled. "No."

He laughed and pulled her to him with a hand

on each of her arms. "It's okay. I'll enjoy torturing you with the suspense even more knowing that. Now, come on. There are gifts to buy and cocoa to drink."

Nathan stuck by his resolve and didn't tell her the secret. Not during their day of shopping. Not after she plied him with rum-spiked eggnog. Not even when she tried to pry the secret out of him with what she considered to be some pretty creative sexual persuasion.

The man only smiled and shook his head when she pushed him for an answer. And then told her to keep trying since he was enjoying her methods.

It was infuriating. He was able to withstand anything she came up with. But he was also adorable and sexy as hell.

The more she got to know him, the more she realized she was already half in love with this man.

Maybe more than just half.

By the time the day of the party dawned, Noelle was ready to give up trying to discover whatever his surprise was.

Besides, she had bigger worries. It was Christmas Eve and she still had no gift for Nathan.

They'd spent hours together over the past few days, but no idea for a present seemed appropriate. Not for the man who completed her.

Finding Nathan was like discovering the final piece of a puzzle that had been missing her whole life.

She was bemoaning her lack of inspiration, listlessly stirring her second cup of coffee of the day with a candy cane, when her cell buzzed.

"Happy Christmas Eve!" Nikki's chipper greeting had Noelle sighing.

Noelle drew in a weary breath. "Yeah. To you, too."

"What's wrong with you?" Nikki asked.

"I still have no clue what to get Nathan." She pulled out the candy cane and popped the end into her mouth.

"Well, you'd better hurry. The clock is ticking."

"Thanks, but I know that." Noelle scowled.

Why couldn't she think of anything? She was an expert shopper. A Christmas aficionado. This should be easy.

"Are you getting here early to help set up?" Nikki asked.

The question elicited a fresh wave of guilt. She usually helped decorate for the party. This year, between the drama of George and the whirlwind of her romance with Nathan, she hadn't lifted a finger to help her family.

Nathan was meeting her at the party, so she was free to go over early. "Yes. Let me get myself together and I'll be over."

She glanced at the time display on the microwave and sighed. The morning was almost gone already. She'd been up late with Nathan—again.

Noelle had no complaints about spending time with him, but it meant she'd woken late.

How was she supposed to help set up for the party, shop for a gift, and get ready for tonight? It would be really tight. The stores were going to be crazy. The traffic, the lines . . . but it didn't really matter since she had not one idea of what to shop for anyway.

"Okay, good. We can brainstorm what to do about a gift when you get here—not that I'll be much help since you won't let me meet him until tonight. Oh, and pack your makeup and outfit for tonight and we can get dressed here together the way we used to."

That was actually a good idea. And right about now, Noelle needed all the good ideas she could get.

Nathan checked the address on the mailbox and
pulled his car along the curb in front of a house
festooned with garlands of fresh greens lit by tiny
white lights and tied in big red bows.

Noelle's love of Christmas must be hereditary.
Her parents' house looked amazing all decked out
for the holiday.

Eager to see her, he grabbed the bag he'd stashed
on the floor behind his seat and then slammed the
door.

He made his way up the path and had just raised
his fist to knock when the door opened. Two guys,
each a head shorter than Nathan, stood in the
doorway holding bottles of beer in their hands.

"Uh, hey. I'm here for the party," he offered
when they didn't move to invite him in.

One frowned and looked him up and down,
clearly sizing him up. "Who are you?"

Not exactly a welcoming committee, were they?
He answered anyway. "I'm Noelle's boyfriend."

"Uh, no, you're not. She's been dating our brother, George, for years."

If these two clowns were his brothers, Nathan couldn't wait to get a look at George himself. "She *was* dating your brother. They broke up."

"No way." The one guy turned to his brother. "They broke up and he didn't tell us?"

The other guy shrugged. "I don't know."

Still, no one had made a move to let Nathan in. "So I'm gonna come in now."

He didn't give them a chance to argue with that as he turned sideways and slipped between them and into the foyer.

The inside of the house was even more elaborately done up than the outside, with garlands draping the staircase, doorways, and chandelier.

A fire crackled in the fireplace in the room to his left.

Next to the hearth was a sight that had Nathan smiling. She stood speaking to an older man seated in a chair. In her red velvet dress with white fur cuffs and collar, she fit perfectly with the decorations. It was all like a scene from some bygone era.

Noelle turned. Her eyes lit when she spotted him in the hall and she rushed forward. "Hi. You're here."

"I am." No thanks to the tag team of bouncers at the door. He leaned in and dropped a much-too-quick kiss on her lips, since there was no way he could kiss her the way he wanted to here. "You look beautiful."

"Thank you." She dropped her gaze away, looking shy and making him want to take her somewhere to prove to her he spoke the truth.

That would have to wait for later. Instead he handed her the shopping bag. "For you."

She took it, looking surprised. "What's this? We didn't agree to exchange gifts tonight."

"I know, but I've kept you in the dark for long enough. It's the surprise I promised you. Remember? The one you were so eager to hear about." He smiled, recalling some of her more creative efforts. "Open it."

Her eyes widened. "Now? Okay."

She moved to the side table and set down the bag. Reaching in, she pulled out a bottle of champagne. She put it down on the table next to the bag and glanced up at him.

"Keep going. There's more," he prompted.

Reaching inside, she drew out a box containing two champagne glasses.

Still looking confused, she glanced at him again and said, "Thank you."

He laughed. He'd made her suffer long enough. "Those were my clues, but apparently they weren't very good ones. The surprise is that I called command and asked to have my leave extended through January second—and they approved it."

"So you'll be here for New Year's Eve?" Her eyes widened.

"Yes, and for your birthday, too."

He grinned as she leapt forward, tackling him where he leaned against the doorway. "Thank you."

That was more the reaction he'd been looking for. He laughed. "You're welcome."

Leaning in, he dared a kiss that was a little bolder than the last one.

"Who the hell are you?" The male voice broke through Nathan's consciousness as he kissed her.

He lifted his head and saw that his two new friends from the doorway had been joined by a third.

"That's George and his brothers." Noelle's hushed words only confirmed Nathan's suspicions.

"Ah." He turned to face the trio, but left his arm around Noelle's shoulders. "I'm Nathan."

One of the brothers tipped a chin in his direction. "He said he is Noelle's boyfriend."

Noelle moved to step forward, but Nathan kept her firmly tucked beside him as he turned his attention back to George's flushed face.

Nathan took more pleasure than he should at the fact he could easily bench-press the man and not even get winded. "George. I've heard a lot about you."

George scowled and turned to his brothers. "I need a beer."

When the other two Stooges followed George out of the room, Nathan let himself relax.

Next to him, Noelle blew out a breath. "Oh my God, I need a drink. I thought you were going to end up in a fistfight against all three of them."

He let out a snort. "No worries."

If they had been rude enough to start something in the middle of her parents' party, he could have taken out all three without any problem at all.

"You really are perfect."

Nathan let out a laugh at her comment. "No. I'm far from perfect."

"To me you are." She heaved out a sigh. "And I have a confession to make."

He stilled. "The last time you had something to

tell me, it was that you'd texted me by accident and had thought I was someone else the whole time."

"I know. This confession is bad, but not quite as bad as that."

Nathan drew in a breath and braced himself. "Okay. Go on. I'm ready."

"I hate that I have to say this, but there's no way around it. I mean, the stores are all closed. It's going to be Christmas morning in just a few hours, and I have no Christmas gift for you. And it's not for lack of trying, I swear. I racked my brain, but nothing seemed good enough." She frowned when she saw his smile. "You're not disappointed?"

"Disappointed? No." He shook his head while holding her hands in his. "Not at all."

"You're really hard to buy for. I don't know why that is, and I swear I'll learn and get better at knowing what you like. But until then, maybe you can give me a hint of something you want?"

He swallowed hard, as it was clear what he needed to do. "I know exactly what I want for Christmas."

It was crazy. It was too soon and there was a very real chance she'd say no, but he was going to ask the question anyway.

Life was too short. He'd seen that firsthand. Now that he'd found the woman he loved, he wasn't going to waste a moment of time he could be with her.

Nathan dropped down on one knee and heard the collective gasp of those nearby, followed by hushed whispers in the room, which had gone quiet.

"I wasn't planning on this tonight and I don't have a ring, but I know it's what I want. I love you and I want to spend the rest of my life with you. Noelle, will you do me the honor of becoming my wife?"

"What the fu—" George's exclamation was cut off by his brother's backhanded slap to his gut.

Nathan struggled to ignore George and focus on the only person who was important. Noelle.

"I know I'm putting you on the spot. And I know it won't be simple or easy while I'm stationed in Virginia and you're—"

"Yes." Her word interrupted his list of reasons why she should say no. A list he should have probably kept to himself.

"Yes?" he asked, afraid to believe it.

She swallowed and nodded as her eyes filled with tears. "I love you, too, and I want to be with you, so yes."

He got up off his knee and drew her into his arms. "We're doing things a little backward, but I suppose I should meet your family now. Huh?"

Noelle nodded, smiling through the tears.

"Before we start with the introductions . . . It seems we're under the mistletoe." Wrapping his arms around her waist, he glanced up. In light of the emotions filling him, he could really use a kiss.

"Looks like. I guess you'd better kiss me."

"Gladly."

Now and every year for the rest of their lives.

ALL I WANT FOR CHRISTMAS IS . . .

KATE ANGELL

CHAPTER I

"I want you to buy me a Christmas gift, as a final test of your taste and your understanding of mine," Daniel Hayes, CEO of Hayes Global Financiers, addressed the three women seated in a crescent of club chairs before his heavy mahogany desk. "Whoever shows the most originality will become my personal shopper. Questions?" His tone was dry, reserved, as if he didn't anticipate any. He expected the applicants to take responsibility and think for themselves.

Riley Tyler hadn't heard a word he'd said during the thirty-minute group interview. He'd started out by introducing them to his company, one of the largest global associations of financial institutions, with nearly five hundred members in ninety countries. The firm provided economic and financial analysis to its members, developed industry proposals on global regulatory issues, and represented the members in discussions with the public sector on global economic and financial policy issues. His words went over her head. He'd lost her.

Her mind shut down, and she stared at him. There was something about Daniel that both fascinated and unsettled her. He was tall, she'd noticed when he stood as the women entered his suite. Dark-haired and eyed, sharp-featured, and serious, he hadn't smiled once. A sense of humor was important to her.

He was impeccably dressed. He wore the clothes; they didn't wear him. Black suit, white shirt, burgundy tie. She wondered why his previous personal shopper had left such a lucrative position, one with ideal hours as well as company benefits.

Daniel observed her now, his gaze hard. She'd never had anyone look at her and through her at the same time. She closed down. Forgot to breathe. He glanced away, and she drew a breath, too deep, too rapid, and accidentally snorted. No change in his expression. He made no comment.

Applicant Caroline Baker sat on Riley's left. Riley admired her geometrically styled hair, pale skin, and exotic features. She had amazing almond eyes. Stylishly dressed in a cashmere, camel-colored skirt suit and matching suede pumps, she crossed her legs and dared to ask, "How personal should we get? Clothes, jewelry, gourmet foods?"

"You decide what's appropriate." Daniel sounded bored.

"No hints whatsoever?" Lauren Lovell pressured. She sat one chair over, a natural beauty attired in a gray, long-sleeved wool dress with a wide leather belt. Her brown hair was so long, she was sitting on it.

The corners of his mouth creased. "If I gave

you hints, I might as well purchase the gifts myself. Do your best."

"Price range?" Lauren once again.

"Check in with Jean Norris in Accounts Payable on your way out. Whatever you spend won't be out-of-pocket. Jean will give you a prepaid debit card."

Riley scrunched her nose. They'd be purchasing him a gift, and he'd foot the bill. The sky appeared to be the limit. Life was overpriced. Bargains were far and few between. But win or lose, she wouldn't take advantage of the man.

Cutting his gaze to her, Daniel raised an eyebrow, asked, "You're quiet. Good to go, Riley?"

The arch of his brow captivated her. He appeared both cynical and wicked sexy. Intense and intriguing. She stared overly long.

Until he nudged her. His "Miss Tyler?" held a hint of impatience.

She blinked. Interview over. "I'm set." For what, she hadn't a clue. She wouldn't ask a question if her life depended on it. She would figure it out as she went.

"I'll meet with you in the conference room tomorrow afternoon at four," he concluded. "I'll hire one of you on the spot. Whichever gift speaks to me the most."

Caroline and Lauren smiled, confident and poised, as they collected their handbags and briefcases and stood. Both applicants had portfolios of prominent and influential clients they'd advised and accessorized. They were ready to step into the position. To dress Daniel for the holidays.

He escorted them to the door, where they conversed briefly. Riley rose more slowly. She held her red envelope clutch purse in one hand while tugging down the inner sweater of her faded lavender cardigan twin set with the other. The hem was slightly stretched and hung below the outer sweater. Her herringbone slacks had wrinkles, but then so did her life. Nothing seemed to go smoothly.

She took a moment to look around his office, on the thirtieth floor of the Landmark Tower in downtown Minneapolis. Masculine and magnificent, she thought. Old money.

The corner suite had an amazing view. Wide arches of multi-paned windows faced north and west. Fat snowflakes swirled, silver against overcast skies. She felt as if she were standing in a snow globe. She circled his desk, and, unable to resist, skimmed her fingers over the soft leather on his chesterfield chair. Butter-cushy.

Financial periodicals were stacked on one corner of his desk. She fingered the edges, then flipped through the pile. Three magazines down, she found Daniel looking at her from the cover of *Twin Cities Metro*. Attired in a tuxedo, he was featured as Minneapolis–Saint Paul's Man of the Year, and one of the cities' ten most-eligible bachelors. The man enjoyed both popularity and prestige. He was desired by women. Admired by men.

Still no smile.

She appreciated the Tiffany lamp, central Oriental rug, and century-old world globe bar on wheels, complete with internal drinks cabinet. The globe opened at the equator, and she peeked inside. Satin banked aged liquors, vintage wines, cut-crystal tumblers, and bubble glasses. She wondered how often Daniel entertained in his office. How late the parties ran.

An enormous black-and-white photograph hung on the east wall. She assumed it was an aerial view of the Hayes Estate on Lake Minnetonka. Steeped in history, the two-story brick and stone mansion commanded the major share of the lake's most prominent point with its three-hundred-sixty-degree water views. The landscape coupled mature pines and aging evergreens with new planting. A narrow path wound from the main house to the dock. The sun glanced off the lake, so still and clear, it mirrored two large watercraft.

Then came the bookcase. Tall and wide, and filled with economic and financial books, binders, and guidelines. A grandfather clock stood in one corner. The pendulum swung with mesmerizing precision. By Riley's watch, the stately clock was off by three minutes. Either that, or her own Timex was running fast.

A crease in the wood paneling caught her eye, just beyond the clock. Shaped like a door. But there was no handle. Mysterious, she thought. Daniel didn't give her time to discover the secret.

He cleared his throat, asked, "Taking a detour?" He leaned against the door frame, arms crossed over his chest, giving her the eye.

Her cheeks warmed. "You have an office to be envied."

"Think so?"

"Don't you?"

"My grandfather and father established a comfortable work environment. I'm holding to tradition. Little has changed."

A personal admission. He seemed almost human. She approached him then. It seemed a long walk across the room to the door. A brass coatrack stood in the corner. His black cashmere coat was hooked over one arm. A dozen vintage railroad caps and hats hung from the remaining three. She recognized them all, thanks to her grandfather Ed. He'd been a train buff, and shared his knowledge with her.

The key feature of each brimmed cap was the badge attached to it. Made of brass or copper, the badges identified the railroad line and the specific job of the wearer. The passenger lines included the Great Northern, Burlington, and Northern Pacific. The jobs: conductor, station agent, brakeman, and ticket taker. Apparently Daniel liked the rails, too.

She might have asked about his love of trains, had he not swept his arm and motioned her out. He blocked part of the doorway, and she brushed against him when she left. Solid, she thought. His cologne was subtle. She couldn't believe she sniffed his shirtfront.

Neither could he. He stepped aside, said, "Starch and Acqua di Gio."

She scooted by him. She was halfway across the reception area when he called to her. "Baby Gap." He referred to her by the company where her previous position had been. "Your experience is limited. You've dressed newborns and toddlers—what makes you think you can handle me?"

"Most adult men are boys at heart," she reflected. "It shouldn't be too difficult to put big boy clothes on you."

Had the corner of his mouth lifted? A hint of a smile? Doubtful. He turned back into his office before he gave too much away. Closed the door.

With his Christmas gift foremost in her mind, she walked to the bank of elevators. She had a couple of ideas. She had only to pick the perfect one. No credit voucher needed. A grin from him would be payment enough. Surely the man had teeth.

Daniel left his suite shortly after Riley. "I'm headed to Personnel," he told his administrative assistant, as he passed her desk in the outer office.

Roxanne nodded, but didn't look up from the computer. The lady could multitask better than anyone he knew. She absorbed facts and had amazing recall. She'd been with the company for six years now. He made a mental note to give her both a Christmas present and a substantial bonus this year. Perhaps his new personal shopper could offer suggestions on a gift.

He paused for half a second and tapped his fingers on one corner of her desk. "You've met the three applicants?" he asked her.

She kept typing. Her manicured fingernails flew over the keys. "Briefly."

"First impressions?" He valued her opinion.

"Hire Caroline Baker."

"Why?" He needed more.

Roxanne looked up. Her half-frame reading glasses sat low on her nose; she eyed him over the rims. "She's poised and perfect with a thick portfolio. She's selected wardrobes for high-powered executives and international businessmen. She likes gourmet foods. A classy lady."

"She's definitely qualified."

"Lauren Lovell is new in town, from New York

City. I overheard her speaking with Caroline, and she's established strong contacts with local tailors and designers. She's vegetarian."

He liked a good steak now and again, but that wouldn't affect his decision about the personal shopper. He waited for Roxanne to mention Riley, but she did not. She went back to work. So he brought her up, "Riley Tyler?"

His secretary talked and typed. "She needs her own stylist, don't you think? Not that I'm being critical. A personal shopper is a liaison between you and your closet. Do you want her own taste in clothes rubbing off on you?"

"What was wrong with how she dressed?" It wasn't like Roxanne to be catty. She always stuck up for the underdog. And Riley was barely in the running for the job.

"She's her own person," Roxanne observed.

There was nothing wrong with a nonconformist.

"She . . . stares."

Which he had noticed, too. She hadn't taken her eyes off him during the thirty-minute interview. Light blue and flecked with gold, they reminded him of lake water when the sun glanced off the surface during the summer. Her expression gave nothing away. He couldn't tell if she found him interesting or boring. Handsome or lacking in looks.

"Furthermore," Roxanne continued, "you're accomplished, reserved, and serious. She . . . smiles, when she's not staring."

"I smile."

"Once a month."

"More often."

"I keep track."

He glared at her. "Not enough work, Roxanne? You have time to count my smiles?"

She grinned at him. "You've locked your jaw, boss. No points for today."

"You have lipstick on your teeth."

She didn't, but he had her reaching for a mirror and Kleenex in her middle desk drawer. "Not funny, Daniel," she said, once she'd checked her teeth.

He smiled to himself. That smile put a point on his mental scoreboard. He moved on, making his way down the hallway. Glass walls caught his reflection. The plush gray carpet cushioned his steps. He nodded to those he passed. Spoke to a few.

He stopped before the door marked DIRECTOR OF PERSONNEL. He needed to speak with Georgia Pettibone. She'd been with the financial firm longer than Daniel could remember. His grandfather and father had trusted her. She had high morals and was a good judge of character. She intuitively knew whom to hire for what position. Employee turnover was minimal.

He knocked, entered, and found her perched on a high cushioned stool beneath a hardwood framed project table, in lieu of a desk. The wide surface area rested on counter-height file cabinets, facing out. The perfect workspace for her.

Daniel knew her to be seventy, yet she never seemed to age. She wasn't ready to retire, and he wasn't ready to see her go. She brought stability to the company. She wore pantsuits and pearls. She had an undeniable air of authority. She spoke her mind. Never minced words. He listened.

She took a sip of tea from a floral china cup. Orange pekoe scented the air. "Good morning,

Mr. Hayes," she greeted him, always respectful of his position.

He'd prefer that she call him Daniel, but she favored the formality. He never pressured her to change. She'd known him through diapers and short pants. She'd picked him up when he was four and had fallen off a chair, trying to sneak gumdrops from a crystal bowl on a shelf in her office. She'd given him a pocketful, taken his hand, and walked him back to his father's suite. She'd never tattled on him.

"Got a minute?" he asked her.

"Always time for you." She motioned him to join her. "Tea?" she offered.

He shook his head. "I'm good."

Reaching her, he unbuttoned his suit jacket before straddling the stool across from her. He rested his elbows on the table. Steepled his fingers. He felt a moment of concern. "I've now met the three applicants you selected for personal shopper."

"And?" She looked at him expectantly.

"Two were strong contenders. One, I'm not so certain."

"Who didn't work for you?"

"Riley Tyler."

"Ah, I see. I should've told you beforehand that Riley was fourth on my short list of shoppers. The lady ahead of her was offered a job at Saks Fifth Avenue. She jumped at the opportunity. I'd promised you three applicants. Riley rose to fill her slot."

That made sense, Daniel thought. He might never have met Riley had the third woman not found employment elsewhere. His chest tightened. Inexplicably.

"Do you plan to cut Riley before receiving her Christmas gift?" she questioned.

Presenting him with a gift had been Georgia's idea. To see which lady's taste matched his own. Georgia believed a lot could be revealed about a woman on a shopping spree, spending someone else's money. The gift would indicate how each perceived him.

"By the way," she noted, "Janine in Accounting just sent me an e-mail. Lauren and Caroline picked up their debit cards. No sign of Riley."

Puzzling, and mildly disappointing. "Perhaps the position didn't interest her after all and she walked away," he said.

"Riley was polite at the initial interview," Georgia pointed out. "I think she'd call if she'd crossed you off her list."

Crossed *him* off? That didn't set well. "Can you contact her? See if she's coming back?"

"Of course, but only if she's a true contender for the position. Otherwise, why get her hopes up?"

Why, indeed? Because he'd like to see her again, as odd as that seemed. "She's qualified, otherwise you wouldn't have scored her at four. Confirm, please."

"Will do. She fit your qualifications. Although her experience is with kids, not adults. Good references. Clean background check. Stable, she's lived in Saint Paul all her life. She has her own transportation for running errands. Most importantly, she has a boyfriend."

"She does?" he blurted, then wished he could recall his words. His curiosity had gotten the better of him. He sounded interested.

Georgia didn't judge. She merely repeated his rule. " 'No inner office dating. Relationships take away from company time.' Rumor has it that Sandra Rule, Senior Policy Advisor, Regulatory Affairs, is involved with Donald Walsh, an engineer in Network Operations. I've yet to confirm or catch them having sex in the copier room. Until I do, I won't pry into their private lives."

He ran one hand down his face. "Ignore the gossip." Both executives were exceptional. Career-minded and valued. He'd hate to replace them.

Georgia eyed him, inquired, "Do you ever regret firing Judith?"

"I haven't given her a second thought."

Judith Evans had been his previous personal shopper. They'd worked well together for four years, up until the previous week, when she'd confessed her love for him. He hadn't seen it coming, hadn't realized she cared. He'd never led her on. His life consisted of sixteen-hour workdays. He had little time for socializing, unless it was business-related.

Floored, and unable to return her feelings, he'd tried to let her down easy. She'd shouted. Cried. Stomped her feet. Here was a side of her he'd never expected. It hadn't been pretty. Scary, actually.

In the end, he'd given her three months' severance pay. Offered a reference. Then left for a Chamber of Commerce luncheon. He'd expected her to clear her desk while he was away, and be gone when he returned.

She'd left alright, but only after taking scissors to the twenty suits in his executive closet, located off his office. Shirts were torn. Buttons flew like bullets. Ties, shredded. His wingtips and loafers, stabbed. Fortunately, there was no blood. Security had removed her from the premises. He'd taken out a restraining order on her.

He was in desperate need of a new wardrobe.

Despite the fact he could bring countries together for an economic summit, shopping for clothes went beyond his comfort zone. Mixing and matching colors confused him. Ridiculous, he knew. If it was up to him, he could wear the same suit every day of the week, identical white shirt, different tie, and be happy with his wardrobe. It wasn't to be. His father had set high standards to which Daniel and his administrators adhered. They projected a polished public image.

Truth be told, he was embarrassed by his lack of style, and the fact that he needed someone to help pull his act together. He hoped to hire a new personal shopper by tomorrow afternoon.

"You'll meet with the ladies once more," said Georgia, "for the presentation of your gifts. Hopefully one will stand out from the others."

He hoped so, too.

They sat quietly. She sipped her tea. He stared into space. Until Georgia asked, "How are your parents?"

Daniel grew thoughtful. Franklin and Lenore had met forty years ago at an art exhibition, where she was the artist. His dad courted and charmed her by buying every painting on display. He'd won her heart. In the early days, they had loved beyond measure. An ideal marriage.

Until Franklin took success as his mistress. His days were long and his time limited. He withdrew into the city. He took over the office next door, and turned it into an efficiency apartment. Small but comfortable, it was perfect for early business meetings. No commute.

After Daniel was born, Franklin pushed himself even harder. Mother and son needed him, but Franklin was too busy to notice. He never took a vacation. Celebrated few holidays. Daniel grew up the man of the house. Responsibility weighed heavily through his youth and teenage years. Under his father's wing, Daniel learned from the best. He interned at Global Financiers during high school, then college, attending the University of Minnesota. Franklin pushed Daniel as his own father had pushed him. Nose to the grindstone. Visible at the corporate forefront. There was little time for extracurricular activities. For fun.

A corporate mastermind, Franklin maximized investments and shareholder value. Achievement was the measure of his life. No one was more admired, respected, or accomplished in the world of finance. Daniel walked in his footsteps.

He matched Franklin's vision and wisdom, until dementia stole his father's awareness and weakened his body. Franklin returned home. He presently had round-the-clock nursing care, and a wife who sat by his bedside and held his hand. She read to him. Shared photo albums and memories long past. She protected him.

"My mother is my father's strength," he told Georgia. "Dad forgets more than he remembers, but he still recognizes her. Me, too, on a good day. He sporadically comments on the early years of their marriage." Decades less complicated.

She understood. "Life is tricky. Reality fades, and the past feels safe. A gentler time, perhaps."

A comfortable silence settled between them, the unspoken communication of two people who knew each other well. "Christmas," she finally initiated.

"What about it?"

"It's two weeks away. I've had several people inquire about decorations. We hang wreaths on office doors each year, but it's been ages since we've decked the hall, trimmed a tree."

The idea and her enthusiasm surprised him. He shrugged. "Fine by me. Who plans to take charge?"

"No one's volunteered." Pause. "I'm suggesting your personal shopper. Once she's gotten you ready for your business trip to London next week, she can turn her attention to decorating. The job description for personal shopper extends to 'duties specified by employer.'" She made finger quotes. "Those duties could include holiday decorations, Secret Santa, and the office party."

Daniel narrowed his gaze. "You came up with this—when?"

"Crossed my mind with my second cup of tea."

"The caffeine kicked in."

She took a last sip of orange pekoe, and wrapped up. "Let me know which one of the applicants you hire tomorrow, Mr. Hayes. The employment forms are filled out. I only need insert a name. I'll be curious."

He pushed off the stool, stood. "No more curious than I am."

CHAPTER 2

Riley Tyler entered Lattetude, a gourmet coffee shop and bakery within the same block as Hayes Global Financiers. She sought a caffeine boost, and ordered a double espresso from the barista. Added a merry-berry scone. She looked around for a place to sit. Found a table near the window. Once seated, she shrugged off her wool coat and watched the traffic pass. The snow fall. Professionals from the financial district drifted in and out, pink cheeked and red nosed. Fat, fluttery flakes whitened their cashmere and leather coats. Slush marred their designer boots.

Finance was a world unto itself, she thought. She'd gone brain-dead when Daniel spoke extensively about his company. Economics, investments, funding—it made her eyes cross. Figures and the future were not her strong suit. She was lucky to balance her checkbook. Most times, she deducted the amount of a check by rounding up. Five dollars and forty cents became six dollars. She was then sixty cents ahead, and never overdrawn.

She'd applied for the personal shopper position, not a job in finance. She was a realist. Her chances were slim to none that Daniel would hire her. Lauren and Caroline were stiff competition. She took a bite of her scone, brushed the crumbs off the front of her sweater. A too-big sip of espresso burned the tip of her tongue. She reached for her glass of ice water, drank deeply. Cooled her mouth. Then returned her thoughts to the day ahead.

She had two projects to accomplish. A boyfriend came first. Daniel's Christmas gift second. She sighed heavily.

Georgia in Personnel had digressed into conversation during the interview. She'd mentioned that Daniel kept his work relationships formal, hinted that he preferred a candidate who was not single. Needing the job, Riley had managed to drop the mention of a boyfriend into their talk.

Now her options were few. She hadn't seriously dated for several months. And she couldn't think of a friend who would play the part of suitor.

One idea came to mind, though, outlandish as it seemed at first. The Build-A-Boyfriend app. She'd recently seen it advertised online. She could create a make-believe man for a mere twenty-four dollars and ninety-five cents a month. His hair, eye color, and career fell to her imagination.

He would pursue her, without personal involvement. She could schedule his texts, an occasional voice mail. Flowers, a gift or two, could arrive by courier. Their involvement would last only as long as she needed him. Cancelation of the app was the perfect breakup. There'd be no broken hearts.

She dug her iPhone from her purse. She glanced about to make sure no one was looking, then located and downloaded the app. She made her selections. The setup took longer than she'd expected. After reviewing her choices, she realized she'd portrayed Daniel as her ideal man. That shook her a little. She barely knew him. She went back and altered several details.

On further reflection, she smiled to herself. She'd made her match. A blond-haired, green-eyed pediatrician from Saint Paul. Andrew Reynolds traveled with Doctors Without Borders, an international medical humanitarian organization that worked in more than sixty countries, and treated people with the greatest need. He was as believable as a pretend physician could be. Gentle, kind, dedicated, and ministering abroad.

She breathed easier now. It was time to move on. She needed to select Daniel's gift. She'd left Landmark Tower minutes after Caroline and Lauren. She'd stood on the sidewalk and watched them cross at the light, then part ways. Caroline entered Luxe Jewelry and Lauren went into Organza Gallery, which specialized in fine art, pottery, and sculpture. Expensive and cultured gifts.

Riley pushed back her chair, stood. She slipped on her coat. The bottom button was loose, ready to fall off. She'd sew it tonight. She tossed her trash in the recyclable bin, and walked toward the door. Her thoughts returned to the CEO and his office suite. She visualized his desk, the world globe, the photo of his family's compound, the bookshelves, the—

Intuition struck, and she immediately knew what to buy.

It felt right. Perfect, actually.

She hoped he would see it that way, too.

The next afternoon arrived with a blustery wind that nearly knocked her off her feet. The snowfall thickened. A blizzard warning had been issued. The windshield wipers on Riley's MINI Cooper were set on high, but barely kept the window clear. Her car was a lightweight in a land of Hummers and four-wheel-drive SUVs.

Holding the steering wheel in a death grip, she cautiously entered the Landmark Towers parking garage and drove up six flights before finding a spot. She popped the trunk and dragged out a large box. Daniel's gift. Sections of the cement were slippery, and it became a balancing act to walk and hold on to the box. She took the elevator to the thirtieth floor.

She'd called ahead and purposely arrived an hour early, 3 p.m. Requiring access to his suite, she conspired with a reluctant Roxanne, who indicated Daniel was away, meeting with investment bankers. He wouldn't return until four.

Riley had an hour to set up her present.

Roxanne's eyes widened at her choice.

Riley could only hope she'd selected wisely.

Ready, set, go. Once Riley finished, Roxanne directed her to the conference room. Down the hall, and on the right. The door was glass, revealing an enormous rectangular table, brown leather chairs, a coffee station, and water cooler. Caroline and Lauren preceded her, their Christmas presents ex-

pertly wrapped and placed at the head of the
table. They sat on either side of the CEO's chair of
distinguished black leather. Riley wandered to the
far end, distancing herself from the competition.

The women had slipped off their coats. They
were so impeccably dressed, they could've been mannequins in Lord & Taylor's store window. Riley kept
her coat on. She'd decided there was no point in
taking it off; it was almost certain Daniel would dis-
miss her.

He arrived at four sharp. The man was prompt.
"Good afternoon, ladies," he greeted them, his
voice deep, hoarse, as if he'd contracted a cold. He
sneezed, confirming the diagnosis. He shrugged off
his coat and sat stiffly in a dark gray suit, white
shirt, and black tie. Professional, but drab. He
drew a breath, made eye contact with each applicant. He raised his eyebrow at Riley, requesting a
reason for her sitting down the table.

"I don't want to catch your cold," she impro-
vised.

"I just arrived. How'd you know I even had
one?"

"The box of tissues."

His expression was unreadable.

A moment later, Georgia from Personnel knocked
and entered. She passed him a chunky ceramic
mug. "Hot green tea, lemon, and honey. I didn't
remember you having a handkerchief. Tissues, as
needed." She left.

Daniel's face softened for half a second. He appeared appreciative of her concern for his health.
The water steamed, and the tea bag steeped. The
air was scented with the aroma of lemons.

"The weather is worsening," he informed them.

"Let's get down to business. I will open my gifts, and hire one of you. In advance, I thank you for the time, thought, and effort you put into choosing the presents."

"Mine first," requested Caroline. Seated on the edge of her chair, she leaned forward and nudged the silver foil box toward him.

Riley noticed her long fingers, a pianist's hand. Mauve polished her nails. Also long. Lovely and feminine. Riley's own nails were buffed and filed short. She hadn't wanted to accidentally poke a child while working at Baby Gap. Toddlers squirmed when trying on clothes. She'd like to grow her nails out now.

Anticipation collected in the room as Daniel slowly unwrapped his first gift. Lauren seemed especially interested in what Caroline had chosen, probably hoping it wouldn't trump her own. Riley sat back, kept to herself. Since money was no object, she assumed the gifts were expensive.

She was right. Daniel now palmed a satin Rolex box. Inside, timeless luxury. A watch designed for professionals and serious travelers. To be worn on formal occasions.

In Riley's mind, the watch didn't quite fit the man. He was handsome, polished, yes, but if she looked beneath the surface, he had rugged depth. She might have gone with a sportier style. A Tag Heuer, with black dial, compass, stainless steel, wide leather band. Adventuresome. That was her opinion only. Perhaps she'd misjudged him.

The look on Daniel's face showed appreciation of Caroline's gift. He seemed satisfied. The corners of his eyes crinkled. His lips tipped, pleased, but he didn't fully smile.

"Thank you," he acknowledged, a man of few words.

Lauren gave him her gift next. The opaque wrap revealed something tall, narrow, and shiny. She beamed, believing her gift would outshine the others.

Riley leaned back in her chair and watched as Daniel took longer than was necessary with the wrapping. He had big, strong hands. His motions firm and decisive, he lowered the opaque paper. So slowly, time seemed to stop. Lost in the reveal, she forgot herself. She became in tune with him. Sensation fluttered in her belly. Her imagination took hold. Mental foreplay. He stroked her. Undressed her. Down to skin.

Her breathing deepened; her stomach was tied in a sexual knot. She shivered, shook herself, embarrassed. Shifting on her chair, she bumped her knees beneath the table, drawing his attention.

He raised an eyebrow questioningly. "Everything okay down there?"

"I was merely trying to get a better look at the sculpture," she assured him. It was magnificent. A sleek marble configuration of a couple entwined. Intimately.

"It's a VanValdi," Lauren said. "*The Mating*."

Riley recognized the Swedish sculptor. She'd seen the titled piece on display in the window at Organza. A prestigious purchase. Unique. Costly. She thought the gift far too personal for a man they barely knew, one who was to be a boss not a boyfriend. It was unsettling.

Daniel ran his hands over the marble, and Riley once again felt his touch. Goose bumps rose on her arms and chest. She was thankful for her coat. It covered her tingles.

He took a sip of his tea, approved the gift. "There's never enough beauty in the world. An intriguing sculpture. Thank you."

Lauren and Caroline were all smiles, each believing her present would win her the coveted position of personal shopper. Their gifts were extravagant, with astronomical price tags. They hadn't minded spending his money, whereas Riley had stuck to a modest budget. She'd spent eighteen dollars and forty-two cents at Value Mart. Her gift had been on sale.

Daniel eyed her now. "Are we waiting for Santa?" he asked her, wondering about his gift.

"I've yet to hear the *click-click-click* of reindeer hooves on the roof," she returned.

"I hope they didn't get waylaid by the incoming snowstorm."

She couldn't put him off any longer. "I believe I heard them in your office."

"Not much room for a sleigh and eight reindeer."

"Nine, including Rudolph."

"My office then?" He finished off his tea, stood. He held the chairs for her competition. They picked up their presents. Riley got up on her own, circled the table, and left ahead of them.

Momentarily awkward, she tugged her coat about her, safeguarding her feelings. What she'd originally thought a great gift now seemed insignificant, even inappropriate, compared to those already given. Daniel had told them to buy a present that represented the way they saw him. She had. She wondered if he'd see himself the same way.

Roxanne was clearing her desk when they ar-

rived. She shut down her computer. "Whiteout
conditions are forecasted," she told them. "Security wants the floor cleared within the hour. I'm
heading home now."

"We're not far behind you," Daniel assured her.

Roxanne looked pointedly at Riley. "The lights
are dimmed. The switch flipped. Go on in."

Daniel reached around her, opened the door.
They stepped inside. Approached his desk. Clickety-
clack, *woo-woo*, the North Pole plastic holiday train
ran a figure-eight track on his desktop. Santa engi-
neered the battery-operated express that pulled
three passenger cars packed with presents and a
red caboose. Tiny lights flashed at the railroad
crossing. The decorative village included a general
store, church, post office, and station house.

Silence held sway in the darkened office. No
one made a comment. Riley's stomach sank. Had
she made a mistake? Had she read Daniel wrong?
Intuition had pushed her to buy the train. Her gut
feelings were never wrong. Not until today.

She swallowed hard, waited for someone to say
something. Anything. Good or bad.

Caroline spoke first, her tone scoffing. "A train
set? Really?"

Lauren gave a nervous laugh. "Is this a joke?"

Riley bit down on her bottom lip. "I thought it
appropriate," she replied, her voice barely audible.
The train had seemed a good idea—yesterday.

Lauren's lips twisted. "Suitable for whom? A six-
year-old?"

Daniel edged closer to Riley. He stood so close,
she felt his body heat, breathed in his cologne. He
tensed up slightly, but his expression wasn't disapproving. She took a chance, looked up as he looked

down; their gazes locked. Damage done, she awaited his criticism. Which never came.

"Six or sixty, trains are timeless," he said, commending her gift. "Nice choice."

Daniel felt a pit open up in his stomach. Almost painful. A heartbeat later his chest warmed. For a split second, he recaptured his boyhood. A youth that seemed all too distant and short-lived. He'd been an only child in a formal household. His father had encouraged maturity in him early on.

Groomed to take over Hayes Global Financiers, the kid in him had sat in the corner until now. Riley had seen his need to play. The train was the perfect gift.

He'd promised to pick the present that spoke to him. The express chugged, whistled, choo-chooed, making the sounds of Christmas. He circled his desk, stood behind it. He leaned his palms on the edge so the train track was within the stretch of his fingers. He suspended his thoughts, his decision, as he watched it pass, once, twice. The arms on the crossing sign rose and lowered.

He was a logical man. Analytical to a fault. Both Caroline and Lauren had extensive résumés and celebrated clientele. Caroline's attention to the mayor of Saint Paul's suits and ties had landed the politician on the nationwide Capital Cities Best Dressed List. Lauren selected wardrobes for international playboys, movie stars, and sports figures.

He was impressed by the Rolex. The statue would have been more appropriate for a lover than an employer. Still, it was a toss-up between the two.

Then there was Riley. Recently employed by

Baby Gap. She had experience with children, but
not with adults. Carter's and Gerber were not his
style. He momentarily closed his eyes and listened
to the chug of the plastic train. It lulled him.
There was an uneven link of track where the train
went clickety-clack-*crack*. Precarious, but it didn't
derail. If the train could hold together, so could
he. After all, how hard was it to choose a personal
shopper?

The whirl of the wind slammed snowflakes
against the arched windows. A menacing sound,
causing him to blink. The afternoon sky was midnight dark. The weather was worsening. He needed
to send two of the ladies on their way while there
was still time for them to clear downtown and
reach home safely.

He gazed at the three. Caroline and Lauren
were dressed professionally, appropriately, for the
position. Riley still wore her coat. She clutched it
tightly about her, a protective layer of wool against
cold temperatures, him, and disappointment. The
office air was dry, and strands of her dark blond
hair stuck out from static electricity. Hope shone
in her blue eyes, tempered by acceptance that he
would probably choose another.

"Why do you want this job?" he questioned her.
Her response would be the deciding factor.

"I need to grow my life." Her words sounded
more like an admission than an answer.

She wanted to mature.

He wanted to play with trains.

They would meet in the middle.

His inner child made the decision for him.
"Caroline, Lauren, I appreciate your interest in
the position. I've decided to hire Riley."

Caroline's expression tightened.

Lauren's mouth pinched.

Riley was disbelieving.

He next dialed Security, alerting the guards to the fact that two ladies were on their way down. He requested they be safely escorted to their vehicles in the parking garage.

Caroline had the class to shake hands; pass him the watch. She glanced at Riley, and he swore she rolled her eyes before wishing him well.

Lauren's huff and stiff spine walked her out. She set the sculpture on a bookshelf near the door.

The women returned to the conference room for their coats.

His suite was suddenly so quiet, Daniel could hear himself breathe. Could feel the beat of his heart. Overly fast. For a man of authority, quick judgment, and action, he was suddenly lost for words. He waited for her to speak. To thank him for the job. She did not.

Instead she bit down on her bottom lip and asked, "Are you sure?"

"Questioning my choice?" He was taken aback.

"Why me?" she asked, sounding vulnerable.

She'd bought him a simple plastic train, and coaxed him out to play. He'd liked feeling six. Finance was serious business, and he'd followed in his father's footsteps when it came to the intensity with which he pursued it. He was a Hayes. Long hours, little social life, unless it was business related. He kept his head high. His jaw tight. Focused.

Until Riley. She wasn't perfect for the position. Far from it, but he'd take his chances. He flicked the switch on the train's engine and watched it pull to a stop before the station. He picked up the post office from the figure eight, palmed it. Procrastinating.

"You have potential," he finally managed.

"You're handing your wardrobe over to a shopper with potential? Dangerous, don't you think? I could dress you like a clown."

A clown would be preferable to Judith and her vengeful scissors spree. He was objective. "You're out to prove yourself. You'll do your best by me. I meet and am seen by hundreds of people every month. Your name will be noticed along with the labels you choose."

She let it sink in. "Custom-made by Brooks Brothers, chosen by Riley." She scrunched her nose. "I don't always buy designer." She pointed to the toy train. "Not Lionel, O gauge, or Thomas the Train. It's plastic Value Mart."

One corner of his mouth tipped up. "You didn't break my bank." The other two applicants had overspent. To impress him. They had not. They'd taken advantage of him. Of his wealth. He'd developed an early discipline that was very lean and mean in terms of spending money. The Rolex and sculpture would be regifted. Or perhaps auctioned at a charity event.

"You'll need to set up an appointment with Stella Mayer in Accounts Payable. She'll explain my clothing account. You're free to buy anywhere. My only request, don't skimp on my underwear. My preference, Hermès woven boxers. Front pleat and separate storage pouch."

A hint of a blush. "Your boxers . . ." She sounded uncertain.

"You'll be dressing me skin-out."

"I . . . knew that."

No, she had not. He almost smiled. He was dealing with a virgin personal shopper. He sensed she would manage his formal suits, shirts, and ties just fine. She'd have no problem with his casual attire. His pajamas and underclothes . . . to be determined.

Thickening snow and a wailing wind now beat against the glass. He looked out and couldn't see the high-rise across the street. A flash of lightning lit up the room, causing Riley to jump. Seconds later, thunder boomed. Thundersnow. Rare, dangerous, and leading to reduced visibility. The wintry blast was about to hold them hostage. They needed to leave the building. Immediately.

Too late. A knock on the office door, and they were interrupted by a security guard. "George," he acknowledged.

"I wanted to give an update on the weather, sir, ma'am," he added, including Riley. His gaze was curious.

"My new personal shopper," Daniel said to clarify. "George, meet Riley Tyler. George has secured the building for as long as I can remember."

"A pleasure," said Riley.

"All mine," from George.

"We were on our way out," Daniel told the guard.

"Sorry, but it's no longer safe for you to leave. The storm hit faster than expected. Harder than anticipated. Possibly the worst blizzard in twenty years. The city's at a standstill. Transportation, including air travel, has shut down. Law enforcement's restricted all but emergency vehicles."

Riley startled. "We're stuck here?"

"Until the brunt of the storm passes," said George.

"Passes . . ." she repeated.

"I've taken a head count, and there are two bankers, an attorney, and a techno team on lower floors who will also be spending the night," George informed them. "They'll be bedding down on office sofas. Hopefully, the electricity will hold, and we'll have heat."

"Heat . . ." Riley's tone hinted of panic.

"You'll be fine," George reassured. Then, tongue in cheek, he added, "You're inside, safe, even if the snow drifted thirty floors."

"Safe . . ." She didn't sound relieved.

"I'll check on you later, sir."

Daniel searched his coat pocket for his iPhone. Started to text his mother. "Anyone you need to reach, before we lose connectivity?"

"I should check my messages." She settled on a club chair, searched her purse for her phone. She mumbled something he didn't understand.

"Pardon?" He wasn't sure if she was talking to him or to herself.

"I had three messages from my boyfriend."

"Boyfriend?" caught his attention.

"Andrew Reynolds," she told him. "He's a pediatrician with Doctors Without Borders," she relayed. She tapped the screen on her iPhone, moving to the next message. "He's headed out on a mission. Planes were delayed due to the weather, but he managed to catch the last international flight out." She sighed her relief. "He's in the air." She went on to check her remaining texts. Sent a few responses.

She was involved with a physician. Somehow that didn't surprise Daniel too much. The man treated children, and she had worked at Baby Gap. Kids all around them.

"Did you tell Andrew that you're stuck in the city? Where you'll be spending the night?" he questioned. Would Andrew care that she'd be crossing midnight with another man? However platonic the situation.

She shook her phone. Glared at the screen. "Dead," she said. "I was only able to tell him I had a new job. No more."

"Where's he headed? How long will he be out of the country?"

"Nigeria. One month."

"What happens to his practice when he's gone?"

She took a moment to respond, longer than seemed necessary. She was involved with the doctor. The answer should be simple. She finally said, "He's established at the Saint Paul Medical Center when he's in town. A medical partnership. Other doctors see his patients when he's away."

"He's gone a lot?"

Pensive once again. Time stretched. "Eight months out of the year, give or take."

"Engagement in your future?"

"This spring . . . sometime."

"Long-distance relationships aren't easy."

"We've made it work."

"For how long?"

Pause. "Two years."

He shrugged. "Whatever works for you." He should've been relieved that Riley had a significant other. It would prevent a repeat of the Judith disaster. Yet there was a heaviness on his chest, a tightness to his gut. Uncommon. Unexpected. Unexplainable. A first for him.

He shrugged off his dark suit coat and draped it over the back of his desk chair. He next loosened his tie. Undid the top button on his white dress shirt. Pushed his sleeves up his forearms. He drew a deep breath, released it. The tension didn't leave him. Instead it expanded. Like a stretched rubber band.

"Take off your coat," he suggested. "You might as well be comfortable. We're here for the duration."

"How long is the snowstorm expected to last?"

"Longer than you want to wear your coat."

He managed to make her smile. A small smile that had her shrugging off her coat and hanging it on the brass coat hanger near the door, beneath the railroad caps. She looked nice in a cream-colored sweater and brown slacks. She fingered a loose thread on her sweater, gave a tug. It only lengthened. She tucked it beneath the hem. Saddle shoes? He'd only just noticed them. Did they bespeak a Catholic school background or cheerleading? Perhaps a fashion statement. He had no idea. They seemed to fit her.

"The blizzard should ease by morning," he went on to say. "But then it will take some time for the streets to be cleared."

"Do I stay here with you?"

He nodded. "A good idea. George would prefer you didn't wander the building. You don't want to get stuck in an elevator if we lose electricity."

"No, I don't," she agreed.

Riley moved toward the bookshelf. She stood and stared at its contents, debating which one to choose. She ran her fingertips over the spines. Scrunched her nose. None appealed. "*International Financial Management, The Blue Chips,* and *Global Money and Finance.*" She read several titles. "Sounds like heavy reading."

"Not always reader-friendly. More an intellectual exercise. The subject matter can be dry."

"How many books have you consumed?"

"On my own, dozens. Although my father read them to me as bedtime stories."

"Not your usual fairy tale."

"Happy endings came with deeper deficit spending." She looked blank, so he explained, "It's a fiscal policy tool to help stimulate an economy in recession."

"Got it." But she hadn't. Her eyes glazed over.

"What authors do you enjoy?" He found conversation easy with her.

"Those who write mystery cozies, mostly. Light, curl-up-on-the-couch-with-a-cup-of-hot-chocolate mysteries. I like the red herrings, and often solve the murder before the end."

He raised a brow. "Red herrings?"

"Something that appears to be a clue but in fact is not."

He knew what they were. Giving her a chance to explain put them on even footing. He wanted her relaxed around him. Talking mysteries seemed to put her at ease. "I remember my mother reading Agatha Christie. Jessica Fletcher, *Murder, She Wrote.*"

"Both wonderful. The book bin at Goodwill often has used copies."

She didn't buy her books new. A sign of her finances? Was she just frugal or low on cash? His stare must have given his thoughts away, because her cheeks heated. She responded with, "Frugal. I read several books a week so I'm always looking for deals."

"Smart on your part."

"Not everything has to be brand new. Books, clothes, I've bought used or vintage. Everywhere from pawn shops to garage sales. I think of it as recycling. That's good for the planet."

She had a point.

"You, however, have an image to uphold. Only the best for you. Promise."

"How do you see me?" slipped out. He wasn't certain if he was asking about suits and ties or something more personal.

She crossed from the bookshelf to stand before his desk. "Always dress to accurately convey who and what you are," she said. "I see my position as identifying trends, gauging style, and developing overall looks that work for you. You're a serious man, and dark, tailored suits fit your position. White dress shirts are practical, but starchy. A hint of color would make you more approachable. On occasion, an abstract, geometric, or striped tie, so you stand out in the crowd. Snappy."

"*Snappy*" worried him a little. He stood out by being CEO of Hayes Global Financiers. He'd never associated wardrobe with promoting his image. He was a corporate warrior; he wanted his clothes to be clean-cut, practical, suited for meetings and travel. Those in his financial circle dressed similarly. Riley wanted to take him out of his comfort zone. Make him more congenial. To whom? His executives and staff? His international peers? They already addressed him without fear.

His brow creased. He wouldn't voice his concerns, not now, at least. He'd see what she had to offer, and, if necessary, request she tone it down a bit. Oddly enough, he didn't want to hurt her feelings.

She sensed his doubt. "You don't trust me, do you?"

"Trust is cultivated."

"I take my job very seriously," she said with conviction. "Wherever you go, whatever you do, I want you to look your best. You're a man of stature, and wear clothes well."

A man of stature. Her first compliment. Not that he was counting. He'd wondered what she thought of him. He appreciated her honesty. Stature was a start.

She eyed him speculatively, and he knew what was coming. "What happened to your previous personal shopper?"

"She fell in love with me."

Her eyes widened. "You fired her for loving you?"

"I didn't return her feelings. The situation grew awkward."

"How awkward?" Riley liked details. Putting two and two together, the way she did with her mysteries.

"Scissors-to-my-wardrobe awkward."

"Fascinating and frightening."

"More scary than intriguing, trust me."

"This time around, you had Georgia subtly screen the applicants, didn't you? You preferred to hire someone already in a relationship."

"Correct," he admitted. "I knew you were involved."

"I am. Deeply so."

"We're good to go, then." Somehow he didn't feel so great. He should be pleased she had a boyfriend. A soon-to-be fiancé. Yet a part of him felt he'd met her too late. Doctor Andrew Reynolds had found her first. Lucky man.

CHAPTER 3

Riley was fortunate to have eaten a big lunch, but by six o'clock, she was once again hungry. She'd done laps around Daniel's suite, getting some exercise. It was a good-size office, and, with each turn, she stopped at the wide arch of windows and looked out over the city. Sheets of snow fell. She could hear the wind howl when she pressed close to the glass.

She crossed to Daniel's desk. He sat, shifting through a stack of papers needing his attention. He had a strong presence, even sitting at a desk chair, she noted. Wide shoulders, thick chest. He'd taken off his tie. Deep in thought, he'd run a hand through his hair and mussed one side. She liked him looking less than perfect. She remained quiet until he looked up, raised one eyebrow. The wicked-sexy brow that fascinated her.

Her breath caught. She stumbled through, "Is there a vending machine on the floor? Candy bars, sodas?"

He closed the file he'd been reading, set it neatly on the stack, and rose. He rolled his shoulders, stretched his arms over his head, and his shirt separated from his slacks. Skin. Four inches of sculpted abdomen. Riley couldn't help herself, she stared.

She had admired his height, his stature, his professional attire, but she had no clue what lay beneath his suit coat and starched shirt. Purely on speculation, she'd imagined him fit. There was a big difference between fit, ripped, and toned. He was all three.

His slacks slipped an inch, exposing his black Hermès waistband. The boxer briefs with the separate storage pouch. He shifted beneath her stare. Jamming his hands in his pockets, he turned away from her. But not before she'd glimpsed the swell beneath his zipper. Her heart skipped a beat. An erection? From her stare?

He spoke to her over his shoulder. "I can do better than junk food," he offered. "How about a sandwich? Roast beef and Swiss on rye?"

"Where will you find a deli open in this weather?"

"Better than a deli," he said, again facing her. "My kitchen."

Her eyes widened. "Where?"

"Follow me."

She grabbed her purse and was on his heels.

He crossed to the bookshelf, to the outline of a door she'd seen the previous day. It blended into the woodwork so perfectly, it was barely noticeable. He lifted a secret latch, the same color as the wood. Twisted it left. A door opened. He reached around the frame, flicked a switch. Lights came on.

"After you." He nudged her forward.

Stunned, she stepped into an apartment. Small, but nicely furnished. "Where am I?" she asked.

"My father's home away from home. A convenience. He often worked late hours, and instead of commuting to the lake house, he converted the adjacent office, and slept here. It made his life easier."

"How did your mother feel about him staying in town?"

He contemplated before saying, "She decorated the apartment for him. At the end of the day, I think she would have liked to see more of him," he said honestly. "But she accepted the fact that global finances was his second family. His life centered on the company."

"A lot of responsibility, I imagine."

"I'd go into detail, but—"

"It would go over my head," she finished for him. "I'm more right brain than left."

"My mother's right, too. Intuitive, imaginative, creative, an artist."

She assumed, "You and your father are left brain. Rational, logical, and intellectual."

"More or less."

He went to check out the food in the refrigerator, which allowed her time to look around. She viewed the night through tall, narrow-paned windows. Mother Nature shivered. The chill off the glass had Riley rubbing her arms briskly. A long navy upholstered couch and two overstuffed chairs edged a hand-woven wool rug of vibrant blue, gold, and cream hues. A pale blue glass coffee table appeared liquid.

Spectacular artwork decorated two of the walls. Oil paintings, one of ice skaters on a frozen lake;

the other, farmland and homestead covered by drifting snow. Lenore Hayes had signed the paintings. Daniel's mother. She had talent and a gift for detail. The chipped blade on an ice skate. The bleakness of a bird sitting on a bare tree branch. The hint of wind on a weather vane. Inspiring.

"Something to note, Riley," he informed her. "My personal shopper buys the occasional groceries. There's a list in the top right drawer of what I keep on hand. I often take lunch here. Saves time."

She liked to grocery-shop. "The closest store or marketplace?"

"I like Ridgeway Square. Six blocks east. Traditional and gourmet. They have an open-air market when the weather warms."

She made a mental note. She'd be forced to drive to the square in the winter, but come summer, a stroll down the sidewalk held appeal. The sun on her face. Breezy blouses and gauzy skirts.

"Can I help you do something?" she asked Daniel, as he removed packets of meat and cheese from the refrigerator. Then pulled a loaf of rye from the bread box. Scored a bag of wavy potato chips from the cupboard. Located paper plates.

"You can fix your own sandwich, if you like. No lettuce or tomato, but there's mustard and mayonnaise."

She worked beside him at the Indian blue granite counter. Swirls of gold and silver made the counter seem three-dimensional. She ran her hand over the surface. Very cool. An eighteen-inch color television fit beneath the kitchen cabinet, tucked flush against the wall. Next to a single-serve Keurig.

An easy silence stretched between them. They

shared a surprising familiarity and compatibility considering they'd known each other such a short time. She didn't overanalyze, merely went with it. She fixed her sandwich with a slice of beef and one of cheese. He stacked his own mile-high. She slipped her hand into the bag of chips and took a handful. He then shook half the bag onto his plate.

"Soda, iced tea, or bottled water?" he next asked her.

"Tea." He reached in the fridge and handed her an Arizona raspberry tea. Then snagged a Fiji for himself. Napkins. "Dad never got around to buying a kitchen table, so we'll sit on the couch."

He set his plate and water on the coffee table, then returned to the kitchen. He opened and closed cupboard doors until he located several jar candles and a book of matches. He returned with them to the sofa. He dropped down, two wide cushions away from her. "You don't want to catch my cold," he said. Considerate on his part. He then clustered the candles at one end of the coffee table. Matchbook in the middle.

She side-eyed him, and he explained, "I'm not setting the mood. The candles are merely precautionary so we'll have light, should we lose electricity."

She liked a man who planned for emergencies. She breathed easier. Took a bite of her sandwich.

He ate alongside her. Napkin over his lap. Mannerly. He kept their conversation going. "Tell me about Riley Tyler," he requested. "Something not on your résumé. Other than the fact you have a boyfriend."

What to tell? How much to tell? "Born and raised in Elmwood, North Saint Paul." Middle class.

He took a drink of his water, said, "Elmwood City Council has yet to pass the fiscal budget for next year. Continued debate on taxes and revenue."

He surprised her. "Obviously you follow all the news, both global and local." She was impressed.

"I follow finances. The smallest town's financial base can affect international economics."

Another bite, which she chewed slowly. Moving on, she said, "My parents own a local café, Tyler's Corner. I have four sisters and two brothers. I'm the youngest."

"The baby." The corners of his mouth curved. "Protected by your older siblings?"

"Stifled, sometimes. Loved, always." She then asked him, "How about you?"

"Only child."

"You never had to share toys or wear hand-me-downs."

He shook his head. "No, I did not."

"With a large family, you learn to appreciate 'new.'" She used finger quotes. "I always looked forward to Christmas, when I would get a gift just for me."

"Did you have a favorite present as a kid?"

"Two, actually." Both memories made her smile. "When I was ten years old, Santa brought me a jigsaw puzzle of a ballet recital. So beautiful. Pink leotards, gauzy tutus, and satin ballet slippers. It was a gift to put together, take apart, and assemble again. Until my older brother Jared stole several inside pieces, then couldn't remember where he'd hidden them. I never got them back."

"That's too bad."

"Especially as the missing section formed the ballet slippers. My dancers no longer had feet."

"Did you ever take ballet lessons?"

She crunched a potato chip. "No, too expensive. But I'd often stand outside on the sidewalk of Miss Rose's Studio and peer in the window during classes. I didn't have to participate to appreciate the beauty of dance."

"The Metropolitan Cultural Center is featuring *The Nutcracker* over the holidays."

"Have you priced the tickets?" Once the words were spoken, she blushed. Cost would matter little to Daniel. It only had bearing on her. Her bank account was not that flush. Even for mezzanine seating. "Someday." She left it at that.

She removed the crust on one corner of her sandwich, contemplative. "The Magic 8 Ball was my second favorite present. At age twelve, it ruled my life. I'd ask a question, shake the ball, and take every answer to heart."

He appeared amused. "What did you ask?"

"Did I have to do my homework? The answer: *It Is Certain.*"

He chuckled. "Understandable."

"Romance was always a biggie. Did Ryan Moran like me? *My Sources Say No.* How about Luke Epps? *Better Not Tell You Now.* Will Lake? *Yes, Definitely.* Which wasn't quite true. He liked me, but he liked my school lunches more. My mom packed a great lunch box. Thick peanut butter and jelly sandwiches, a bag of Fritos, fruit, and, best of all, Hostess Ho Hos. Two to a package. I loved the pinwheel inside."

He knew the outcome. "You shared your Ho Hos with Will."

"Until Mom replaced them with oatmeal cookies. Not Will's favorite. He then moved down the lunch table, sat next to Sally Young. She had Twinkies."

"Fickle young boy. Did he break your heart?"

"For about a minute. Not much bothers me. I bounce back fast."

"Resilience is good."

After a sip of her iced tea, she asked, "How about you? Best Christmas gift ever?"

He was slow to answer, finishing off his sandwich first. "Monopoly," he finally said. "I was eight. I always chose the car. My father turned the board game into a way to teach me commercial theories. Domination of a market, economic rewards, trade and developing properties with houses and hotels, collecting rent from opponents. Driving players into bankruptcy."

Her jaw dropped. She stared, disbelieving. The man was cutthroat. "You and I played two different games. I played for fun, you played for fiscal dominance."

He eyed her. "Bet you spent a lot of time in Jail. Landed on Income and Luxury Tax often, and lost all your money in the first thirty minutes."

How did he know? "The dice were not my friend." She daringly asked, "Your first train?"

He rubbed his forehead, thoughtful. "My sixth Christmas, my parents got me a LEGO deluxe train set. A bit old for me, but my father felt I'd grow into it. He helped me set it up on the hardwood floor in the library. There were"—he thought back—"curved, straight, and switching rails. An electric-powered engine. A flatbed and boxcars. The red caboose fascinated me most. I wanted to play with it separately. My dad explained that the caboose provided shelter for railroad crew, who were required for switching and shunting, and to keep a lookout for load shifting, damage to equipment and cargo, and overheating axles. I hooked it back on the train."

"You were six," she couldn't help but say. "How could you possibly grasp the purpose of the caboose?"

"No photographic memory, but I have exceptional retention."

She pursed her lips. "Your father must be a detailed and disciplined man."

"He once was. Not so much now. Dementia."

"I'm sorry."

He looked at her, then questioned, "How would you have handled the caboose?" Seemed important to him.

"I would've let you push the caboose by itself. All over your big old house. We would've named the caboose together, maybe Chug-Chug or Charlie. You could've taken it to bed with you."

He exhaled. "You'll make a good mother someday."

"My kids will be able to do and try most anything, and learn from experience."

"You say that now, but I bet you'll be very protective."

"No parent wants to see his child hurt. I'd try to shape awareness and sensibility. Foster kindness. Wisdom. Understanding."

"I'd contribute logic and deductive reasoning. Business acumen."

"Our kids would be balanced."

"Stable and capable."

"Happy . . ."

Together. The wind slammed against the windows, a reality check, reminding them of the reason they were there in the first place. A rampaging blizzard. They'd gotten way ahead of themselves. Sounding like a couple, yet they barely knew each other. He was her boss. She, just his personal shopper. Then there was Andrew Reynolds, her pretend boyfriend. She would never have gotten the job had it not been for the good doctor. She kept that in mind.

They came back to reality at the same time. She hugged her stomach. He rubbed the back of his neck. Awkwardness sat between them. Seconds pushed into a minute. Daniel rose from the couch. He collected their paper plates and bottles. Crossed to the kitchen. He turned on the television beneath the cabinets. The screen was fuzzy, and the meteorologist's words were choppy. They listened intently.

"Zero visibility. Thirty inches of snow. Gusts up to eighty miles per hour. Wind chill minus fifty. Stay indoors."

The lights blinked. Held. Daniel moved down the counter to the Keurig. "K-Cups," he offered. "Colombia coffee or salted caramel hot chocolate?"

"Hot chocolate." Warm and comforting on a snow-blown night.

The Keurig brewed quickly, and he soon handed her a red and white mug, striped like a candy cane. "My father wasn't always home during the holidays, so my mother brought Christmas to him at Landmark Tower." He poured his steaming Colombia Roast into a mug with a melting snowman on the side. The heat of the coffee liquefied Frosty down to his black top hat, charcoal eyes, and carrot nose.

Whimsical, she thought. She leaned back on the sofa, crossed her legs. She had a question for him. "Does your staff decorate for Christmas? Their offices? The hallway? The elevator? Outside of the wreath on the door of Personnel, the floor is pretty stark."

Glaringly bare, Daniel agreed. He was pleased the conversation had shifted to decorating. Minutes ago, he'd been stunned silent by how strongly they'd connected on a child's train set and sense of family. He liked her perspective. He was certain her children would be free-spirited. There would be laughter in her home. A loving warmth. Her little ones would bounce through summer, barefoot and hugging sunshine. Winter, they'd dress like Eskimos for sledding and snowball fights.

Once again, he thought Andrew Reynolds a lucky man.

"I have a tentative schedule for you, from now until the first of the year," he informed her.

She sat up straighter, alert, interested. Staring.

"I'll need five dress suits before week's end," he said. "I'm leaving for London next Saturday. An upcoming international conference. I'll return the following Wednesday."

"Not much time for tailor-made. You'll travel off-the-rack."

"I'm fine with that."

"Your sizes, measurements?"

"I have a binder with all my info." His thoughts shifted. To having her touch him. He would've enjoyed her measuring his chest, his inseam. He had watched her watch him when he'd unwrapped the statue in the conference room. She'd stared at his hands, her lips parted, her cheeks flushed, as if imagining his fingers on her skin. He'd gone purposely slow. Tightening her arousal. Until she'd jerked in her chair, embarrassed by her own wayward thoughts. He continued with, "Judith kept a wardrobe journal. One she left behind. The only thing she didn't destroy in her temper tantrum. I'll get it for you."

He set his mug on the coffee table, crossed to one of two doors on the far side of the room. "Bedroom, bathroom," he cast over his shoulder. He entered the bedroom, eased back the pocket doors on an empty walk-in closet, and located the journal on a top shelf above the shoe rack. He brought it to Riley. Sat back down. A bit closer to her on his return. Despite his cold.

She weighed the journal on her palms, then fanned the pages with her thumb. "Thick as a dictionary," she commented. "There's long lists of designer contacts, phone numbers, web pages, photos from fashion shows—Saint Laurent, Michael Bastian, Vivienne Westwood Men's Collection—along with seasonal updated trends, and page after page of your personal likes and dislikes."

She drew a breath, scanned a section. "Shoes and sandals. No, to flip-flops, slide sandals, Crocs, or clogs. Yes, to shoemakers John Lobb, Berluti, and A. Testoni." She gave a soft whistle before lowering her gaze to his wingtips. "Royal Black Berluti, according to the catalog picture. You paid a king's ransom."

"I pay for comfort."

She slowly closed the journal. "You in a binder.

Very helpful. I'll get started on Monday." She hesitated. "Will I have a desk?"

"I thought you might work from the elevator."

"A day of ups and downs."

She had a sense of humor. "You'll have an office."

Her eyes closed, and he swore she sighed. Looking at him again, she said, "A small space would be amazing."

"It won't be a suite like mine, but you'll be comfortable."

"I don't need much."

"You'll have whatever you need."

"Thank you," she said softly. Sincerely.

Her appreciation touched his heart. His chest warmed.

She licked her lips, asked, "Do I check with you first on all wardrobe purchases?"

"Not necessary. Just don't take off for New York Fashion Week without letting me know first. Judith went last year, without a word."

"No travel plans."

"I do, however, leave shortly. Have a suitcase packed and ready to go by next weekend. Professional attire. Five suits."

"Will you have downtime?"

"Minimal. A dinner possibly with the representatives from our London office. I keep entertaining to a minimum."

Her eyes widened. "Why?"

He was honest with her. "Socializing crosses the line between professional and personal. My father taught me to keep my distance, not to become too friendly. I don't need to be anyone's best friend. I avoid wives and children's names. I prefer it that way. My primary concern is that each man upholds his position to the highest standards."

He heard her mumble. "I didn't hear what you said."

She dipped her head. "Best you didn't."

"Don't be shy, Riley. I won't fire you for speaking your mind."

She blew out a breath. "Good to know, since I've only been on board three hours."

"So?" he pressed.

"You could let it go."

"Not if your comment concerned me."

She clutched the journal to her chest, as if protecting herself from him. Meeting his gaze, she spoke formally. "Very well, Mr. Hayes. I said, 'How sad for you.'"

"Sad? How?" He didn't fully understand.

"To have executives and staff busting their butts for you, making financial history, and you don't have time to know one personal thing about them."

He was stunned by her assumption, however true. He had worked with these people for ten years. They'd sat in boardrooms all over the world for days straight, discoursing on immediate and far-reaching economic issues. He was aware of their qualifications, but he knew nothing about them beyond the facts on their résumés.

She faulted him for that. He set his jaw, irritated by the fact.

"I didn't mean to offend you."

"I'm not offended, but I do feel judged. I'm in charge, and can't let my guard down. I don't have the freedom for friendships."

"Detachment is your friend."

Detachment? He cared. In his own way. "Tell me about your boss at Baby Gap," he said stiffly. "Were you buddies?"

"Baby Gap is a world apart from global capital. We're very human there."

And he wasn't?

"My manager was an older woman," she said with feeling. "Myra Ronan shared pictures of her grandchildren with everyone who entered the store. There was no separation of company and clientele. Being personable, caring, built our sales." She next rattled off Myra's husband's name, listed all her children and grandchildren. The schools they attended. Their teachers and grades on report cards. Their extracurricular activities. She covered the dogs and cats, and a goldfish named Glimmer. "The assistant manager—"

He held up his hand. "One big, happy family. I get it."

"We were close, no denying. That closeness made for a comfortable work environment."

"You think I'm a stuffed shirt?"

"More of a tight ass. You wear pants well."

He blinked. Riley jumped topics so fast, it took him a second to catch up. She'd censured him, then complimented his butt. He didn't have a comeback.

"I'd never criticize you, Daniel." Her tone was apologetic, sincere. "You are who you are. You're aloof, and I'm open, a people person."

"There's not a lot of socializing here, Riley," he cautioned, not wanting her feelings hurt. "Don't be offended—"

"If I'm ignored? Should someone blow me off?"

"We have a lot of work to accomplish each day. My executives pack sixteen hours into a ten-hour day."

"I'm grateful for my job. I can fade into the background. I won't approach anyone for coffee or conversation."

He felt like a heel, discouraging her from making friends. But he liked things the way they were. He prided himself on organization. The offices ran smoothly. Everyone kept his nose to the grindstone. He sensed there might be something about Riley that would prove disruptive. He suspected she had that kind of personality. Positive and personable, she would touch lives. Look what she'd done to him with the train. She'd recognized his youth. Made him feel like a young boy. Intuitive, she saw people from the inside out.

She set the journal beside her on the sofa. "I will have you packed and ready to travel, easy-peasy."

Easy-peasy. He'd never heard the expression. He assumed she'd accomplish the task.

"What are my responsibilities while you're gone?"

"How do you feel about Christmas decorations?" He awaited her reaction.

She told him what he hoped to hear. "They make the season bright."

"You were hired as my personal shopper, but there might be additional duties."

"Whatever you need."

He appreciated her enthusiasm. "The firm hasn't decorated for years. Do you have any experience?"

"I did the store windows at Baby Gap."

He pictured garland-wrapped strollers. Ornaments hanging from the rails of a baby's bed. Holiday sippy cups. He hoped for a more mature theme, but refused to discourage her before she even got started.

"Meet with Georgia once I'm gone. You'll be starting from scratch. Buy whatever you need. There's friendly competition between the floors, so let's let everyone know that the best decorated floor wins a catered deli lunch. George in Security is the impartial judge."

"I'm already tasting pastrami on rye. Those big deli dill pickles." She pursed her lips, had one final question, "Any restrictions?"

"No live animals."

"So much for the reindeer."

He nearly smiled. Nearly. They were back in sync. It felt good. Outside, the world disrupted them. The windows shuddered with the force of the wind. Snow plastered the glass. The electricity flickered, held, failed. They sat in darkness.

Daniel didn't hesitate. He reached across the coffee table, found the book of matches. He began lighting the candles. Flames jumped, then settled into an intimate glow. The room was cast in gold and orange hues.

"The television's off," he said.

"Too difficult to read by candlelight."

He relaxed enough to say, "Care to play a board game?"

She shut him down. "Not Monopoly, you'd kick my butt. I don't want to spend the blizzard in Jail."

"How about Daytrader?"

"I'm not familiar."

"Monopoly meets *The Wolf of Wall Street*."

She scrunched her nose. "Financial markets?"

He nodded, rubbed his hands together, and

gave her an idea of what to expect. "You get jobs and make money, then start trading in the companies you work for to accumulate enough cold, hard cash to retire. When it's time to cash out, you try to make it to the bank for the win before the volatile market sets you back." He let the concept soak in. "Care to play in my world?"

"The game's right up your alley, not mine. You'd have an advantage."

"Give it a try—what do you have to lose?" He retrieved the boxed board game from the bottom dresser drawer in the bedroom. He'd played the game often as a kid. He'd only beaten his father once.

"We'll use the coffee table as our trading floor."

"I can hardly wait." She was less than enthusiastic.

He laid out the game, then ran through the rules with her, keeping them as simple as possible. He finished with, "You'll need to make fast decisions. Don't get greedy and overtrade. As far as money management, beware of the volatility of stocks. Got it?"

"I'm processing." Her eyes were glazed.

They both leaned forward, ready to play.

Thirty quick minutes passed. She fell back on the sofa, her face pinched. "You won."

That he had. She hadn't proved much of a challenge. It was the quickest game he'd ever played. "You came in second."

"There were only two of us playing."

"The game was new to you. You'll do better next time."

"If there is a next time."

"Surely you'll want a rematch."

"My game next time."

"Whenever."

"Now."

She reached for her envelope purse. "How about Connect Four? I carry a miniature version with me. I haven't emptied my bag since Baby Gap."

He'd played so few kids' games, and wasn't acquainted with her choice. "A brain game?"

"You have to think fast."

He had a quick mind. "I accept your challenge."

He soon learned Connect Four was similar to tic-tac-toe. The object of the game was to connect four of a player's colored discs so they formed a line in a horizontal, vertical, or diagonal direction.

She chose the red discs and he went with yellow. He had big hands, and the playing grid was only six by six inches. The discs were tiny, and they slipped off his fingertips. They alternated turns, and she played hard. Riley bit down on her lip, all wide-eyed concentration. He paid more attention to her than the game. She had a sweet mouth. Full, gently curved. Kissable. The thought distracted him. So much so, he missed a turn or two.

She beat him twenty-one of twenty-two games.

He held up his hands in defeat.

She laughed out loud. Grinned from ear to ear. Crazy-happy at beating him. A game meant for ages six and up. He was thirty-five and she, thirty. They were on the older side of Connect Four.

Still, her delight touched him. Warmth spread from his gut to his chest. His smile came easily, and hers faded. She stared at him. A stare he now recognized as being either astonished or simply dazed.

Completely awed, she placed her hand over her heart, and slowly said, "Total transformation, Daniel Hayes. You're a handsome man, but when you smile, you're a lady-killer."

CHAPTER 4

Riley couldn't forget Daniel's smile. Fleeting and astonishing. His dimples flashed, deepened, and she forgot to breathe. She'd never seen a better-looking man in all her life. She felt a moment of sadness that he was so serious. A grin from the CEO, and world economic leaders and his own executives would see him as more than a financial genius. The lean hardness of his face had shown his character. His smile portrayed both charm and strength. A man of depth. He was so much more than a suit.

She took apart the game grid, scooped up the discs, and tucked Connect Four back into her envelope purse. To be played another day. A sharp knock on the apartment door, and Daniel rose to check on the arrival.

A flashlight swept the room. "Last pass of the night, Mr. Hayes," George from Security said, sounding out of breath. "Climbing stairs has worn me out. I wanted to make sure everything was secure before I headed back to my station in the lobby."

"We're fine," Daniel assured him. "Can I make you a sandwich to go? How about an iced tea?"

The guard shook his head. "Thank you, no. My wife sent me to work with a grocery bag of food. She anticipated the snowstorm long before the weatherman."

"How is—" Daniel's brow creased.

"Hannah, my better half?" George supplied.

"Yes, Hannah," Daniel slowly repeated, as if storing her name in his memory.

"She retired from teaching, sir. Her days are filled with grandchildren and knitting. A neighborhood coffee klatch. Thank you for asking."

"She's safe during the blizzard?"

"Hannah's staying with my oldest son and his family. My boy recently built a new home. Two fireplaces. The garage is stacked with wood. Everyone will be warm and out of harm's way."

Daniel nodded, nothing more. His attempt at personal small talk was short, but obviously appreciated. George stood taller.

"I'll see you after the storm passes." The guard quietly closed the door.

"He's a nice man. Conscientious," Riley said once he was gone. "Climbing all those stairs had to be strenuous."

Daniel mused, "George is known to take the stairs on occasion. Keeps him in shape, and he swears he beats the elevator when it stops on every floor."

"His wife's name is Hannah."

He came back to the couch, stood over her. "So he told us."

"Because you asked him."

"I was being . . . polite."

"You showed interest. Most people love to talk about their families."

He shrugged. "It's not a big deal."

"It was to George." Pause. "And to me."

"Why you?" he asked.

"I like compassion in a man."

"Don't read too much into our conversation."

"You know his wife's name, and next time you can ask about his oldest son."

His jaw tightened. "We'll be all business when I see him again. He'll be running Security and I'll be dealing with finances."

"That's that."

"It is what it is, Riley. The way it's always been. We work hard and smart, proving to the financial world that we're serious. We stretch ourselves. We don't let each other down." He pinned her with a look. "Change can be confusing."

"I think you're in a rut," slipped out. She kicked herself for once again speaking so bluntly. It wasn't her place. Being confined with the man, playing games by candlelight, had skewed her perspective. He was powerful, influential. He'd hired her, he could just as easily fire her.

Regret prompted her apology. "Open mouth, insert foot."

He crossed his arms over his chest, and calmly said, "Twice you've apologized to me now."

"You're keeping count?"

"I'm good with numbers."

"Two is memorable."

His expression was unreadable when he said, "You're too new to Global Financiers to understand our spectrum of personalities, and how each person settles into the company."

"Like human puzzle pieces?"

"We fit."

She wondered if there was a space open for her. Doubtful. A personal shopper was not a key player. She'd never take a seat in the boardroom. Too starched and stuffy. She might never make a friend. She would do her job. Stay out of everyone's way.

She unexpectedly yawned. Her day had been full, emotional, as she'd awaited Daniel's decision on who would win the role as his personal shopper. So few hours had passed since she'd presented him with the train set. Since he'd chosen her. Now they faced a night together on the thirtieth floor. Fatigue claimed her.

She placed her hands on either side of her thighs, gave a bounce on the sofa cushion. The couch was comfortable. She had no expectation that Daniel would give up the bedroom. Toss her a pillow and blanket, and she'd sleep tight. The sofa was long enough that she wouldn't get a crick in her neck from the armrest.

"You look tired," Daniel observed.

She rubbed her eyes. "I'm fading fast."

"Bed, then."

Bed? "The sofa is fine."

"You'd be more comfortable in the bedroom."

"Where will you sleep?" she asked cautiously.

She met his gaze. Heat darkened his eyes. She flushed. The walls closed around them. Intimate and embracing. Awareness thickened the air. Unexpected. Unintentional. But tangible. He released a slow breath. She barely managed to draw air in.

His nostrils flared ever so slightly. Her lips parted. Expectancy swelled amid the shadowed flames. A sudden longing lodged in her chest.

Unfamiliar territory. Two people riding out a snowstorm. Attraction tugged, awakening feelings and possibilities. She hadn't seen it coming. The sensation jarred and scared her.

He had graciously offered her his bed. His own sleeping arrangements, undecided. They'd shared a hot look. One that drew her nipples to points and dampened her panties.

He was equally affected, she noted. An erection was difficult to hide. He slid his hands into his pockets and made a discreet adjustment.

Candlelight flickered over his face. His expression appeared as confused as she felt. All because of a stare. They hadn't even touched.

Imaginary or not, she had a boyfriend. Andrew Reynolds was an implied prerequisite to her employment. A man not to be forgotten. She lowered her gaze, clasped her hands on her lap. Waited for the moment to pass and the air to clear.

"I'll take the couch," he decided. "There's bedding in the closet. Plenty of pillows and comforters. The building temperature may drop, but not significantly."

She lifted her gaze. "No shivers or chattering teeth?"

"I'll make sure you stay warm."

His body heat reached her. Surrounded her. Embraced her. He held out his hand, and she took it. He pulled her to her feet. She bumped into his side. Sensed his strength. Felt protected. She slipped her hand free, and pulled back. He picked up two jar candles, passed her one. Then maintaining a platonic distance, she followed him to the bedroom.

He held the door for her, and she entered. She took two steps, and stopped. Holding up her candle, she squinted against the light. She made out a dresser with a mirror and a double bed. Unmade. She set her candle on the built-in shelf in the headboard. The room softened to a bedtime glow.

"The closet connects the bedroom and bathroom," he told her. His trip into the closet produced a stack of bedding. He helped her make the bed. Man and woman. A silent closeness. Spreading and tucking cotton flannel sheets. Smoothing the goose down comforter. Plumping feather pillows. Her stomach tightened when their fingers brushed. Their heightened familiarity was as warm and comforting as a wool blanket. Their closeness felt uncanny.

The bed was soon made, and her stomach softened with appreciation. She stood aside as he collected his own bedding, tucked it under one arm, then turned toward the door. He still held his candle.

"There may be enough water pressure to wash your face and hands," he cast back. "I wouldn't advise a shower. You'd end up soapy. There should be a new toothbrush and toothpaste in the cabinet. Feel free to use what you need."

Her throat tightened at his kindness. "Thank you," was barely audible.

"You may find me serious and harsh," he said from the doorway. "In my own way, however conflicting with yours, I do look out for those in my employ. That includes you, Riley, on this blustery night." One corner of his mouth curved. "A better day tomorrow. I'll cook you breakfast if the electricity's back on. Otherwise, it's dry cereal." He left her.

She missed him the moment he closed the door. Their rapport had touched her deeply. It had come on so suddenly. An indescribable longing. She believed he felt it too. Maybe not as strongly as she did, but still, his gaze had shone with interest. Unimaginable as that seemed. He was somebody. She, a nobody.

Had it not been for the blizzard, they might never have spent any time together. Never gotten acquainted, beyond her purchasing his wardrobe and awaiting his approval.

She tamped down her feelings. Her position with him was personal shopper. Nothing more. She would school her features, detach. Downplay her emotions. The last thing she wanted was to get fired, one day into the job. Still, a small part of her anticipated seeing him the next morning.

With a quick trip to the bathroom, she freshened up to the best of her ability with the meager water supply. Returning, she let the candlelight play across the walls of his executive closet. The masculine look was carried out in hardwood floors and cedar paneling. Chrome bars with luxury wooden coat, suit, and pant hangers. Tall shoe trees and tie racks. Not a stitch of clothing remained. Vengeance by Judith Scissorhands. Because Daniel hadn't loved her.

Riley stepped from the closet and rounded the foot of the bed. Went to sit on the side. She slipped off her shoes and slid into bed. Fully clothed. She snuggled into the cocoon of flannel and goose

down. She blew out the candle. She closed her
eyes, and her breathing slowed. She slept deep.
Ten hours straight.

A knock on her door had her blinking. She
rubbed her eyes. Ran a hand down her face. She
felt momentarily disoriented. Until the previous
day came into focus. The blizzard. Daniel's office
apartment, his bedroom. The warmth of the comforter against the cooling air. The electricity had
yet to be restored, she realized. She faced dry cereal for breakfast.

She pushed up on one elbow, called, "Come in."

Daniel cracked the door, and a crease of light
shot across the bed. Morning followed him into
the room. She glanced in the mirror atop the
dresser next to the bed. Inwardly groaned. Sleep
had not been kind to her. Bed head. A pillow
crease on her cheek. Sleep in her eyes. Her lips
were dry. Her knit sweater hung off one shoulder.
She needed mouthwash and deodorant.

Daniel, on the other hand, had never looked
more handsome. She liked his rolled-off-the-couch
look. Sexy, and romantic. Stubble darkened his
jaw. His shirt was untucked, but not wrinkled. He
stood in sharply creased slacks and his socks. He
rested one hip against the door frame. Sipped a
bottle of water.

She wiggled her butt up the mattress, and the
comforter fell across her thighs. She straightened
the neckline on her sweater. Tugged down the hem
that had snuck up beneath her bra. Then leaned
against the headboard. Met his gaze.

"Good morning," he initiated.

"How good is it?" she asked, referring to the weather.

"Snow is still falling, but less wind. I can see the skyline."

She breathed a little easier. "Snow removal?"

"No snowplows or trucks that I can see."

"Soon," she said hopefully.

"I imagine the government center, banks, and most of downtown is shut down. Schools will be closed, too. Students will have a snow day."

She grinned. "I loved those days. School buses were unable to run, but we could still go outside and sled, make snow angels, and build snowmen."

"Sounds like a good time." Pause. "My father always found a way to bring a tutor to the house when schools were closed."

"No fun there." She bit her lip for being so blunt.

He shrugged. "Education was important to my dad. He believed we should never stop learning. Even on a snow day."

"I'm sure he had your best interests at heart."

"He did," was what he said. What she heard was, *"A day of play would've been nice, too."*

She let it go. In her mind, learning was important. Experiencing life, equally so.

"Breakfast?" he offered.

"French toast, scrambled eggs, bacon, bowl of fresh fruit."

"Dry cereal."

"Captain Crunch, Honey Nut Cheerios, Lucky Charms?"

"Muesli or Bran Flakes. Healthy."

"Yum. Fiber."

"No milk, but there's honey."

Despite the scarcity of choices, she was hungry. "I'm in."

She pushed back the comforter, sat on the edge of the bed, put on her saddle shoes. Stood and stretched until her back cracked. Her sweater rose with her arms, over her abdomen, closer to her satin B-cups. She remembered that she'd worn her lucky bra to the final interview. Sheer black satin demi-cups edged with lace. A super-sexy bra. It gave her confidence. She flashed him. Her face heated.

Daniel's gaze lowered to her breasts, and his own color heightened. He blew out a breath. His jaw tightening. A gentleman, he looked away.

She lowered her arms. Swallowed. Reached for her purse on the dresser, searched for a comb. "I'll be with you in a minute." She kept her voice light. "Hair and teeth."

He nodded, made a slow turn out the door. Side view showed his protruding zipper. A significant ridge. Based on her breasts. Her heart would've burst with happiness at any other time in her life. Instead she lowered her expectations and reminded herself she had a boyfriend. However pretend.

Hair combed, her teeth brushed—a drizzle of water, and the taste of toothpaste lingered—she next made the bed. Then found her way to the living room. Daniel had set the coffee table with two boxes of cereal, plastic bowls and spoons, paper towel napkins, a squeeze container of honey, and two bottles of water.

She crossed to the sofa, dropped down. He

came to sit beside her. Closer this morning than the night before. "How's your cold?" she asked.

"Better, I think."

She was a human thermometer. Without thinking, she touched her fingers to his forehead to check if he was overly warm. His brow was as cool as her fingertips. He arched one wicked-sexy eyebrow questioningly, and heat crept up her neck. She explained, "Mothers came into Baby Gap with cranky children, some were ill. I was often asked to feel foreheads for fever. Sorry, Daniel. Knee-jerk reaction. You're fine."

A smile played about his mouth. One corner tipped. "Thank you."

"For what?"

"Your concern for my health."

"We can't have the boss sick, can we?"

"I'm not a good patient. I get ornery when I don't feel well. I'm known to growl."

"More than usual?" Again, inappropriate.

"I'll let that one slide."

She'd forgotten herself. They sat so casually on the couch, so at ease with one another, that it was hard to remember he was the CEO of Global Financial. Influential in economic circles. Respected in the community. A desired bachelor in the Twin Cities.

She suddenly wondered whom he had dated when he had social obligations or downtime. The question was on the tip of her tongue, but she bit it back. His cultural circle was out of her league and none of her business. Still, she wondered how often he brought a woman to his apartment. Her stomach knotted with the thought of him and a lover in the same bed where she'd spent the night. She licked her lips. Sighed.

Riley's expression spoke to Daniel. She was easy to read. He felt she had more on her mind than cereal. He side-eyed her several times, and with each glance, found her staring at the bedroom door. Intently. He wasn't sure why.

He was analytical. A few questions, and he'd have his answer. "Did you sleep well?" he began.

She nodded. "A deep sleep. One of the best I've had in ages."

"You were warm enough?"

"Toasty."

"I've always slept well there when I've spent a night in town."

"Do you stay in the city often?"

"Not as often as my father. Mostly when I have a social function."

She hesitated. "I'm sure you're a man in demand. Cocktail parties, charity dinners, fund-raisers, you and your . . . date."

Date? He'd tapped in to her thoughts. She was curious as to the ladies in his life. Possibly even wondered how many had shared his bed. He'd never explained his personal life to anyone. There'd been no reason. He sensed her distress at having slept on another woman's sheets. A vulnerability. A part of him needed to clear the air.

"No other woman has spent time in my apartment." He kept his voice even. "Other than Judith. And that was only when she organized my closet or dropped off groceries. She was never here longer than an hour. That was my rule. This is my private space, my sanctuary. A place where I can breathe when I need to escape. Where I crash when the day's gotten away from me."

Her face softened. Her eyes brightened. He'd eased her mind. She looked at him as if he'd righted the world. She cleared her throat, said, "I hadn't meant to pry, but I felt awkward—"

"In a bed where I'd made love."

Her cheeks pinkened. "More or less. You were voted one of the Twin Cities' most eligible bachelors."

"I like being single," he stated. "My wealth and heritage put me in the public eye. I work more than I date. I've never met that special someone to share my life with. Not like you and the doc."

"Andrew . . ."

He heard the breathy catch in her voice. Such throatiness could only be love. He didn't want to dwell on the relationship she had and the fact that he'd never been seriously involved.

He moved on, pointing to the boxes of cereal. "Your choice."

"Muesli. It's like granola."

He went with Bran Flakes. Adding honey, they scooped and ate. The crunch of her eating the granola cereal was the only sound in the living room. He heard every oat cluster and nut. He smiled to himself. He enjoyed having breakfast with her.

"Plans for today?" she asked between bites.

"Global Financial is expanding. We're hoping to merge with Fredericks International, a progressive corporation outside Washington, D.C. They would complement our long-term operating balance of current assets and liabilities with their short-term focus on managing cash, inventories, and borrowing and lending."

Riley looked lost. So he modified, "I'll be bringing the founder to visit our home base here in Minneapolis closer to Christmas. I need to formulate an agenda. Show him how the company is run."

"Is he as formidable as you?"

"Equally so. Perhaps even more so. Geoffrey Fredericks is an economic Einstein. He has tremendous ability and foresight. He's had a rough year. His wife passed away unexpectedly. He has a small son, Christopher. They will travel together when the time comes."

"Personal shopper, holiday decorator, babysitter," she assumed.

"Would you mind terribly?"

"I love kids. Perhaps a movie or a trip to the toy store. I could help him pick out a Christmas present for his dad."

"I'm appreciative. Christopher is six."

"Six is a great age. Six-year-olds are vulnerable, yet expectant. They still hug without being embarrassed."

She finished off her first bowl of muesli, and went for seconds. She used her spoon to sift through the cereal box, picking out the dried fruit. He could only stare. The next time he poured out a bowl of granola, there'd be no dried cranberries, apricots, or raisins. He shook his head. She had a hearty appetite.

Riley slowly came to realize what she was doing. The spoon even with her lips, she blushed, "I-I've eaten—"

"I know."

"Why didn't you stop me?"

He shrugged. "It doesn't really matter. I prefer the nuts and oat clusters over the fruit."

"Really?"

"A single raisin might've been nice."

She looked down at her spoon. Piled with raisins. Instead of pouring them back in the box, she ate them. Right in front of him. She chewed, swallowed, added, "They are good." She scooped through the remaining cereal and found one raisin. She held it up for him. "You're in luck." She rolled the raisin off her spoon and back into the cereal. Then resealed the box. Her grin broke. "Happy now?"

"Thanks for sharing," he said with a hint of sarcasm.

"I'll get a new box when I grocery-shop for you."

He'd eaten the same cereal for years. A change might be nice. "Choose something similar to what I've been eating, but slightly different."

"How different? Puffs, Chex, colorful circles, frosted, fruity, chocolate, cinnamon, Cookie Crisp, stars, marshmallows?" she rattled off. She knew her children's cereal.

"Nothing too sweet."

"Maybe a peanut butter crunch."

"Maybe . . ." He was hesitant. "Use your best judgment. I'm into nutrition. And I do like raisins."

"Raisin Bran has two scoops of raisins."

They'd both finished their breakfast. She rose, disposed of the plastic bowls and plastic spoons. Daniel leaned back on the couch and appreciated her backside as she stood on tiptoe before the cupboard and replaced the cereal and honey on the top shelf.

Riley Tyler was a small woman. Curvy. Cute. Full of energy and suggestions. She spoke her mind. He liked that best about her. No one had ever criticized him before. Unless it was behind his back. She was frank, and gave it to him straight. He didn't mind her candor.

He stood, said, "I'll be working at my desk if you need me."

She crossed to the coffee table, lifted his wardrobe binder. "I'll be sitting in a chair facing you. I'm a visual person. I'll be making up a mental color palette. I want to go page by page and imagine you wearing the clothes. I'll take notes, and once the electricity is restored, I'll call in rush orders for the necessary purchases."

Color palette? Made him nervous. He felt compelled to remind her, "There's nothing wrong with dark suits and white shirts."

She gave him a thumbs-up. "I'm with you. Conservative yet fashion forward."

That stopped him cold. One corner of his eye twitched, and his jaw clamped. "Riley . . ."

"I'm playing you, Daniel."

"Not funny."

"It is if you could see your face."

He glanced toward the arched windows and caught his reflection. Creased forehead, tight-lipped, stiff-necked. He had the look of his father. A man set in his ways. Stern and serious. Inflexible.

Daniel released a slow breath. He respected his dad. Always had, always would. Franklin had conformed to traditional dress. Old-style suited him. Daniel, too. There was nothing wrong with basic and bland.

A hint of sunshine contradicted him. Pushing through the clouds, shades of pale yellow and gold streaked the dark hardwood floor, bringing warmth to a drab day. He watched the hues come alive, sparkle, and dance.

"Whimsical." Riley stood behind him. "I won't go full kaleidoscope on you, Daniel, but color can be flattering, if only in a tie."

His face relaxed. His expression was once again his own.

Riley walked ahead of him into his office, the big binder in hand. "I'll pull those pages for clown and circus trends. No Bozo for you."

Daniel chuckled. Half-smiled.

Riley heard him. Grinned back.

Humor. They connected in that moment. A first for him with any woman. The ladies in his life went out of their way to impress him. To please him. Flirty, flattering. Phony. They tried too hard. Riley was her own person. Funny and quirky. Her comments uncensored.

He liked her.

Liking her stopped at friendship. He'd never pursue another man's woman, even if Andrew was halfway around the world. That relationship would never be compromised. Decency was ingrained in his DNA.

He was soon seated behind his desk. No computer. No laptop. No connection to the outside world. He withdrew a legal yellow pad from his top desk drawer. Located his favorite Parker ink pen, a gift from his mother. It weighed nicely in his hand. He started outlining a schedule.

Riley flipped through the binder pages, the sound mildly distracting. Daniel worked best quiet and alone. Ten minutes passed, and he sensed her gaze. He glanced up. She sat in the middle club chair and faced him squarely. She openly stared. Direct, intense, thoughtful.

He set down his ink pen, steepled his fingers, asked, "What's on your mind, Riley?" Better to know now than later.

"I was wondering what your favorite color is."

"Why?"

"For your wardrobe color wheel."

"Explain."

"Choose a color and I'll build your closet around it."

"Black." That would keep his suits dark and conventional.

"Limiting, but workable." She rose off her chair slightly and reached across his desk, stealing his pen. His *favorite* pen. She began taking her own notes. Then afterward went on to say, "I have a few more clothes questions, if you don't mind."

"Aren't your questions answered in the binder?"

"All notations by Judith," she returned. "I want to start with a clean slate. You telling me your preferences."

His preferences. Difficult to say. He'd always depended on his personal shopper. That's why he had one. "Perhaps a bit later," he stalled.

"I have all day." Her gaze pinned him once again.

She would stare at him until he responded, he was sure of it. It was as amusing as it was annoying. He'd talk to her, if talking got his pen back. He nodded. "Let's do it now. You have five minutes."

"Might take ten."

"Seven, max."

Her grin told him longer. Much longer. However much time she needed to dress him. A part of him liked the fact she was paying so much attention to him. Even though their discussion made him uncomfortable. He had no personal style.

"Run with it."

She did. "My Qs are relevant to you, the man."

"I'm listening."

"Let's start at the top and work down. The collars on your dress shirts: point, spread, or button-down?"

He touched his collar. "Point."

She made a notation in the binder, then tapped his pen against her chin. A rather stubborn chin, he realized, and one she lifted to get her way. It was up now. "You have a wide chest." Her gaze touched on his shoulders, skimmed his torso. "We'll go regular over slim fit." She jotted it down. "Until I order tailor-made. Fabric, Daniel. Royal oxford cloth, poplin, herringbone twill, white pique cotton?"

He hadn't a clue. Royal sounded good. "Oxford cloth."

She nodded approvingly. "Nice choice. Shirt cuffs: French, barrel, or button?"

He vaguely recalled Judith mentioning that French cuffs added a touch of masculine elegance. A richness to his wardrobe. "Button." He didn't want any memories of her in his closet.

"Ties. Striped, checked, paisley, retro swirls."

"Solid." He expected her to say "boring." She surprisingly did not.

"Belt or beltless pants?"

He'd always worn a belt. "Belt."

She moved to winter trousers. "Wool or heavy cotton?"

"Wool," sounded logical.

"Do you chafe?"

What kind of question was that?

She caught his confusion, and explained, "A silky lining works best if your thighs rub. Even if they don't—"

"They don't," he felt compelled to say.

"—the silk helps retain the shape of the slacks, and upholds the integrity of the fabric."

"Fine."

"You're fit and won't need an expandable waist-band."

He had a home gym. Worked out.

"Flat front or pleat?"

"Flat."

More writing. He was about to tell her enough was enough. She was a major distraction. Not only to his workday, but in the way her soft brow creased in concentration. How she bit down on her bottom lip. Then flicked the tip of her tongue to the corner of her mouth. She unconsciously pressed his pen against her lips. He half-expected her to suck the end. His reaction to the idea left him hard. He shifted on his chair.

"Socks next. I'll deal with your shoes later."

They were winding down. He breathed easier.

"Mid-calf or knee-length?"

"Calf."

"Cashmere or silk?"

"Cashmere."

"Socks that stay up on their own or sock garters?"

His father wore sock garters; he never had. "Stay ups," he said, adding, "Socks should match my trousers," or so Judith had said.

"For formal occasions, yes. More casual, perhaps argyle. Traditional, professional, yet adds flare."

She finished her notes, looked up. Her expression was serious. "Why do you need a personal shopper?"

He had a logical explanation. "My father had one, and since I don't have a great sense of style, he advised me to hire one, too. Business runs my day. It's time-consuming to shop. Left to my own devices, I'd wear the same suit month to month."

"I doubt that." She glanced down at her notes. "You know what you like. A good tailor could easily outfit you. Rotate your suits, shirts, ties by season."

Truth be told, he'd debated a tailor after Judith's tirade. He hadn't been certain he could deal with another woman's emotions. Georgia insisted he try again. Then came the interviews. And Riley. He hadn't been sure about her then. Still wasn't certain now. But the personal contact between them appealed to him. He liked their interaction.

He cleared his throat, asked, "Are you talking yourself out of a job?"

"I want to be sure you truly need me, that's all."

Her concern touched him. "I require your assistance for more than my clothes. A tailor wouldn't shop for my groceries, decorate for Christmas, or babysit a potential corporate partner's son." He surprised himself by adding, "I want you here, Riley."

"Here to stay."

Good to hear. "You will be, once the blizzard passes and you settle into a routine."

"Routines are dull. Mind-numbing."

He liked order. "You can create your own schedule," he relented.

"I'll keep you apprised of any and all fittings. You'll need to try on the clothes I buy before you leave for London. No point in boarding the plane with a suitcase full of shoulder-sagging suits or baggy trousers. Too tight shoes." She finalized, "I'll also help you pick out ties."

Ties. An unexpected image flashed before his eyes, and held. One he couldn't control. One that affected his groin. Intense and magnified. He pictured her naked with designer ties about her neck. The ends barely concealing her nipples. The point of one extra-long tie arrowed low. Sexy. He scooted his chair fully beneath his desk. Before she saw he'd posted a boner.

He returned to work, without his favorite pen. The day progressed, and he didn't get nearly as much accomplished as he'd planned. Not with Riley sitting across from him. Not with her casting him looks from beneath her lashes. Picturing his palette.

Color him hot and bothered.

CHAPTER 5

Riley found herself staring at Daniel time and again over the next week, as she gathered his travel attire. It had taken the Twin Cities several days to dig out from the blizzard. Once the electricity was reinstated, she made dozens of calls. She found voice contact far more efficient than e-mails or texts. She liked the personal touch, talking to an actual individual on the other end of the line, and not just reading messages on her iPhone or computer screen. She was pleased with all of Daniel's purchases. She hoped he would be, too.

The highlight of her week came when his suits were delivered, and he tried on each one. There were five total. The man was born to wear a suit. Tall, lean, solid, he looked spectacular.

He gravitated to black and deep navy. Her favorite was Cambridge gray. Lighter than charcoal, and darker than a dove's wing. The most versatile, in her opinion. She'd paired the suit with a blue-

and-white-striped shirt and dark blue tie with flecks of nickel.

She'd purchased and positioned a standing floor mirror in one corner of his bedroom, so he could check his appearance and get the full effect. His dresser mirror cut him in half.

His administrative assistant, Roxanne, had brought him paperwork to sign as he stood in his new gray suit beside his desk. She'd gaped, then closed her mouth so fast, she bit her tongue. She'd set the papers on his desk and admired, "Nice change from black."

"I like black," he'd returned.

"Gray likes you more." Roxanne disappeared.

Riley kept him comfortable with her selections. Minimal color. He hadn't complained once. Not even over the Santa Claus tie she thought might add to the spirit of the season once he'd returned to the office.

Late Friday afternoon she packed for him. He would be traveling abroad on the corporate jet, a Citation CJ3+, she'd learned, with three other executives early Saturday morning. She laid out his leather duffel and garment bag on the bed in his office apartment. New masculine luggage she'd chosen after hearing Judith had poked holes in his previous Tumi Alpha.

Daniel joined her after his meeting on safeguarding the integrity of principal-agent relationships and supervisory functions. She couldn't discuss the subject. She was lucky to have remembered the topic. For that alone, she was proud of herself.

He now stood in the doorway to the bedroom, a

shoulder to the jamb, and watched her. "I received the schedule you drew up of your projects while I'm away. You'll be busy."

Purposely so. "Lots to accomplish." She would force herself to complete a number of tasks. Otherwise she'd think of him. He'd be away for four days, returning on Wednesday. She would miss him. More than she wanted to admit. He'd helped her adjust to a new work environment, and made sure she was comfortable in her office. Her own space at the end of the hallway. She had plenty of room, high-end furniture, and more technology than she'd use in a lifetime. Her favorite chair was an overstuffed swivel. She spun for fun. Daniel caught her, and had lifted his wicked-sexy eyebrow. The arch that stopped her heart. Tingled her tummy. And left her knees weak.

"Last suit," she told him, stretching over the garment bag and attempting to hang the rotating hook over a short bar. She pinched her finger, pulled her hand back.

He crossed to her. "Let me help," he offered.

He bent behind her, leaned down, just as she flattened her palms on the mattress and pushed up. She planted her bottom in his groin. Startled, she shifted her hips, driving her deeper into him. He grabbed her waist, stilled her, but didn't let her go.

Sex presented itself. The air grew heavy.

She gasped.

He groaned.

Neither moved.

She heard her heartbeat in her ears. Felt it in her throat.

He inhaled sharply. Raw. Sexual.

She quivered.

He thickened. His dick pressed the crease of her ass.

A compromising position. One of carnal intent.

He recovered first. Jerked back. "Damn," he muttered. His expression was as hard as his erection. "Sorry, Riley," he said, shouldering the blame.

She straightened, managed to say, "Takes two." Turning to the side, she motioned him to finish hooking the hanger. He did so. Without her being in the way.

"Shaving kit," he said, his voice rough. He cut through the closet to the bathroom, walking stiffly.

She zipped the garment bag. Awaited him to fill the duffel with personal items. Her heart, still beating crazy-fast, had yet to settle from their encounter.

Daniel returned, his shaving and dental needs and cologne in hand. A muscle in his jaw worked as he stowed each item in its own compartment. He soon finished. He looked at her then. A banked heat darkened his eyes.

She stared back. She couldn't help herself. She was drawn to the man. Warmth spread, from her chest to her sex. Temptation thickened the air. The walls closed in on them with the suggestion they step closer. Until they were mere inches apart. Her breasts brushed his chest. Their hip bones touched. He was about to kiss her. She wanted him to.

"Riley . . ." His voice was deep, rough. Wanting her.

"Daniel . . ." No more than a whisper.

He curved his hands about her shoulders, unhurried, patient. Giving her time to embrace their intimacy. To accept their need.

She was ready for this man. Until her iPhone vibrated in her cable sweater pocket. An insistent buzz in the silence. The sound couldn't be ignored. She went to shut it off, but the caller's name on the screen stopped her cold. "Andrew . . ." A scheduled call from the Build-A-Boyfriend app. Ill-timed? Or saving grace? Had she kissed Daniel, she would've cheated on her doctor. Andrew Reynolds had gotten her this job.

She read his text, a loving message that was to serve a purpose. Proof she had a significant other, however imaginary.

Hello, sweetheart, flashed, and Daniel immediately released her. He stepped back, frowning, while eyeing the text. *Working long days. So much sickness. Headed into surgery. Miss you. Love you.*

The app awaited her return text. Her fingers shook as she typed, *You are always on my mind. Be safe. XOXO.* She shut off the phone.

She heard Daniel swallow. "We nearly made a mistake." He sounded hoarse. Sad. For once, his face revealed exposed emotion. Deep and impassioned.

"Nearly . . ." She'd lost herself in him. Now desire left her defenseless.

"Never again."

She watched him leave the bedroom, her heart heavy. What might have been, might never come around again. What had she gotten herself into with her pretend boyfriend? She had lost a real man. She cared about Daniel. Yet she needed Andrew to stay employed. A catch-22.

His back was to her when she passed through his living room. He stood at the sink, head bent. She needed to clear the air. To say something that

would bring them back on an even footing, so she
wouldn't have to tiptoe around him. "Have a safe
trip. You won't recognize the thirtieth floor when
you return. We'll be holly-jolly."

"Don't go to extremes."

"You know me, Daniel. When do I ever do anything in moderation?"

"Practice a little restraint."

She already had. With him. She wanted nothing
more than to fall into bed with him, but she'd held
back. Her job depended on it.

Christmas was Riley's favorite holiday. She con-
sulted with Roxanne and Georgia before she made
her purchases, but in no time decking the halls
took on a life of its own. She'd gone all out, and
when countless boxes of decorations were delivered and stacked in the middle of the wide hall,
she realized she might have gone overboard. They
filled the space. A maze of cardboard bracketed by
two tall evergreens in tree stands that flanked the
bank of elevators.

The boxes and trees drew stares from the executives. The curious stopped and checked them out.
The decorations became conversation starters with
the staff. Riley knew most by name, but hadn't said
more than a few words to any of them. Hoping to
know them better, she proposed Ho-Ho Tuesday
to get everyone involved in the decorating process.

"Daniel would never approve of staff stopping
work to decorate," Roxanne had said, worried, earlier that morning when Riley suggested the entire
floor participate in the festivities.

"How about shifts?"

"How about you, Georgia, and me?" Roxanne countered.

"How about sending an e-mail invitation and we'll see who shows up. It could be one person or the entire floor."

"Daniel would kill me."

"He won't be back until tomorrow. He'll never know. The offices will look amazing. We'll win the building decorating contest and have a catered deli lunch."

"You'd risk Daniel's disapproval for a pastrami sandwich?"

"For the big dill pickle."

Roxanne grinned. "You're a sneaky personal shopper."

"Today I am a decorator, filled with Christmas spirit."

Riley stood over Roxanne's desk chair, and, together, they composed a jovial e-mail.

Ho-Ho Tuesday! Let's get jolly! It's time to deck the halls, trim the trees, and draw for the Secret Santa exchange (twenty-dollar limit). The office party won't plan itself. We're open to suggestions. Meet us in the hallway! The more the merrier. Bring your Christmas spirit. Fa-la-la-la-la! Signed, The Elves

Roxanne sighed when she hit Send. "This is far and above anything we've ever done before. Previous years, the only decoration in the hall was a wreath on Georgia's door."

It was time to expand from the wreath.

Roxanne straightened her desk and set her voice-mail message. The two women walked together to the center hallway. Riley's eyes went wide. Daniel's executives and staff were fifty strong. From what she could count, over half were already gathered, opening and peering in boxes. One woman shook out the branches on the trees. The scent of pine drifted in the air.

Roxanne leaned close, kept her voice low. "Can't believe Eric from Strategies and Martin from Technology came to play. Two somber, solemn men. Unbelievable."

"Christmas brings out the kid in all of us." Riley's thoughts turned to Daniel. She wanted the boy in the man to enjoy the holidays. A week of merriment never hurt anyone. She wanted his heart to beat with happiness. Wanted him to smile. His serious side would wait for him in the New Year.

She looked around now, as the people assembled. Most were excited; a few, hesitant. She raised her voice to be heard over the chatter. "There are lots of decorations, meant for the hallway and your individual offices. Take what you want. If we run out, I'll order more."

Nods and smiles spread the excitement. Joy took hold as everyone tore into the boxes. Ornaments, poinsettia wreaths, garland, red velvet bows, and silver bells were discovered. A handmade weathered wood sleigh appeared with a seat and enough space to stack presents for their Secret Santa exchange. The sleigh would remain in the central hallway.

Within minutes, a life-size soft-stuffed Santa and Mrs. Claus stood free of the cardboard, as did a six-foot fiberglass nutcracker soldier in a red and gold uniform, a big Russian hat, and handheld saber.

"I'm claiming the nutcracker," Darrel from Liquid Markets announced.

"We'd like Mrs. Claus," two ladies in Payroll called out.

"All yours," Riley returned. "Santa?" She offered the pair.

"Jolly Belly is mine," came from a territorial female executive in Legal and Regulatory Frameworks. "I need a man in my life." Laughter rippled.

Decorations continued to appear. Pudgy snowmen came adorned in red cable-knit sweaters, hats, mittens, and a glitter finish. Smaller white furry polar bears, snowy owls, and aluminum-cast reindeer could be used as desk displays.

Roxanne chose a snowman. "Perfect for the corner of my desk." She cut Riley a look. "What should go in Daniel's office?"

Mistletoe, unspoken. Riley planned to hang a sprig in the doorway to his bedroom. This she kept to herself. Along with the fact that she'd canceled her Build-A-Boyfriend app. She only awaited the termination notification. Andrew Reynolds was no more.

She'd weighed her decision while Daniel was away. Unsure, then sure. Afraid, yet brave. Was she jeopardizing her job by breaking up with her pretend boyfriend in hopes of connecting with Daniel on a more personal level? Right or wrong, good or bad, she was officially single. She wanted to spend time with her boss. That included a night together. She was willing to take the chance, despite Daniel's rule of no office romance.

He'd almost kissed her before he'd left for London. Almost taken her to bed. There'd been no mistake he wanted her. His body didn't lie. She hoped their separation would lead to a strong reunion. He'd be back tomorrow.

Daniel returned a day early. He'd wrapped up business sooner than expected, and instead of touring London, he ordered his pilot to fuel the plane. The three executives traveling with him hadn't questioned his decision. A choice he could not fully explain. It went beyond logic, was based instead on emotion. A first for him. He missed Riley Tyler.

He'd considered their relationship from every angle. Boss and personal shopper. Man, woman. Yet there were further complications. She was involved with the doctor. Still, he sensed her feelings for him. They had stood in his bedroom, so close, they exchanged breath. The pulse at her throat had raced as fast as his heart. He'd lowered his head; her eyelids were shuttered, and her lips parted. Her body had eased into him as if she were coming home, all soft and warm with desire, right before her iPhone buzzed. A buzz that reminded him she had a boyfriend.

The interruption of Andrew's text had brought Daniel to his senses. He'd been about to seduce a woman who belonged to another man. A decent man, given his profession. Could a woman care for two men simultaneously? Possibly. He'd spent the last few days evaluating all possible scenarios.

Still, she confused him. How had he fallen so hard, so fast, and in so few days, with a quirky lady who challenged and contradicted him, then grinned her apology? Inexplicably, Riley was good for him.

They suited each other well. He just had to convince her of that fact.

Over the course of his trip, he came to the conclusion it would be best to talk to her on his return, to be open and honest; to sort out their feelings. He would tell her how he felt. At the end of their discussion, should she pick Andrew, he'd step back and live with her choice. However it might kill him.

Now he rode the elevator to the thirtieth floor, next to the president and founder of Fredericks International and Geoffrey's son, Christopher. The young boy was shy, and after shaking Daniel's hand, he hid behind his father's pants leg.

Daniel had texted Roxanne, twice, announcing their arrival. No response, which was highly unusual. She seldom left her desk.

The elevator had been full when they'd gotten on in the lobby. Gradually emptying on the slow rise. There'd been few words exchanged between the CEOs. Each respected the other's professionalism and privacy. Daniel was hoping Fredericks would finally agree to the merger, once Geoffrey witnessed the polish and work ethic of Global Financial. It mirrored that of Fredericks International.

The elevator came to a stop, and the doors slid open. Daniel stepped into a winter wonderland. Christmas cheer and commotion echoed in the hallway. He might have thought he'd gotten off on the wrong floor had he not seen Roxanne and Georgia stringing garland between office doors.

"Wow!" came from Christopher, his expression full of childlike wonder. He released his father's hand and moved into the fray to get a better look at all that was going on.

Geoffrey craned his neck as well, looking down the full length of the hallway, which was crammed with financial advisors and economic strategists. Accountants and attorneys. Daniel had agreed to let Riley decorate for Christmas. He'd never expected her to bring the North Pole to Minneapolis.

Daniel cleared his throat and spoke formally to Geoffrey. "I apologize—"

"For what?" The man kept an eye on his son. "The holiday mood?"

"For appearing disorganized."

"It's allowed once a year, don't you think?"

Knowing Riley, it could be a weeklong distraction.

Christopher soon returned to his dad, his small face flushed. His coat was unbuttoned, revealing a young man's suit beneath. "They're cutting out silver snowflakes in the conference room. Might I join them, Father?"

"Are you barging in or were you invited?" asked Geoffrey. Obviously, manners mattered to the man.

"I stood outside the door until I was asked in."

"Did you introduce yourself?"

The boy nodded. "The lady's name is Sullivan."

His father frowned. "You shouldn't call her by her last name."

"Sullivan Shore," Daniel explained. "An unusual name for an exceptional woman. She oversees our Domestic Accounts."

"Accounts and snowflakes. I'd like to meet her." Geoffrey patted his son on the shoulder. "Perhaps

I should also make a snowflake. We can find the perfect place to hang them. Together." He addressed Daniel. "Excuse us, please."

The Frederickses left Daniel staring after them. The father walked slowly, formally. The boy's steps had bounce.

"Riley, can I have these blue ice skates to hang on my wall, until after the holidays?" Daniel heard Avery from Asset Allocation request.

Riley's reply was muffled. It sounded like a yes. Daniel located her outside his office, bent over a box labeled HOLIDAY WORD ORNAMENTS. He was close enough to see that each one was marked with vintage stamping: SANTA, JOY, BELIEVE, HO-HO-HO. She wiggled her bottom, reached deeper, and withdrew FROSTY THE SNOMAN. Straightening, she smiled at her discovery.

Her smile faltered when she saw him. Her hair tie had loosened, and strands fell across her face. She peered at him, one-eyed. She'd moved casual Friday to blue-jeaned Tuesday, he noted, adding a sweatshirt designed with a goofy-looking reindeer. On her feet, she wore scruffy lavender tennis shoes.

He forced himself to remain aloof, his expression tight. Otherwise, he would have grabbed the woman and hugged her close. He was that glad to see her. Instead he jammed his hands in his winter coat pockets, widened his stance. Appeared the formidable CEO everyone expected.

Confrontation stood as a third party between them. Silent and tense. Roxanne and Georgia found their way to her side. The director of personnel placed her hand on Riley's shoulder. Roxanne appeared to be joined at Riley's hip.

Something had obviously shifted during his absence. Roxanne had initially been critical of Riley; Georgia iffy, as well. She'd fourth-slotted her for the interviews. Yet now they stood all for one. Clearly, they liked her. Could it be they had handpicked her for him right from the start? Was he the last to know?

Several of his top executives circled about her, too. Protectively. Which amused Daniel greatly. The men had taken off their suit coats and loosened their ties, while the women had removed their high heels. Whatever he was about to say to Riley, he could say to them, too. They would share in his censure. Almost laughable. He employed them, paid their six-figure salaries, yet they seemed to be siding with the personal shopper who'd wrapped them up in Christmas spirit.

She licked her lips. "You're back."

He refused to be distracted by her moist mouth. "You've been busy."

"We're decorating."

"That I see. You've involved everyone."

"Group e-mail. The more, the merrier."

What he'd said before he'd left for London, and what she'd heard were two different things. He'd expected that she would do the decorating, not involve the entire floor. But if he were to send everyone back to their desks now, he'd appear to be a Scrooge, despite the fact that world finances could crash and no one would be at his computer to warn of the fact. They'd be trimming the trees. Decking the halls. Hanging wreaths and stockings. So be it.

At that moment, he decided, he didn't much care. It was all about Riley. She stared at him, wide-eyed and hopeful. "We have a good chance of winning the decorating contest, don't you think?"

Daniel weighed his words carefully. What he said next could make or break his relationship with her. "I think you have it in the bag."

She leaned toward him, raised, then lowered her arms, as if she was about to embrace him. She did not. She hugged her middle instead. All those around her cheered. Daniel wouldn't have believed it, had he not witnessed the moment himself. Riley was their holiday hero.

Off to the side, stern-faced investment consultant Calvin Jacobs high-fived reserved Phillip Greenfield in Product Management.

Quiet, often passive, wealth relationship advisor Arnold Otten pumped his arm. Exuberantly.

Rumor had Sandra Rule, senior policy advisor, Regulatory Affairs, involved with Donald Walsh, an engineer in Network Operations. Evidence of their relationship now surfaced. He openly held her hand. Sandra blushed.

Daniel nodded in their direction, let it go. Who was he to knock relationships, as long as his company continued to run smoothly?

Tapped on the shoulder, Daniel turned to find the Frederickses and their snowflakes. Christopher's smile lit his face when he asked, "Where can we hang them?"

Daniel looked at Riley, who took over. "I have the perfect place," she said. "Follow me."

Father and son were right behind her. They didn't go far. Daniel could still see them from where he stood. They decorated his office door with two silver snowflakes, one covered with glitter, the other gold stars.

Riley stood back to admire them. "The most beautiful snowflakes I've ever seen."

"Have you seen many?" asked Christopher.

"Both real and cutout," she told him. "Yours do Christmas proud."

Daniel came to join them. "I'm honored to have them on my door."

Christopher scrunched his nose. "Can I have mine back . . . someday?"

"Of course," Riley was quick to say. "I'll get your address from Mr. Hayes, and mail both to you."

The boy grinned, reassured.

"Perhaps mail won't be necessary," his father said. "We'll be traveling to Minneapolis often, once the merger takes place. You can pick it up the next time we're in the city."

"The merger?" Daniel had tried repeatedly to bring Fredericks to the table, but hadn't been successful. Not until that moment. After he and his son had made snowflakes together on decorating day.

"Your company is more than finances. There is a human connection here," said Geoffrey, his voice muted. "I'm impressed by the balance. When my wife unexpectedly passed away, I decided I want a strong future for my son. One where living fully is as important as banking millions."

Riley dipped her head, dabbed at her eyes. Geoffrey's admission touched her. Daniel, too. His own throat tightened.

"I've been approached by several firms who wish to buy a controlling interest in the stock of my corporation," Geoffrey added. "I want the negotiations to have minimal impact on my family. We will discuss the acquisition after Christmas."

"My comptroller and legal team—" Daniel stopped himself. "I'll be in touch, Geoffrey." They shook hands.

"Mr. Hayes." Christopher wound between Daniel and his father. "Would you help me decorate a tree?"

Daniel looked at Riley. "My decorator and I would be happy to join you." He shrugged off his winter coat, and her eyes rounded in surprise. He wore his navy suit, a pale yellow shirt, and paisley gold and light blue tie. She'd included the shirt and tie as alternatives to his staid white shirt and solid navy tie. He'd gone snazzy.

"That reminds me," Geoffrey commented. "I'd like to meet the personal shopper you mentioned. Perhaps she'd have suggestions for me as spring approaches."

Daniel brought them together. "Geoffrey, Riley Tyler."

Riley extended her hand, her cheeks pink. She'd dressed down for the day, never expecting a formal introduction to a prospective client. "I'd be pleased to give you some tips," she said.

"The tree." Christopher nudged them back to the hallway.

One of the two evergreens had already been decorated. Coats came off, and they went to work on the second. Riley and Christopher bonded immediately. She offered suggestions and let the boy make the decisions.

Christopher pulled a face when she collected a tiered red and burgundy ruffled tree skirt. It was too frilly and feminine. He gave in, allowing her one concession.

"Lights, ornaments?" she asked him. "We have strands of white, multicolored, or tiny twinklers."

The boy was quick to respond. "Multicolored."

Riley pointed to a nearby box, and Daniel retrieved it. He and Geoffrey unwound the long strand. The men went high with the lights, and Riley and "Chris," as she now called him, went low. His father didn't object to the shortening of his son's name. Chris seemed to like it. A lot.

She let the boy plug the lights in a nearby outlet. Green, red, white, and blue bulbs brightened the branches.

"Ornaments?" Riley next asked. "We have a little of everything. Peek inside the container against the wall and make your choice."

Chris didn't just look, he emptied the entire box. Close to a hundred ornaments. All shapes and sizes. Wood and metal. Glass and glitter. Antique and crystal. Vividly colored balls and decorations of every description. Sleds and snowmen. Angels and cherubs. Cars, trains, and planes. Winter animals.

The adults stood back as Chris made his selections. There was no organization as they hung the ornaments. The tree was decorated with a child's eye. An eclectic blend of old and new.

"Icicles or tinsel?" Riley questioned finally.

Chris pursed his lips, took his time. "Both, please."

Both it was. The icicles sparkled; the tinsel shimmered.

Riley climbed a short ladder and topped off the tree with a big, red velvet bow. All in all, it was one magnificent evergreen. By anyone's standards.

Chris puffed out his chest, proud. "Take a picture, Father," he requested. "Could we have the same tree at home?"

His father located his iPhone in his suit jacket pocket. He snapped a photo of son and tree.

"I'd be happy to order a similar box of ornaments for you," Riley offered.

"Great!" Chris went in low and hugged her about the hips.

Riley patted his shoulder.

"I'm hungry," the boy next said. He'd worked up an appetite.

"Can you recommend a family restaurant nearby?" his dad asked.

Daniel blanked. He'd hadn't a clue. He could recommend a five-star restaurant, but family-friendly suggestions eluded him.

Riley came to his rescue. "The Dinner Table. Burgers, fries, pizza. Five blocks east. It's cold outside, so you won't want to walk. Take a cab."

"Better yet, take my Town Car," Daniel offered. "I'll call my driver. He'll meet you at the main lobby door. Roger will wait while you eat, and drive you back to your hotel afterward."

"Appreciated," said Geoffrey. Father and son retrieved their outer coats, then took the elevator down to the lobby.

Daniel glanced down the hallway, which was now fully decorated. Christmas blossomed in wreaths, garlands, big silver bells. Snowflakes. Red and pink poinsettia plants lined the walls. Four straw reindeer guided the old-fashioned sleigh. They appeared ready to fly, to deliver Santa's presents.

"Looks good," he told Riley.

"I'm glad you approve."

He did. The decorating was done. It was now time for them to talk. He nodded toward his office. "Got a minute?"

"You're the boss."

Roxanne was back at her desk. She glanced up as they passed. "Hold my calls," Daniel requested. She nodded.

He held the door for Riley, and she preceded him inside. Her decorating had extended from the hallway to his suite. Strands of gold mercury pinecones adorned a desktop tree, along with blue, red, and burgundy glass balls. Off to the side, tall, striped candy canes filled a pair of ceramic Santa boots. In front of the bookshelves, a painted orange and gold blaze burned in a cardboard brick stand-up fireplace. His own personal stocking, embossed with his name, was hooked on the coatrack.

What caught his eye and held his interest as he took in the room was the plastic sprig of mistletoe tacked to the frame above his bedroom door. Had Riley anticipated that he would be dating over the holidays? The sprig would end an evening with a good-night kiss and possible lovemaking. But the only woman he wanted in his bed was her. He was about to tell her so.

He shrugged off his suit coat, loosened his tie. Unbuttoned his cuffs and shoved up his sleeves. They stood close, but not touching close. He'd never struggled with words before—until that moment. He spoke haltingly, the fear of losing her strong. "I like you." Lame for a highly educated man, but a starter, nonetheless. It was all he had.

"I like you, too, Daniel."

Her response relaxed him a little, until he forced out, "You love Andrew Reynolds."

He made her uneasy. It was evident in the way she clasped her hands, squeezed her knuckles white. Blew out a breath.

"You can tell me, Riley. It's something I need to know."

"Why?" The word was whisper-soft.

"Because I'm attracted to you. I sense you feel the same. But we can't act on our attraction if you're planning a future with your doctor. I don't believe in one-night stands or affairs. And I'd never go after another man's woman."

She was staring at him with the same look of confusion that came across her face when he explained corporate finances. How much more could he simplify their discussion? Did she care for him or not? Had he misinterpreted—

Her iPhone rang. His gut tightened. It could be only one person: her doctor. The man was about to disrupt the most important conversation of Daniel's life. He couldn't let that happen.

He closed the distance between them. Took the hand that held her phone. "Don't answer it, Riley." He kept his voice firm, even, despite the jumble of emotions that threatened to choke him. "Be with me. I never wanted you to fall in love with me, and I never planned to fall for you. But I have. Choose me."

"Choose you . . ." She still looked dazed.

He drew her hand to his chest. The iPhone screen flashed over his heart. A short text caught his eye. No doubt private. He didn't care. He read it once, twice, before releasing her hand, unable to wrap his head around the message.

"Build-A-Boyfriend termination. Andrew Reynolds canceled," he repeated. Confusion punched. Anger ground his teeth. *What the hell?* The app was familiar to him. The company's owners had done an interview on one of the morning shows months ago. He'd watched, shaken his head over some people's need to deceive. Had Riley misled him? "I'm listening." He awaited her explanation.

It came with a finger poking his chest, and a whole lot of attitude. She stood up to him. "This is all your fault," she declared in defense of her actions. "You and your stupid rules. I'd never have deceived you had there been another way. You required a personal shopper, but Georgia hinted it had to be someone in a relationship. I needed the job, so I downloaded an imaginary boyfriend." She huffed, "Be mad if you will, Daniel, then get over yourself. Fast. I'm a free woman. I want you. I'll give you ten seconds to meet me under the mistletoe."

He arrived in five. His heart was suddenly light. He fixed his gaze on her and never looked away. The emotion between them built silently as he gazed into her eyes. She lit up from the inside out. He saw love in her gaze, and conveyed his own for her. He kissed her. Stirring and satisfying. Stealing her breath and curling her toes. His teeth teased her lower lip. He nipped her chin.

He walked her backward, into the bedroom, straight to the bed, never breaking their kiss. There, they slowly broke apart. Only to rapidly undress. Naked, he bent down and lightly kissed her brow, the curve of her chin, then her breastbone. Gentle. Tender. He palmed her breast. Rolled her nipple between his thumb and forefinger. Her pulse quickened.

As one they sank to the bed. Cool sheets at her back. Hot man atop her. Touching Daniel seemed right. Perfect. Riley wasn't tentative. She trusted him. She ran her hands through his hair, then drew her thumbs across his cheekbones. She traced the powerful set of his shoulders. Circling his neck with her arms, she pushed herself flush against him. She felt every inch of his maleness. Sculpted and symmetrical. She loved the texture of his skin, the underlying flex of his muscle. Strength and passion. His sex was stiff and substantial. A man in his prime.

He stroked his hand down her rib cage, at first with infinite care, then with male craving. His long fingers stretched and searched, his palm pressing hotly into her abdomen.

She feathered her fingers over his chest hair, scraped a nail across his abdomen. He inhaled sharply. She went on to give his erection the attention it deserved. She fondled, and his penis heated in her palms. His low groan pleased her.

Clutching her hips, he let his thumbs tease her belly. He plied her wetness, then inserted the tip of his finger. She lifted her hips, as intense pleasure reached deep down inside her.

Aroused and anxious, he raised himself slightly, and hunted for a condom in his bedside stand. Scored a packet. Stripped the foil and sheathed himself.

He parted her knees, and she rocked her hips, as ready for him as he was for her. He entered her then, with one slow stroke. Streamlining. Her body accepted him.

He pulsed inside her.

Her stomach quivered.

A shift of his hips, and he set their sexual rhythm.

Sensation filled her. Warmth, closeness, love.

In sync, they soared. She was close to coming and so was he.

Sharp pants of pleasure escaped her lips.

His breathing was ragged and rose from his gut.

She surrendered.

And his control broke.

The very air around them seemed to explode.

A hard, racking shudder convulsed her.

One last thrust and he gave himself up to his climax. He followed her to the end. And after.

Spent, he collapsed on his side, then rolled off the bed and disposed of his condom. Returning, he drew her to face him.

He stared down at her, gently brushing strands of damp hair off her face and neck. Cupping her chin, he caressed her cheek. She kissed his palm. He took her lips in a kiss that promised forever.

"All I want for Christmas is you," he told her. "Marry me, Riley."

"Marry me back, Daniel."

Hearts joined, they sealed their lifetime pledge to each other.

He was the CEO of Global Financial.

She kept her position as his personal shopper, now that she could both dress and undress him. He looked as good naked as he did in a suit. The man had one fine body.

Christmas neared, and the first-place ribbon was awarded to the thirtieth floor for best holiday decorations. Security guard George was unbiased. He shook Daniel's hand, and Roxanne ordered their deli lunch. There was much celebration.

Riley ate both a thick pastrami sandwich and two dill pickles. Daniel appreciated the way she savored her food. Her low moans would always do it for him.

They exchanged their gifts a week later.

Riley gave Daniel a Lionel Santa Fe train set for the boy inside the man. Extended track and extra cars. He hadn't stopped smiling. The train would be handed down to their sons and daughters. She'd promised him a big family.

He gifted her with a magnificent diamond ring, which fit her finger perfectly. Followed by tickets to *The Nutcracker*. Balcony box seating. Lastly, a Magic 8 Ball, which she immediately shook. The first question she asked: Would they live happily ever after? The ball answered: *Yes, Definitely.*

HER
FAVORITE
PRESENT

ALLYSON CHARLES

CHAPTER I

"We didn't meet our targets again this month." Gabe Harrison looked each of his managers in the eye, trying to impart how seriously he took that fact. "Each of your departments has shown a slow decrease in output, and that's even including the fact that we have some new hires who should be bumping up productivity. I want to know what's going on."

His business partner and cofounder of Build-A-Boyfriend, Ben Givens, raised a hand.

Gabe sighed. "Ben, we're not in school. You don't have to raise your hand. Just say what you want."

Ben cleared his throat. "Our sales numbers are still going up. So is our profit." He swiveled in his chair and shared a look with their employees, shrugging. "I'm not sure why you called this meeting."

"Because even though sales have increased, our

profit margin isn't increasing at the same pace as it used to." Leaning forward, he rested his palms on the maple boardroom table. Like almost all the furniture in Build-A-Boyfriend's offices, it was bought secondhand, and didn't match the darker wood of the chairs around it. Both Ben and Gabe had agreed that since customers didn't come into their office, they were better off saving money with used supplies.

"Do you know how many overtime hours we paid out last month? Too many." Settling into his chair, Gabe crossed his arms over his chest. "And even with the increased man-hours, the number of texts and phone calls we placed to our clients went down. Someone explain that to me."

He glared at his four managers. He didn't set targets on a whim. A lot of market analysis and good old-fashioned number crunching went into his quarterly projections, and he expected his goals to be taken seriously. And met.

Gabe and Ben had started the Build-A-Boyfriend app in Gabe's mother's garage their senior year in college. It hadn't taken long for Gabe to realize that his idea to rid himself of a persistent ex-girlfriend by pretending he had a new one had moneymaking potential.

He and Ben had worked long days and even longer nights growing the business until their offices now took up the top floor of the MacArthur high-rise in downtown St. Louis. His dream of taking his business public was within sight, and he wasn't going to let an avoidable slowdown take him off track.

Harry, a software developer who'd been with

them almost since the beginning, frowned. "Our people aren't working slower. The amount of time needed to process the requests of each client has gone up. Where we used to spend about ten minutes total work time per day on each client, that number has now increased to about twenty-five minutes per client." He scratched his round stomach, a faded and wrinkled Mario Brothers T-shirt stretched tightly across it. "Dude, we're lucky our overtime was as low as it was."

Gabe stared at a stain on his employee's graphic tee. Grape juice? Marinara? With these guys, who the hell knew? As the only man to wear a suit to the office, he sometimes felt like the one adult in the room. "Are these premium service members? Even with the added time of ordering flowers once a month—"

"It's not the flowers," Harry said. "It's the people. They're not happy with just getting a text every once in a while. Now they respond. They want a little back-and-forth. It takes time."

"It's the same with the voice mails," Ben chimed in. "When our clients first subscribe, they're given the number of their fake boyfriend, and told if they want to get a voice mail, not to answer calls from that number." He shrugged. "A lot of them are answering. They want a conversation in front of witnesses."

Gabe stared at his oldest friend. "How do you know this? You're the behind-the-scenes computer guy. You don't work the phones."

While Build-A-Boyfriend had originally been Gabe's idea, it never would have found life if not for Ben. A brilliant computer programmer, he'd designed the app and developed a program to automatically generate text messages tailored to their clients. Both men had made several million dollars from their idea, but whereas Gabe was always striving to make Build-A-Boyfriend bigger and better, Ben seemed content to enjoy the status quo.

His friend flushed a bright red. "I've been manning some of the phones when it gets busy. And until I figure out how to automate texts that respond appropriately to our clients' incoming ones, I help John's group reply to the overflow of text messages."

Gabe cocked his head. "I don't get it. Why would you want to talk to our loser clients? You have your own job to do."

"They're not losers!" Ben's pink cheeks flushed even darker. He scratched at a mark on the table. "A lot of them are just . . . lonely."

Gabe frowned. "Of course they're lonely. They're too pathetic to get real dates, so they use our service. But we're just supposed to give them the appearance of having a boyfriend or girlfriend, something tangible they can wave in front of their parents' or friends' faces to prove the lie that they're in a relationship. If our employees are now having conversations with them on the phone, that goes a step beyond what our service provides."

Ignoring the glower on Ben's face, Gabe steepled his fingers. "Of course, we could make that part of a new premium package. An upgrade to pay for." He mulled that over. He'd have to talk with marketing. Run some projections. But until then . . . "Right now, that's not part of our service. We're wasting too many hours interacting with our clients. If they need their hands held, they should call their priests. Or a 900 number. We need to get back to basics."

"So, what?" Harry asked. "We just ignore their texts? Hang up on our clients if they answer our calls?"

"Yes."

Harry whistled, and everyone else shook their heads.

Ben shifted to the edge of his seat. "I wouldn't do that to . . . I mean, our employees have gotten to know some of our clients. Like them. They're not going to hang up on them." Tilting his head to one side, Ben narrowed his eyes. "Besides, that kind of customer service could give a company a bad reputation. Think about what that could do to our chances for a successful IPO."

As someone who prided himself on his skills of manipulation, Gabe recognized that little salvo for the strategy it was. He eyed Ben with new respect. He hadn't thought his mild-mannered friend had it in him.

Too bad it didn't solve his problem.

"Well, we won't go public wasting time talking to our clients, either. They know what they get when they sign up. One hundred texts a month, ten voice mails, and a handwritten note. That's it. If they want more, they need to find themselves some real boyfriends." He snorted. "What am I saying? They use us because they can't."

Harry propped his right foot up on his left knee. "When's the last time you worked the phones, or sent any texts? I know when you started the business, you got your hands dirty. But I think you've forgotten that our clients are real people."

Ben spoke before Gabe could tear his employee a new one. "He's right. We provide a service to our clients, take their money, but you seem to think they're lower than dirt. It's not right."

Gabe looked at the men around the table. Each one eyed him with varying degrees of pity and disgust. The turkey sandwich he'd had from lunch, leftovers from Thanksgiving with his mom and Ben, turned to stone in his stomach. When did it become a crime to want to make money?

"We started a business for people to lie about significant others." Gabe tapped his fingers on the arm of his chair. "I don't know how else you're supposed to think about our clients."

"If you'd get to know any of them," Harry said, "I think you'd see that most of them are really nice."

"And funny," Ben chimed in. Not meeting Gabe's eyes, he slid lower in his chair. "I'm just saying you should get to know our clients before you judge them."

Gabe cleared his throat. Time to get this meeting back on track. They could all think he was a dick if they wanted, as long as they got their productivity numbers back up.

Ben's spine popped straight. "Hey, that's a good idea."

"What is?" Gabe tried to keep the growl out of his voice. He didn't know where his friend was going, but he knew he wasn't going to like the destination.

"You. Getting to know a client." Ben held up a

finger before Gabe could protest. "Just one client. You should handle one of our accounts. Get to know the woman behind the credit card number that you so happily charge. Maybe we could even arrange for you to meet her in real life."

Harry hooted. "This will be awesome. Gabe, Mr. One-Night Stand, as one of our boyfriends. Get ready to kiss that IPO good-bye."

Even though he had no intention of taking his friend up on his challenge, he couldn't let that one go. "Hey, as you pointed out, I used to do some of the grunt work around here. I do know how to text a woman and leave her a nice voice mail."

"Sure," Ben said. "Back when it was still anonymous. When texts and voice mails just went into a void. But now that you have to interact with the client more, it's a little different."

"I can *interact* with women just fine." He didn't bother keeping the bark out of his voice this time.

"So you'll do it?" Ben asked. He raised his eyebrows. "You'll take over the account of one of the clients me and the boys pick out for you? See for yourself that our customers are decent people who just might need a little cover until they find the right person for them?"

Gabe examined his choices. Saying no was the obvious one. Hell no, more like it. But at the varying looks of excitement and hope on his employees' faces, and Ben's, the businessman in Gabe took over. A happy workforce was a productive workforce. Besides, he could use this to his advantage.

"All right. I'll do it." Crossing one leg over the

other, Gabe watched as his managers shot excited looks at Ben. "I'll even throw in a little Christmas present. If you're right, that our clients are normal women, not pathetic losers who can't get their own dates, then I'll take what was supposed to have been my own Christmas bonus and divide it up among you four managers."

Jaws dropped. The four men leaned forward and started thanking him profusely.

Ben knew him better. "What's the catch?"

"No catch." Gabe grinned. "Just the flip side of the deal. If, after playing the part of this woman's fake boyfriend, my assessment of our clients hasn't changed, then I get something from each of you."

Harry flicked a glance at Ben, shifted in his seat. "What?"

"I get productivity levels back up." Gabe pointed at his managers. "If I win the bet, each of you has to put in ten more hours a week, for three months." Gabe's grin widened. "At no cost to Build-A-Boyfriend."

It was so silent in the boardroom that Gabe could hear the faint whir of a printer coming to life in the front office.

"It's a deal," Ben said. The managers started to protest, but Ben held up a hand. "I'll work the extra hours with you if it comes to that. But it won't." He turned back to Gabe. "Because we're going to find the perfect woman for Gabe, one whom even he'll have to admit is a catch."

Gabe met five determined sets of eyes. He wasn't worried. Even if these men picked the most impressive woman out there, they were fishing in a shallow pond. Anyone who needed to use their service was already destined to be a pathetic waste of space.

He laced his fingers together and flexed his palms out, cracking his knuckles.

This was going to be the easiest boost to productivity he'd ever managed. The best Christmas present he could get.

Everything he wanted was just one bet away.

CHAPTER 2

Rachel Sanders juggled rolls of wrapping paper in her arms. One slipped, and she pinned it between her chair and her hip before easing the bundle to the floor behind her desk.

"Thanks for buying that from Sally," Rhonda said. "She came in second for total donations."

"No problem." Rachel smiled at her coworker, and slung her purse strap over her arm. "I'm glad to help out your daughter's school. And I won't gain five pounds from wrapping paper, not like the chocolate I bought from her last year."

Rhonda wrinkled her nose. "That chocolate wasn't very good. I was hoping the school would get a new supplier this year."

Circling her desk, Rachel headed for the office door. "It was chocolate. Even bad chocolate is good."

"I thought that was supposed to be sex."

Rachel didn't admit that it had been so long, she didn't remember whether that saying was true or not. "I'm heading down to the cafeteria. Do you want anything?"

"No thanks. I'm good." Rhonda settled behind her desk. "Remember we have that meeting at two."

Holding up her smartphone, Rachel nodded. "It's on my calendar. See you later."

Bustling to the elevators, Rachel scanned the e-mails on her phone, and punched the Down button. She had twenty minutes to hit the cafeteria on the first floor of her building and get back to her office before the pile of projects on her desk tumbled into a pile of rubble. She loved her job at *Verve,* the premier magazine on family, home decorating, and relationships, but if she didn't stay two steps ahead, she'd be falling behind.

That was just the way it was in the media industry. And she wanted to get ahead. Go all the way to the top.

The doors hissed open, and Rachel stepped inside, frowning over the e-mail from her latest interview subject. Why would the woman cancel no—

She walked into a firm chest, her phone pinned between a man's hard muscles and her own body. Face hot, Rachel jerked back. "I'm sorry." Raising her gaze, she met a pair of arctic-blue eyes. They widened ever so slightly, and Rachel darted a hand over her hair. Her ponytail seemed to still be in place. She'd eaten the last of her emergency chocolate two days ago so there shouldn't be any dark smears on her face. Why was he staring? She swallowed. "I should have watched where I was going."

The surprise faded from his eyes, and he smiled. "What would be the fun in that? Having a beautiful woman crash into me made my morning." Raising an arm, he stopped the doors from sliding closed on her. "Please, come on in. I promise I don't bite." He flashed two rows of even white teeth, teeth that seemed quite able, and willing, to take a nip out of unsuspecting and gullible women.

Rachel sniffed. Good thing she was neither of those anymore. At twenty-four, she wasn't staring down middle age yet, but she was old enough to recognize a meaningless line when she heard one.

Stepping into the cab, she muttered a thanks and turned to stand next to the man. The button for the first floor was already lit, so she returned her focus to her phone.

"Text from your boyfriend?" Elevator Man asked.

Biting her lip, she shook her head. The only texts of that sort she'd been getting lately had been from a fake boyfriend service she'd signed up for seven months earlier. Her phony relationship had succeeded in getting her bosses to accept more of her story ideas, but she wasn't about to admit to a random hot guy that she paid $24.95 a month to receive some texts and voice mails.

And the man was hot. She glanced at his reflection in the metal elevator doors. Thick dark hair brushed the collar of his white dress shirt. A little longer than she usually liked, a bit more product than she thought men should use, but it worked for him. A hint of stubble covered his square jaw, just enough to make him look more bad boy than corporate stooge. The tailored three-piece suit he wore gave her a good idea of the body underneath. He was corded with muscle, big without being bulky. His entire body was tensed like a coil ready to spring.

She sighed. Usually her penchant for bad boys led her to unemployed jerks who rotated their time crashing at their friends' homes and their parents' basements. The naughty businessman fantasy was new for her. It was a good thing for her heart she was too busy to pursue it.

He caught her examining him in the mirrored doors. His smile was slow and knowing. She dropped her eyes back to her phone, cursing her fair Irish skin. Her flush told anyone paying attention when she was embarrassed, angry, or aroused.

The elevator dinged at the thirtieth floor, and she and Elevator Man stepped back to let a tall woman, made taller with her four-inch heels, onto the cab. She held a miniature pinscher tucked under one arm like a clutch. It didn't look happy in its pink leather collar.

Elevator Man's eyes flared. Leaning back in the corner, Rachel shook her head. Put a woman in a tight skirt in front of the man and his attention was already . . .

Whoa. Rachel blinked, but her eyes continued to water. Had the woman swum in a bottle of perfume? The scent was oppressive, obnoxious, and Rachel could taste it in the back of her throat.

Elevator Man pressed himself into Rachel's side. She would have scaled the wall to get away from the sickly sweet aroma if it would have helped, but that corner was the farthest they could go. The woman pressed the button for floor ten.

She and Elevator Man shared a horrified look. Twenty floors of this hell?

He leaned down, his lips a whisper's breath away from her ear. "I don't think I'm going to make it. Tell my mother I love her, and that I want her to go on a world cruise with the insurance money."

Rachel shook her head and smiled. She wanted to respond, but that would involve opening her mouth and sucking in more of the foul air. She dug her nose into the crook of her arm. The cashmere blend tickled, but did little to block the smell.

"Do you think it's her or the dog?" he asked. As if knowing he was the subject of their whispered conversation, the little brown and black dog turned its head, its upper lip curling. Elevator Man glared back. "It's got to be both of them. They bathe together, and this is some horrible flea shampoo bubble bath they drown themselves in."

His words were soft. Her snort, as the visual he planted grew in her head, was not. The woman glanced back at them.

Elevator Man pulled a handkerchief from his front breast pocket and handed it to Rachel. "She just lost her grandmother," he explained.

She dabbed at her streaming eyes, and held the cloth beneath her nose. She probably did look like a grieving woman. Except for the smile hidden beneath the handkerchief. She could just make out the scent of fresh laundry detergent and Elevator Man's own subtle cologne over the woman's perfume. She breathed deep, grateful for the reprieve.

"It was tragic." He wrapped an arm around her waist and pulled her into his side. "A gas leak. She never smelled it."

Rachel started coughing. Her shoulders shook with laughter, and she glared at the man for putting her in this position. He tucked her into his chest and rubbed her back. "There, there. It will be all right, dear."

Her hand fell to his waist, and she dug her nails in. She didn't think her blunt-cut manicure had much of an effect, not through his vest and shirt, but she didn't want him to think she was a complete pushover. He was hamming it up big-time, and why? So he could get a free grope?

But she didn't back away. Burrowing her nose between his jacket and his vest, she sighed. She'd found a little haven, and she'd have to be dragged out of it.

The doors slid open on ten. The woman with the dog murmured, "Sorry for your loss," and stepped out.

When the doors slid shut, Rachel pushed away, but kept his handkerchief pressed to her face. She glared at him over the white linen. "My dead grandmother? Really?"

Pulling a business card out of his wallet, the man tried to use it as a little fan in front of his face. "Your dead grandmother is lucky. She couldn't smell."

She bit back a smile. "Plus, she's fictional."

"I'd give anything to be a fictional person right now if it meant I couldn't smell." He leaned back against the wall. "Why do you women do that? Are you trying to attract men or repel them? No man wants to risk a chemical attack just to get near you."

"Says the man who wears Bvlgari cologne."

"In moderation." Tapping the business card against his chin, he looked her up and down. "You like the way I smell? If you can recognize Bvlgari, you must."

"Right now I'd like the way a sewage treatment plant smells. Anything that is other than this hell."

The elevator light hovered above the number one, never seeming to sink to the level. "God, please open the doors. Let us out of here."

As if hearing her prayers, the elevator dinged and the doors eased open. Grabbing her elbow, the man hustled her out like the place was on fire. About twenty feet away, he stopped and bent over at the waist, hands on his knees. "Stale lobby air and pine never smelled so good."

Rachel had to agree. The high-rise's Christmas tree had gone up last week, and the aroma of fresh pine needles was as soothing to her abused nose as a massage was to tired muscles.

She dabbed under her eyes, and folded the handkerchief. She held it out to him. "Thanks. I'm sorry there's some mascara on it. Make sure to use bleach."

Slowly, he straightened. He was tall, probably stood a half foot taller than her own five-six. Now that they were no longer in a survival situation, she felt oddly shy. His gaze seemed too probing, his smile too familiar. Like he knew all her secrets. Like he could see under her clothes.

His smile was definitely predatory, and her mouth dried up. Reaching out, he grabbed her hand and tugged her toward the cafeteria. "You can buy me lunch to make up for it."

"What?" She tripped after him. The fingers wrapped around her hand were firm. She ignored the light tingle that skittered over her skin. "You made me laugh, which made me cry more. Any stains are on you."

"You're right. I should buy you lunch." He stopped in the middle of the open cafeteria doors and stepped behind her, placing his hands on her hips. Rachel's breath caught in her throat. She could feel the heat of him on her back. His breath slid beneath her ponytail and caressed the back of her neck. "Do you feel like Japanese, Italian, Mexican, or American?" He turned her to face each counter as he asked.

Her mind blanked. Did she like Japanese? She couldn't remember. It had been a while since she'd let a man stand so close, let alone a complete stranger. He really did smell good.

"Mexican," she said. She'd planned on getting a salad for lunch, but nerves overcame her intent. *Verve* had run an article last February. Most men polled said they didn't like it when women ordered salads. Claimed to appreciate a woman who had a real appetite.

Of course, those same men didn't appreciate when a woman had real curves from indulging in that real appetite.

Taking the handkerchief from her grip, he threaded his fingers through hers and led her over to the Mexican counter. She cursed herself the whole way. What did she care what some random stranger thought about her?

The cheese enchiladas did look good, though. Smelled even better. Smiling at the man behind the counter, she pointed at the dish. When he handed her the steaming plate, she inhaled deeply. Her stomach gurgled in anticipation.

Elevator Man took her plate and put it on his tray with his own meal. Okay, that nickname had to change. When he pulled out his wallet at the cashier's station, she laid her hand on his arm. "I can't let a man buy me lunch when I don't even know his name. I think there's a rule about that."

"And do you always follow the rules?" At her raised eyebrow, he sighed. "Gabe Harris—" He cleared his throat. "I'm Gabe Harris. And you are?"

"Rachel Sanders. Nice to meet you." She picked up the drinks that didn't fit on the tray. "Thanks for lunch."

"My pleasure." Gabe nodded his head at a table in the corner, and she followed him over. It was a nice view to walk behind. Better than from the top of the St. Louis Arch. Broad shoulders narrowed down to a trim waist. When he bent to rest the tray on the table, his wool business jacket rose, giving her a glimpse of one very fine ass. High and tight and just begging for a little squeeze.

No, she told her fingers firmly. No touching the tasty stranger's butt. Plopping into her chair, she looked around the table and sighed. "We forgot silverware."

He laid a broad palm on her shoulder and pressed her back into her seat. "Got it covered." Reaching into his breast pocket, he pulled out two napkin-wrapped rolls of plasticware and placed one in front of her.

"What else do you have in that pocket?" she teased. "So far, its contents have been very useful to me."

He smiled, the hint of a dimple appearing in his left cheek. It was the first real smile Gabe had shown her. No flirt, no smolder, just genuine amusement.

It was gone so fast it gave Rachel whiplash. The practiced smile replaced it. Just as pretty. Showed just the right amount of teeth. But it held no true warmth.

Rachel lowered her gaze and cut into her enchiladas with the back of her fork. She hated the pretenses when you first met a guy. Always trying to act like a different, better person. The pressure. Another reason she loved the Build-A-Boyfriend service. The past seven months she'd had a break from the awkwardness of first dates.

But this wasn't a first date. Gabe could be a salesman for all she knew, holding an entire arsenal of fake smiles, and it wouldn't matter to her.

"So, Rachel, what is it you do?"

Crap. Maybe this was a first date. Next, he'd ask what her favorite movie was.

Gabe wrapped a small taco up tightly and took a bite. No sour cream squirting out the end. No salsa dribbling down his chin. Very impressive.

"I'm an assistant editor at *Verve* magazine. We're up on the thirty-eighth floor." She washed down a bite of pepper with a swig of soda. "And you? When you're not telling stories in elevators, what do you do?"

"I work at a company that develops software. I was visiting with a friend up on forty-six." He shoveled in a huge bite, ending that line of conversation.

Rachel's stomach dropped, just a little. He didn't work in the building. She'd probably never see him again. Which was fine. She sawed into the enchilada, cheese spilling out the end. She had to focus on her work. She needed one last great story pulled together before the end of the year if she wanted to nail down that promotion.

"What type of software?" she asked.

He swallowed. "We develop algorithms that aid in communications."

"Like, for phone companies?" Did she even

care? She was never going to see this man again. She didn't need to pretend to be interested in his job.

"Something like that." Leaning back, Gabe crossed his arms over his chest and pinned her with a searching look. "So, Rachel Sanders, any boyfriends?"

"Uh, not currently." Her voice tilted up on the last word, making the statement sound more like a question.

"When was the last relationship you were in? Why did it end?" He swept his eyes up and down her body. There was no heat behind his gaze this time. Just assessment.

Rachel straightened her spine. What the hell? He sounded like her grandmother. Even for awkward first-date questions, those were pretty damn bold. They were definitely more like third-date queries.

She gave him a sweet smile. "Well, in order, none of your business, and really none of your business."

He pinched his lips together. "I'm sorry. I didn't mean to offend you. I just don't believe in beating around the bush."

"You'd rather chuck a grenade into the bush instead?" Rachel mimicked his posture, crossing her arms over her chest. "Those are pretty hot-button questions."

Gabe flicked his eyes to her chest and back to her face. Yes, crossing her arms over her chest did give her some instant cleavage beneath her V-neck sweater. And yes, she knew that would happen when she did it. So sue her.

"I'm a busy man, Rachel Sanders. If you dumped your last boyfriend because he ate a PB&J and you hate peanut butter, I think that's something better known right up front." He leaned forward, resting his elbows on the table. In the bright light, Rachel could see flecks of hazel in his blue eyes. "Not liking peanut butter is a serious character flaw in my book, and I'd want to cut my losses early if that were the case."

She tried to keep her expression stern. "What if he was eating that peanut butter sandwich in bed, getting crumbs all over my new Egyptian cotton sheets? I can't have crumbs in my bed, no matter how good the sandwich. Surely you can understand."

"As long as it's not a general dislike of peanut butter that kicked a man out of your bed." He picked up another taco. "I'll allow for some time and place restrictions."

"That's big of you." A trickle of hot sauce ran down his thumb. Rachel's eyes tracked its path. Finishing the taco, Gabe held her gaze and stuck the tip of that finger in his mouth, sucked the sauce off.

Heat flared in her core and spread through her body, like she'd been the one licking hot sauce. When he smiled, she knew her blush had given her away.

With the thumb that had just been in his mouth, he traced a circle on the top of her wrist. "Like I said, I'll allow for it. But if you don't want peanut butter in your bed, I think you're missing out on some fun."

Did she think she was hot before? She knew her fair skin was as red now as if she'd just eaten a ghost pepper. His damp thumb continued to rub circles into her skin, her pulse leaping to his touch. If he could make her tingle just by rubbing her wrist—

"Rachel!"

Rachel snapped out of her trance and looked around the cafeteria. Her boss waved, and wended her way through the tables to reach them.

"Rachel." Janice looked at Gabe and her eyes lit up. "Is this Trevor? Do we finally get to meet the fiancé?"

Oh shit. As discreetly as possible, she tugged her hand free from Gabe's. He raised an eyebrow, and she looked away, not wanting to see the accusation in his gaze. She'd told him she didn't have a boyfriend, and now he thought she was engaged.

"Hi, Janice." She forced a bright smile. When in doubt, bluff. "No, this is Gabe Harris. Trevor is still out of town. Gabe, this is my boss, Janice Richland."

"Oh." Janice looked between Rachel and Gabe, the lines on her forehead deepening. "And who's Gabe? Just a friend of yours?"

Was there an emphasis on *friend*? Rachel wasn't sure, but the pit that opened up in her stomach told her this could be bad. Gabe already thought she was a liar. That little flirtation was over. But if he told her boss that she'd been coming on to him, and her boss thought that she was cheating on her fake fiancé, she could kiss her promotion good-bye. Along with the respect of all her coworkers. A magazine that prided itself on family values and doling out sound relationship advice wouldn't consider a cheater for the associate editor position, not when there were several other qualified applicants to choose from.

She darted her eyes around the cafeteria, hoping to find inspiration in the tinsel-wrapped pillars and holiday displays.

"No, not just a friend of Rachel's," Gabe said. Rachel's heart sank to her toes. He was going to out her that she picked up random men in the elevator. Everything she'd been working for since college was going to slip through her fingers. Editor positions were few and far between in St. Louis. No other national publications of the same scale were based here. She'd have to move if she wanted to stay in the magazine business. Or look for a job that didn't use her English degree. She'd never realize her dream of becoming the youngest associate editor in *Verve* history.

Gabe rested his elbows on the table and leaned forward. "Rachel, do you want to tell your boss just who I am? Or should I?"

CHAPTER 3

Pink flooded her face and continued down to the alluring shadows hiding beneath her V-neck sweater. Gabe dragged his gaze back up. She did have some beautiful curves, but it wouldn't do to ogle Rachel in front of her boss.

The boss. She was still waiting for an answer. And Rachel looked like she might throw up at any second. She looked so miserable that messing with her stopped being fun. He took pity.

Standing, he held out a hand to Janice. "I'm a good friend of Trevor's." He moved behind Rachel and rested a palm on her shoulder, squeezing. "I just moved to town and Trevor volunteered to show me around, help me find a place to live, all that. But since he's not here . . ." He let the woman draw her own conclusions.

"Isn't that sweet of Trevor? Asking Rachel to fill in for him." The tight pinch to Janice's lips relaxed, and she smiled down at Rachel. Gabe thought it was actually sweet of Rachel. If anything he was saying was true. Not the mythical Trevor who'd just fobbed a friend off on his fiancée.

Fiancé. That was a new twist on Build-A-Boyfriend. What would possess a woman to invent a fiancé? Rachel seemed normal enough, but pretending to be engaged took the pathetic factor of their clients up to a whole new level. He examined her from head to toe. She looked fine. Really, she was quite pretty. That wasn't her problem. Yet he knew for a fact she was using his service.

"You should read some of the texts Trevor sends her," Janice continued. "So thoughtful. And the flowers he sent when he had to miss her birthday last month traveling for his job? Beautiful."

"That's my boy," he said. Well, that *was* his idea. An extra service, and fee, for clients who wanted flowers delivered on special occasions. Warmth flooded his chest. His company was putting out an impressive product. "He's great with the texting."

Janice waved a finger at Gabe. "But tell your friend that work isn't everything. He needs to stop traveling so much and settle down so he can spend more time with Rachel. Do you know he's been too busy to even take her ring shopping?"

Gabe looked down at her bare third finger. Or meant to. The path to that finger took him past the mouthwatering view of her cleavage. Standing behind her gave him a great angle. It would be a shame to pass up the opportunity. "That is something I will definitely get on my friend about. Don't you worry."

Finally finding her voice, Rachel said, "I'll be back up to work in a minute. I'm just finishing up lunch."

Janice waved her concern aside. "No problem. It was nice meeting you, Gabe."

"You too." The woman walked away, and Gabe had no more excuses to stand behind Rachel. With one final look at the pale swells nestled in a blue silk bra, he circled back to his chair. "Well, well, well. Very interesting."

She leaned forward. "Gabe, I'm sorry. I know I said I don't have a boyfriend—"

"Because you don't. You have a made-up fiancé." Could that be a new business venture? He couldn't imagine many people wanting to take Build-A-Boyfriend that far. "I wasn't expecting that."

"Wait. What?" She shook her head. "How do you know my fiancé isn't real? And why aren't you mad?"

Hmm. Would a normal guy be angry in this situation? Probably just wary. And he'd ask questions. "I knew you couldn't be in a relationship, or at least, not a happy one, not with the way you reacted to me." He ignored her narrowed eyes. Facts were facts. "And it's not up to me to judge you on why you're lying to your boss. Seems harmless enough." He tilted his head. "So, do you have a second phone you text yourself from, or do you have a friend do it?"

"I don't text myself." She tugged at the hem of her sweater. "That's ridiculous. I just . . . pay someone else to do it for me." There went that blush again. She was like a glowworm, lighting up whenever she was embarrassed or lied. She'd make a terrible spy. "Lots of people do it. This company has plenty of clients, not just me."

"Company?" He, on the other hand, was rather

impressed with his talent at deception. The way he was leading her on, he could be the next James Bond.

Rachel sighed, and pushed a sugar packet around the table with her finger. "It's called Build-A-Boyfriend, although they make up girlfriends, too."

Gabe bit his tongue. The "girlfriends" made up less than 10 percent of their business. He couldn't dress it up. Women were just more desperate to appear wanted than men.

"I pay a monthly service fee and they send me texts from 'Trevor' "—she made air quotes around the name—"and some voice mails. Even a flower delivery when I ask, with a handwritten card. It's really quite a good service."

"I'm sure it is," Gabe said. It had to be if he was going to go public. Maybe this hadn't been such a stupid idea of Ben's, getting to know their customers. They were still pathetic, no doubt. Even Rachel must be in some way. She just hid it well. But the customer feedback he got could be invaluable to improving Build-A-Boyfriend.

Glancing at her watch, Rachel gathered the trash onto their tray.

"Why did you sign up for it?" Gabe asked.

She stood. "I have to get back to work."

He rose with her, and picked up her phone. He called his own number, waited for the faint ringtone from his pants pocket, and disconnected. "There." He handed her the phone. "Now you can get more texts to add to your inventory." He waggled his eyebrows. "And I'm for free, baby."

She rolled her eyes. But she didn't object to his having her phone number. Of course, he already had it programmed in his phone, but she didn't know that. Now, when he contacted her, he wouldn't seem like a creepy stalker.

And he would contact her. Gabe hadn't figured her out yet, and he needed definite proof that she was just another loser if he was going to get free labor from his managers for the next three months.

With a hand on her lower back, he guided her through the tables and toward the elevator. Rachel seemed like a desirable woman, but he knew the truth would be hidden deep inside her. She must have some fatal problem that drove men away.

A lock of reddish hair slipped from its pins and drifted down to coil around her neck. He tightened his fingers on her back. Her issue must be big to have men ignoring her obvious attractions.

She turned soft brown eyes up to him. "Are you going back up to your friend's office?"

"No." A large group of people filed into the elevator. Taking an elevator ride with Rachel when he had to behave before witnesses just didn't hold the same appeal as their ride down. Placing a hand on the doors to keep them open, he shepherded her in.

She turned back to face him. "Well, thanks again. For everything."

Keeping up appearances before her boss was much more important to her than the lunch he'd bought, he knew. "Glad I could help." And damn if he wasn't. "I'll be in touch."

The doors slid closed, cutting her off from view.

Gabe pressed the Up button and waited for the next elevator. Someone walked up next to him.

"Was that her?" Ben asked. "Did you already find her? We picked that client because she works in the same building, but that was fast, even for you."

"I ran into her purely by accident." The elevator doors slid open, and Gabe stepped back to let people off. "Rachel stepped onto my elevator."

"Rachel." Ben followed him into the cab and hit the button for their floor. "I thought you'd refer to her as client 2375F. That's how you see them, after all. As numbers."

Gabe ground his back teeth together, and glared at the bicycle messenger who was listening to their conversation. Gabe was getting tired of his friend's harping on about that. Like Ben was above profit. Like he didn't enjoy his new sports car as much as Gabe did his. When did wanting to be successful become a bad thing in America?

"So, is she a 'pathetic loser' like you think all the rest of them are?" Ben trailed Gabe off the elevator and toward his office.

"I had one conversation with her." Gabe loosened his tie and strode to the floor-to-ceiling windows that spanned the back wall of his office. The Arch rose a couple of blocks away, and the St. Louis skyline made a pretty picture. A picture that told Gabe he'd finally made it. His years of holding down two jobs while going to school, of watching his single mother break her back waiting tables and taking side jobs to pay the bills, those days were over.

But he knew he was always just one bad business decision away from it all going to hell.

"One conversation wasn't enough for you to see that she was a normal woman?" Ben's brow wrinkled. "Was she a bitch?"

Gabe laid a palm on the cool glass of the window. "No, she was perfectly pleasant." Except for those claws she'd dug into his side. He smiled. He'd deserved those.

"Did she eat with her mouth open? Have BO?"

Rubbing the back of his neck, Gabe dropped into his chair. "No, nothing like that."

Ben crossed his arms over his faded *Star Wars* T-shirt. "And yet you still refuse to admit that you were wrong about our clients. That they're nice, normal women." The creases in his forehead deepened. "Is it that hard for you to see the good in people?"

Gabe tried to suck in a deep breath, but his chest was too tight. Little by little, time had chipped away at his and Ben's friendship. It used to be the two of them against the world. All-nighters spent planning their business, bouncing ideas off each other over beers. When had Ben started looking at him with a hint of distaste?

Gabe clenched his fist against his thigh. "I see people just fine. Some women can hide their crazy better than others. Now, if you'll excuse me, I have work to do."

"I have stacks of work on my desk, too." Ben pushed to his feet. "But work's not everything."

"Part of this work includes texting client 2375F. Since I've met her now, I can't do her voice mails. Jerry will have to remain on point with those." Gabe slid his phone from his pocket. His engineers had set it up so he could text from "Trevor's" number on it, as well as his own. He tapped his fingers along the top of the phone. Ben's disapproval sat in his gut as heavy as last year's fruitcake, and his bet didn't seem so fun anymore.

"Unless you want to concede . . . ?" Gabe lifted

an eyebrow, trying to appear nonchalant. It would be better if this bet were over. He could put all his energy back into work. No distractions. No more peeking down Rachel's sweater. No more inappropriate elevator rides.

Gabe grunted. Her cleavage hadn't been that great anyway.

And if he believed that, reindeer could fly.

"No, I'm not conceding." Ben paused at the door. "I haven't given up on you yet."

And with that absurd statement, he coasted out, pulling the door to Gabe's office shut behind him.

Gabe stared at it. Missing his friend. He saw Ben every day, but he missed him all the same.

Spinning around in his chair, he looked out at the skyline. This view might have cost him more than his blood, sweat, and tears. Their rise to the top had changed his friend. Ben had become soft, distracted.

For Gabe, the view had always focused him. Shown him what hard work and some risk-taking could get a man. Inspired him to work harder so he could have an office with a view of the Manhattan skyline, too. And he'd get it. After going public, a branch office on the East Coast would be the next logical step.

Opening up the messaging function on his phone, he logged in as Trevor. And stared at the little blinking cursor.

And stared.

What the hell should he write? *Hope you're having a nice day, sweetie.* Gabe frowned and hit Delete. After meeting Rachel, such an everyday comment seemed tedious. Damn it, this was what computers were for. Coming up with this bilge automatically.

What would Rachel's boyfriend—*fiancé,* he corrected himself—write to her? His company's past emails to her were too damn boring for his tastes.

A smile tugged at his lips. Leaning back in his chair, he tossed his feet up on a small filing cabinet and crossed one ankle over the other.

He knew what a man would text his fiancée. Especially if she was a woman like Rachel. If "Trevor" was away from her for days at a time, there was only one thing a man would think about.

This bet might be more fun than he'd anticipated.

Just as long as he didn't get his company sued for sexual harassment.

CHAPTER 4

Rachel touched up her lipstick, using the elevator doors as a mirror. Her stomach dropped with the elevator. Why had she agreed to this?

"You look good, honey."

Startled, she glanced over at the older man in the elevator with her. He winked.

"Thanks." She chuckled. "I'm nervous, so that's nice to hear."

"Hot date?" the Santa Claus look-alike asked.

The elevator dinged and the doors slid open with a hiss. Gabe stood in the lobby, a slow smile licking at his lips when he saw her.

"You could say that," she answered. With a smile at the old man, she stepped out on shaky legs, cursing herself. It wasn't like she'd never been on a date before. She'd been on many. Too many. First dates were miserable. But since she'd started using the Build-A-Boyfriend app, she hadn't thought she'd be feeling that swooping feeling in her stomach for a while. The one like that first plunge on a roller coaster when you still didn't know whether the ride was going to be a hell of a lot of fun or two minutes of torture.

"Don't do anything I wouldn't do," the older man said, and waddled to the exit. Since Rachel had no idea what he would or wouldn't do, it wasn't particularly useful advice.

"Hi." Her voice altogether too breathless for her liking, Rachel tried again. "I hope you weren't waiting long."

"Nope." From behind his back, he pulled out a wrapped rectangular package, a little larger than his hand. "I know flowers are more typical. . . ."

Rachel loved presents. She tore through the red ribbon and silver paper with brisk efficiency born from years of practice. And laughed.

"Handkerchiefs?"

A dimple in his cheek played peekaboo with her. "I can't always be in the elevator to save you. I thought I should give you the tools to protect yourself."

"Thank you. I love it." Now she remembered why she'd agreed to dinner with Gabe when he'd called. A drop-dead sexy man who could make her laugh? A fun little holiday fling with him was the perfect present to herself.

Tucking the box into her purse, she fell into step beside him. "Where are we going? I can stop by the garage and get my car, follow you there."

"That won't be necessary." He followed her into the revolving door that led outside, reaching over her shoulder to push the door forward. He walked close behind her to fit in the small space. "I'll drop you back here after dinner."

The cold air slapped her in the face, and she

tucked her scarf into her coat. A bell ringer stood near the entrance, a donation bucket decorated with red garland next to him.

Pulling a knit cap lower on his forehead, the man nodded to them. "Hi, Gabe. How you doing tonight?"

Tucking her hand under his arm, Gabe walked over, pulling out his wallet. "I'm not freezing my ass off standing out here, so better than you."

The bell ringer snorted, and nodded his thanks as Gabe slipped a bill into the bucket. "It is cold. And there are too many kids out there shivering without coats." The man's eyes rounded in innocence. "I just can't stop thinking about the children."

Rachel bit back a smile as Gabe dug out his wallet again.

"Does anyone buy your BS, Charlie?" Gabe stuffed a couple more bills in the bucket. "That was overacting at its worst."

Wrapping his arms around himself, Charlie bounced on his toes. "Only suckers like you." He winked at Rachel. "Have a nice night."

Grumbling, Gabe pulled her down the sidewalk.

"You know the bell ringer?" Rachel slid on a small patch of ice, and Gabe pulled her close to his side.

"He worked in front of this building last year, too." Pulling out a set of keys, he pressed a button and the lights of a silver Audi coupe parked in the loading zone flashed. "When he's not trying to manipulate you into a bigger donation, he's a nice guy."

And Gabe must have put enough in the bucket over the years to get on a first-name basis with him.

She held on to his arm a little tighter. Most people tried to avoid eye contact with the bell ringers, too busy to stop, let alone have a conversation.

She stood to the side as he pulled the passenger door open. "Aren't you afraid you'll get a ticket?"

Gabe gave her that smile, the one that was all charm and no substance. No matter how nice he might be, Gabe was still a player. But since she wasn't looking for anything long-term, she was happy to play the game. "It's a loading zone. I'm loading you in."

"Not the most flattering terminology," she muttered. Sitting down, she turned her legs into the car, a precise operation as her pencil skirt didn't allow for a lot of movement. Gabe headed around the hood, and Rachel took a moment to enjoy the luxury. The cream leather of the seat was smooth beneath her fingers, and she settled back into its firm embrace. The air in the car smelled faintly of Bvlgari. Of Gabe.

He slid behind the wheel. "Where to?"

"You asked me out," she said. "Shouldn't you already have a destination in mind?"

His teeth flashed in the glow from the streetlight. "That's a separate question from dinner. Besides, you're supposed to be showing me around town." He leaned over the center console, the leather creaking. His breath brushed her ear, and she shivered. "Trevor did ask you for that favor."

That wasn't all Trevor had asked her for. The texts she'd received from him today had been decidedly odd.

"I do owe you for covering for me with my boss." Rachel turned to face him, found herself inches away from his face. "And you bought me lunch. Dinner's on me."

His firm lips frowned. This close, Rachel could see the faint silvering of a scar crossing his upper lip. It only added to the aura of restrained power he cloaked himself in. A bad boy poured into a three-piece suit. A low throb pulsed between her legs.

"You pick." He pressed a button, and the ignition purred to life. "I'll pay." Pulling into traffic, Gabe glanced at her. "So, where to?"

Rachel directed him to one of her favorite restaurants. "I hope you like Greek," she said as they were seated at a cozy table in the corner. The walls were painted the blue of the Mediterranean Sea, with murals of island life adorning them. Glass fishing floats cradled in intricate knots of rope hung from the ceiling. "But even if you don't, you'll find something you like on the menu. It's big."

"You're not kidding." He held up a menu that was not only several pages long, but two feet high. "I could wallpaper my bathroom with paper this size."

"I think it's so they can fit all the pictures in." Biting the inside of her cheek, she tried not to laugh at his wide eyes when he took in the photos of all the dishes on the menu. This probably wasn't the typical place he took his dates. Gabe seemed more like the French and expensive type. But he'd change his tune once he took a bite of the food.

The waiter came and took their order. After he left, Gabe settled back, his large frame making the small wood chair squeak. He didn't look concerned. Rachel had a feeling Gabe hid his emotions well.

"Tell me more about this Build-A-Boyfriend app," he said. "Why do you use it instead of just getting a real boyfriend?"

"What, just snap my fingers and have one delivered to me, ready-made?" Gabe probably could just snap his fingers and have a willing woman immediately hanging off his arm. He most likely hadn't had to work at getting a relationship since puberty. "Besides, house-training them can be so difficult. A virtual boyfriend just seemed easier. Less mess."

Rolling his eyes, Gabe stretched his legs out straight, his black leather wingtips nudging her ankles. Rachel glanced at his feet, several inches longer than her own size eights, and blushed.

"Uh-oh. You were thinking something naughty." He tapped her with that foot. "What was it?"

She gulped down some water. "I don't know what you're talking about."

"Your face is like a lie detector," he said. "It flashes bright red when you're embarrassed or thinking something you shouldn't. You're very easy to read." He smiled. "I like that."

Rachel twisted her lips. Of course he'd like that.

Leaning forward, he trailed his index finger up and down her hand, the touch light. All the hairs on the back of her neck stood up, and tingles started in places that hadn't tingled for months.

"I have vays to make you talk," he said, his accent heavy and hokey.

She was sure he did. That one finger could probably make her spill state secrets, if she had any. She was both relieved and disappointed when the waiter came, bearing huge plates of food.

"It's as big as their menu." Gabe looked at his moussaka doubtfully.

"Don't back down from a challenge," she told him, and spun her fork into her plate of noodles, moaning with delight when the spicy marinara hit her tongue.

"If you wanted spaghetti and meatballs, why'd we come to a Greek restaurant?" he asked. He cut a neat square off his eggplant dish. Placing it in his mouth, his eyes lit up. "This is good."

"I know. And their meatballs are better. That's why we came here." She aimed her fork at one of the plump, juicy balls and gasped when Gabe stole it right out from under her.

He licked the marinara sauce off his fork. "You're right. That's a damn good meatball."

"That's theft, that's what that is." She glared at him. "Just because you're buying dinner doesn't give you the right . . . hey!"

He chewed thoughtfully on another meatball. "I think it's the paprika. That's what makes it good." He rolled his eyes at her growl. "Oh, relax." Cutting a wedge off his meal, he forked a slice of moussaka over onto her plate. "Better?"

She wiggled in her seat, her own version of the happy food dance. "Yep."

They ate off each other's plates for the rest of the meal. It felt right. Comfortable. As if they'd known each other for a lot longer than a day.

It wasn't until they were heading back to the office and her car that Gabe brought up the Build-A-Boyfriend app again. "So, why do you use that app? I don't understand why someone like you would need to make up a boyfriend."

The charming flirt was in his voice, the flattery laid on as thick as icing on a gingerbread house. But genuine confusion hid there, too.

Rachel sighed. "It's kind of embarrassing."

"Those are the most interesting stories."

Rachel couldn't see his face in the darkened interior, just shapes, slashes of contour. She focused on the strip at his throat that was illuminated by the streetlights. It was a nice throat, thick and tan with just a hint of an Adam's apple pressing out.

"I joined Build-A-Boyfriend for work." Shifting onto one hip, she faced him. "All the editors at *Verve* are happily married. They're very nice women, but it's like a cabal, with baby pictures, anniversary stories, kids' playdates. The editors don't take my ideas as seriously as they do those of the married women. I don't think they mean to discriminate, but it's a family magazine. The way they look at it, since I don't have a family, I don't know what I'm talking about. I was tired of my story ideas getting passed over."

"So you invented a fiancé for a business opportunity." Rachel didn't hear the disgust she was expecting to. The tone of his voice almost sounded like respect.

"It started with a boyfriend. I just wanted the women I work with to think I was in a relationship. And I don't have time for a real one." She scraped her teeth over her lower lip. "A couple of promotions are going out along with the Christmas bonuses this year. I know one of the assistant editors is going to be made an associate editor. I want it to be me."

Gabe nodded. Flicking on his blinker, he turned into the parking garage of her office building. "I hadn't considered that as a potential use of m— that app. What level are you parked on?"

She directed him to her car. This late at night the garage was near empty.

"And it's working?" he asked. "More of your ideas are being taken seriously?"

"Two of my ideas were accepted for stories in the past two months," she said, smug. "That's more than in the past year combined. If I drag out a long engagement, impress them with the quality of my work as associate editor, then I can break up with Trevor in a couple of months with no one the wiser. It's a perfect plan." She frowned. "Well, it has been. I might have to change services."

Gabe slammed on the brakes behind her car, jerking her head back. "Why would you change services?"

She rubbed her neck. "Because today the texts I received from Trevor got a little weird."

His lips twitched. Was he smiling? "Weird? How?"

Rachel dug into her purse and handed him her phone. "Look. For the past two months it was all 'I love you, I can't wait to see you,' and now this?"

She couldn't miss his smile now. "It's not funny," she told him. "It's odd."

"I don't know." He pressed a button on her phone and started typing. "I'm thinking from a made-up fiancé, that's probably the most realistic text he's sent you."

"'What are you wearing?'" She snorted. "Wait, what are you typing?"

"I'm texting him back."

"What?" She reached for her phone, but he blocked her. Unbuckling her seat belt, Rachel got up onto one knee on the seat, reaching around his shoulder. He slapped her hands away, pressed a button on his door, and got out of the car. Shutting his door, he leaned back against it, his body silhouetted in the window, and ignored her protests.

Rachel yanked on her door handle, but the thing didn't budge. She hit the locks. Nothing. "Bastard child-proofed me," she muttered. She found the release button on his door as Gabe finished up and circled the car. Opening her door, he handed her the phone. She narrowed her eyes as she read. "What the hell!" She jumped out of the car and waved her phone in his face. "Why did you write this? If anyone reads these, they're going to think I'm a freak."

"He asked what you were wearing." Gabe shrugged. "I told him."

"'A low-cut sweater to show off my beautiful breasts. A tight skirt that begs for your hands to caress my ass. And thigh-high stockings just waiting for your teeth to drag down. Hurry home, stud.'" She stared up at Gabe, her mouth opening and closing like a fish out of water.

"I had to guess about the stockings, but a man can dream." He picked up a lock of her hair that always seemed to escape its bonds, and rubbed it between his fingers. "If I was out of town and you were here waiting for me, that's the kind of text I'd want to read. It's the kind of text your bosses would be expecting to see between two engaged people."

Maybe. It was getting hard to think with Gabe standing so close. Rachel's breath fogged the chilled air between them, but she itched to rip off her long coat. Her body was hot—because she was ticked off, she told herself—and getting hotter.

"Do you think"—she licked her bottom lip—"that the app takes into account length of relationship and changes its texts accordingly?"

"It would be smart." His feet nudged the toes of her pumps. When he inhaled, his chest brushed against hers. Even through all her layers, the friction made her shiver.

"What do you think the next text will be?" Her voice was a soft whisper. "I'm not very good at sexting."

His smile was dark, tempting. Like expensive chocolate. Something she couldn't resist.

Bending his head, he whispered, "You just need something good to sext about. Some memories of a hot night you can remind your fake boyfriend about." His lips gently brushed across her ear, and then lower. He placed a soft kiss on the patch of skin just below it.

She inhaled on a shaky breath. Trickles of sweat ran down her back, and she felt like she was going to combust. His lips on her throat made it hard to think.

"I'd need . . . um, someone to stand in for Trevor." She let her head fall back and stared at the flickering fluorescent lights. Her body felt heavy, her limbs too relaxed to even try to take off her coat. If it wasn't for the car at her back, she might have slithered to the floor in a boneless heap.

"I've got the perfect person." Gabe traced his tongue down her throat to the hollow. The heat from his mouth followed by the cold air hitting her moistened skin sent shivers through her body.

"A good friend of Trevor's, in fact. One you're supposed to show around town." Scraping his teeth along her collarbone, Gabe tightened his hands at her hips. "It would only be fair if he shows you a thing or two in return."

Rachel could feel her pulse pounding throughout her body. Her clothes were too heavy, too constricting, just too much against her sensitized skin. She wanted them gone. Rubbing her thighs together, she tried to take the edge off, but she still felt achy. Empty.

Never one to wait patiently for what she wanted, she ran her fingers into Gabe's hair and pulled his head back. Practically throwing herself at him, she wound her arms around his neck and kissed him for all she was worth.

Teeth bumping, lips gnashing, the kiss started out more exuberant than good. He tasted of tomato sauce and red wine, and she licked into his mouth, sliding her tongue against his. She wasn't thinking about finesse or technique, just about getting as close to this man as possible. If she could have crawled into his skin she would have.

Grabbing her under her butt, he lifted until her body was pressed against his. She tried to wrap her legs around his waist, but her skirt was too damn tight. Rachel whimpered. She needed her coat to come off. There was too much fabric between them. Snaking one hand between their bodies, she tried unfastening the coat, but her mind was too unfocused to thread the buttons through their holes. So she started tugging, hoping to rip the damn thing off. His body felt hard and wonderful, and she wanted to rub against that hardness without four layers separating them.

Stepping to the side, Gabe rested her butt on the hood of his car and pressed forward until she was lying back with his body heavy on hers. He changed the kiss, took control, dialed it back from frantic to commanding. He alternated from slow, deep plunges into her mouth, to tugging on her lip. He tightened his hands in her hair until the pull bordered on pain.

Screw her coat. With Gabe lying on top of her, and she wasn't complaining about that, she couldn't unbutton the top anyway. So she attacked the bottom. She only buttoned the top few buttons usually, and the coat spread apart at her legs when she tugged. Wiggling as best she could, she hooked her fingers under the bottom of her skirt and hiked it up. High enough to free her legs to wrap around Gabe.

Rachel arched into his erection. Still too many clothes between them, but this was better. Much, much better.

Gabe pulled his head back, her lower lip sliding out from between his teeth. His breath came out in harsh pants. His arctic-blue eyes, usually as calm as a frozen pond, burned with lust. He looked aroused, wild, and a little surprised.

He could join the club. When Rachel had woken up this morning, she'd had no idea that by nightfall she'd be wrapping her legs around a man she hadn't yet met. Everything about this was shocking. Her body's reaction to him. Her desperation. She couldn't remember ever feeling like this, and she wasn't quite sure she liked it. It was too out of control.

But like it or not, she wasn't backing down. She

needed, and so she took. Rocking against him, she felt the tension build.

"Goddamn." The air fogged before Gabe's mouth. His eyes glittered, and when she thrust against him, he swore again.

He lifted his torso off of her, making sure to keep his hips firmly in place. Looking down, he traced her body with his gaze.

Rachel tried to visualize what he saw. Her auburn hair was half out of its ponytail by this point, a mess around her head. Her cheeks would be flushed bright pink, her eyes glazed. A virtual stranger, a wanton woman rubbing herself all over him. Rachel couldn't remember if she'd ever been a wanton woman before.

She rocked harder into him, a small moan escaping her lips. It felt good. She liked being this woman.

Gabe placed the tip of his finger on her lips. She sucked it inside, enjoyed the flare of his eyes. Using the wet tip, he traced a path down her throat, pausing at her racing pulse point. He traced the edge of her sweater, each inch of skin he grazed burning beneath his touch.

With much more dexterity than she'd shown, Gabe popped the buttons of her coat and pushed the fabric down to her sides. He cupped her breast with his palm, his gaze flicking up to her face to make sure she was still on board.

She nodded, the ability to form words past her. To drive the point home, she tightened her legs around his waist and pressed closer.

He cursed, and Rachel smiled. Gabe had a filthy mouth in bed. Well, on a car.

And then he pulled down her sweater and bra

cup and used that filthy mouth in an extremely filthy way.

Rachel bowed her back, sensation rocketing from her nipple to her core. Her neck arched, and she was looking at the world upside down and through a haze of lust.

Which cleared up right quick when someone stepped out of the elevator and started walking parallel to them.

"Gabe," she hissed. Her hands found his shoulders and she pushed with all her might.

He moved about an inch.

Smacking his shoulder, she whispered his name again.

He lifted his head, his eyes looking delightfully dazed, his lips slightly reddened. "Huh?"

"Someone's coming." Rachel looked over. The woman was about thirty feet away now, head down, looking at her smartphone. Rachel clapped a hand over her mouth. It was Margie, one of *Verve's* editors. She was wearing Lycra and sneakers, obviously having come from using the building's gym after work. And getting closer with every second. "Get off me! A coworker's coming."

Gabe whipped his head around to where she was looking. With a speed that almost gave her whiplash, he dragged her off the hood of his car and took her to the ground. She landed on her purse and something crackled. Gabe covered her body with his own.

Rachel bit back a hysterical giggle. "I don't think this looks any better," she whispered.

"Shh."

She clung to him for what felt like hours, but was only mere seconds, before they heard the beep of a car lock. An engine started. She pushed at his shoulder. "Your car is on the drive. It's—"

"It's not blocking her exit, she can still get around." He frowned when she shifted and a crunch sounded in the air. "Plus, it will block her view of us when she drives past."

Rolling to her side, she looked over her shoulder. He was right. His car did provide a nice privacy wall.

"Will you stop moving around?" he said. "You're making a lot of noise, and if she has her window rolled down, she might hear you."

"I can't help it. I'm lying on something."

Gabe reached for her, then tensed when a car drove toward them. "Wait," he whispered.

After the car drove past and the engine sound faded, Gabe grinned down at her. "I think we made it undetected." He rolled to his feet and took her hand, pulling her up.

Brushing her hands over her bottom, she met something sticky. "Undetected but not unscathed." She turned her back to him and tried to look over her shoulder. "Is it bad?"

"Not if your coat likes spicy meatballs."

Rachel looked down. Next to her purse was her to-go bag. Smashed and torn, the tinfoil swan that had held her leftovers was ripped open in the middle. She shrugged her coat off—her cream-colored, dry-clean-only, wool coat—and examined the damage.

Gabe's lips twitched suspiciously, and she scowled at him.

"If you hadn't thrown me to the ground—"

"Your coworker would have caught us." He took

off his jacket and slid it over her shoulders. Taking her stained coat, he folded it neatly and placed it on the passenger seat of his car. "Besides, you liked it."

"Like hell." She'd loved it. But for some reason, she also liked arguing with him. "What are you doing with my coat? First you ruin it, now you steal it?"

Gabe crossed his arms over his chest. Without his jacket, he wore only his white dress shirt, charcoal slacks, and matching vest. He must have been cold, but he didn't show it.

Rachel bit her lip. The three-piece suit really worked for him. She didn't know why more men didn't wear vests.

"Even though I was saving your sweet ass, it is my fault that your coat was ruined. I'll take it to my dry cleaner. See if he can salvage it."

"Another rescue operation?" Pulling his jacket tight around her, Rachel breathed deep. She was cocooned in his scent. The warmth from his body still lingered in the fabric. As a substitute for his arms, it was pretty damn nice.

He led her to her car, waited for her to unlock it, and pulled the door open. "If that's what you want to believe."

"What should I believe?" She tilted her head back to look at him.

"Truth?" His brows drew down. "I've just made an opportunity to see you again when I return your coat. Don't take me for a nice guy, Rachel. When I want something, I'll play any move to get it."

"And you want me?" Rachel couldn't ever remember being so bold. Something about Gabe drew it out of her.

He stared at her lips. "Parts of you, very much."

Gabe was right. A nice guy wouldn't have said that. But all guys would have thought it.

Sliding her arms into the sleeves of his jacket, she pulled it tight around her, searching for its warmth.

This was what she wanted, wasn't it? A hot and harmless fling. Not a relationship that would distract her from her job. Gabe was perfect fling material, and she'd just walked right into him. She must have been on Santa's nice list, and he was giving her an early Christmas present.

Rocking onto her toes, she kissed his cheek. Loved the rough stubble under her soft lips. "Good night."

Sliding into her car, she waited for him to back his out from behind hers before turning on her engine.

Gabe had confirmed he was on board with the idea of a fling. It should have been enough to make her sing "hallelujah."

She watched his headlights follow her to the exit of the garage before losing sight of him in traffic.

So why did she feel so empty?

CHAPTER 5

The knock on his office door startled Gabe. Shoving his phone into a desk drawer, he called out, "Come in."

Ben popped his head in the door. "Hey. You wanted to see me?"

"Come in, have a seat." Gabe rolled his shoulders. He'd been hunched over his phone texting for too long, but he'd enjoyed reading Rachel's responses. "Since when do you knock?"

Ben flopped into a burgundy armchair. The cushion hissed angrily at the sudden weight. "You're busy a lot and don't like to be interrupted." He shrugged.

Frowning, Gabe picked up a yellow notepad. He tapped his pen against the paper. How long had these walls been cropping up between him and his oldest friend? When was the last time Ben had talked to him about something other than work?

"Uh, have any plans this weekend?" Gabe asked. "Seeing anyone?"

Ben narrowed his eyes. "Why are you asking? Did you hear something?"

Gabe cocked his head. "Just curious." Was his friend dating an ex-con? Or did he just not want to share personal information anymore? He cleared his throat. "But that's not why I wanted to see you. I was rereading the old texts to Rachel"—Ben raised his eyebrows—"client 2375F, and they're all very similar. 'How are you doing today, I miss you,' that kind of thing."

"I know it's been a while since you've been in a relationship longer than a night," Ben drawled, "but those are things people who like each other typically say."

Gabe tapped his notepad harder. "I'm aware of that. But there's no progression. Some of our clients have been members of Build-A-Boyfriend for over six months. Don't you think if you were really seeing someone that long, the texts would change? Become more personal?"

"Maybe." Ben leaned forward. "What's your point?"

"I was wondering if you could change the algorithm. The longer the client has been with us, the more intimate the texts become." Raising a hand, Gabe continued. "And before you say it, I'm not suggesting dirty texts." He bit back a smile, thinking of his last message to Rachel as Trevor. She wasn't like their typical client. She liked a little dirty talk.

"But if a client texts us that she's, I don't know, going to New York for the weekend—"

"We need to text back a relevant question, like 'How was your trip?'" Excitement laced Ben's voice. "Or, 'How's your mom, Mary, doing?'"

Looking at his notes, Gabe twisted his lips. Those weren't quite the sample questions he'd written down. "Sure. But even though we shouldn't start sexting our clients, I do think people in a relationship might ask even more personal questions, like 'What are you wearing?' Or 'Thanks for last night.' The sort of thing you said to your last girlfriend." A small kernel of shame blossomed in his chest when he realized he didn't know who exactly Ben's last girlfriend had been. Janice? Jenny?

He studied his friend. "So, can you do it? Make that program change?"

Staring out into space, Ben blew out a long breath. Gabe knew that look. He waited for the virtual lines of code to run through his partner's head, knowing better than to interrupt his train of thought.

Finally, Ben looked at him. "I think so. I'll start running tests."

"Great." Swinging his legs up on his desk, Gabe smiled. "I love this business. I come up with the ideas, and you do all the work."

"That's bullshit, and you know it." Ben shook his head. "We've had equal sleepless nights, equal risks—"

"And equal rewards," Gabe finished. "I like that we've finally gotten to that last part." They were so close to the ultimate reward. Just a couple more quarters of better-than-expected profits, and he'd be ready to file their prospectus with the SEC.

Leaning forward, Ben rested his elbows on his knees. "It's not just the money. I know in the grand scheme of things our service is insignificant, but we do help some people. A client just e-mailed that because one of her coworkers saw the texts she'd been getting, he finally got up the nerve to ask her out. He knew he couldn't wait any longer without losing his chance, and now they're dating. I like that we helped her."

Gabe placed an elbow on his desk and rested his head in his hand. "Sounds like we just lost a client. Not a win in my book."

"Don't you want to help people?" Ben looked at him with his big puppy-dog eyes, and Gabe almost hated to let him down. But his friend was too sentimental. He had to wise up, for his own good.

"Policemen and firefighters help people. Doctors. We just make money off the losers in the world. When are you going to accept that?" Gabe swallowed, the word *loser* leaving a foul taste in his mouth. Rachel had felt so warm and soft in his arms last night. It didn't sit right to call her a loser. But she was the exception. A client who was using their service to get ahead at work. He could respect that.

Ben shot to his feet, the armchair tipping over backward. "Stop calling them losers," he yelled. "You don't know anything, so just shut up."

Openmouthed, Gabe watched his partner stomp from the office and slam the door behind him. In their eight years of friendship, that was the first time Gabe had ever heard Ben raise his voice. What the hell had just happened?

He turned to his computer and tried to focus on the spreadsheet he should be analyzing. His mind didn't want to concentrate. He stared at his door instead. Should he find Ben, force him to tell Gabe just what the hell was wrong? His friend was starting to act like a chick, all moody and emotional, and it was pissing Gabe off.

Sliding open his desk drawer, he picked up his phone. If his friend was acting like a hormonal woman, maybe he should ask one for advice. He scrolled to his messages and smiled at the last text Trevor had sent. In it, he'd just said that Trevor had been thinking of her that morning. In the shower. With a washcloth. Rachel's two word response made him laugh.

He switched over to his real phone number. *Have a problem with a friend. He's been acting moody lately. Secretive. Any ideas how to approach him?*

Five minutes of drumming his fingers on his desk later, his phone buzzed. *Good morning to you, too, Gabe. I'm doing well, thanks for asking. My co-worker didn't see us last night. I know you were worried about that.*

Gabe rolled his eyes. He knew he'd gone to the right person about Ben. Both he and Rachel took forever to get to the point.

About your friend, since I don't know anything about him, it's hard to give any advice. Thinking back to when he started acting differently, can you remember anything that changed?

Spinning his chair, Gabe stared out at the skyline. Things had been changing between Ben and him so gradually, it was hard to pinpoint when it started. But the blowup, or as much as a blowup as Ben was capable of, had been right after Gabe had called their clients losers.

His fingers flew over his phone. *I've been saying the same thing for years, but I guess it's finally getting to him.*

And whatever you said, I'm sure you were your normal charming self.

Gabe smiled. *Always. Tired of talking about my friend. Let's talk about you.*

You brought up your friend.

And now I'm changing the subject. What are you wearing?

Gabe could almost hear her exasperated sigh from eight floors down. He settled in his chair more deeply and waited. He enjoyed texting with Rachel more than he liked talking to most women.

A turtleneck and baggy pants. Turned on yet?

Some of my best presents came wrapped in ugly paper.

It was a minute before the next message came through.

I'm not your present.

She'd been pretty damn giving last night. If her coworker hadn't shown up, she would have given him everything on the hood of his car. Remembering how sweet she'd tasted made Gabe thirsty for more.

You're the only thing I want for Christmas.

Gabe . . .

At least give me another dinner. Besides, you need to show me the sights of St. Louis. Trevor would expect no less from you.

Gabe's phone lit up, and he whistled, low and long. Rachel had a very dirty mouth. It was a good thing Trevor was imaginary, or else he would have been in a world of hurt from everything Rachel threatened to her fake fiancé.

So is that a yes? he asked.

Yes.

I'll pick you up tonight at your office.

Tomorrow. I'll be working late tonight.

Gabe frowned, then laughed at himself. He was as impatient as a teenager. He couldn't remember the last time he'd been so eager to see a woman. He was sure once he'd gotten inside Rachel, he'd lose his fascination with her. She was just his next conquest, and one that held a hint of the forbidden since she was also a client. It was no wonder he was champing at the bit.

Rubbing a knuckle into his breastbone, he turned back to his desk. There wasn't even the possibility that this thing with Rachel could turn into something. He could never tell her he owned Build-A-Boyfriend. That she was a bet.

The damn bet. He was going to lose. Ben had picked the one woman who used their app for a clever purpose. He wouldn't be able to call Rachel a loser. There went his bonus.

Losing his bonus didn't bother him nearly as much as losing the extra man-hours from his staff. But he knew his employees worked hard, and they'd still be able to make their goals for the IPO.

So why did he feel so shitty? It couldn't be because he knew whatever he and Rachel had going on had an expiration date. That was how he went into all his relationships, and Rachel was no different.

Well, she was different from the other woman he'd dated in some respects. She didn't laugh politely at his jokes all the while doing a web search on their phones for how much his car cost. No, Rachel tried not to laugh around him, tried to stay disapproving, until the giggles just burst out of her.

It was because she didn't know just how much money he had. Seeing a fancy car was one thing. Knowing he was the CEO of the top-grossing company in St. Louis was something else. If she knew just how many zeros were on his bank statement, she'd be exactly like the others, he was sure.

Gabe pounded at his keyboard, printing out the report. He'd take it home and look it over tonight. He couldn't concentrate now, and since Rachel was busy, he wouldn't have anything better to do.

No, Rachel was no different from the others. And even if she was, it wouldn't matter. She'd never forgive him if she found out he'd been playing her this whole time. He'd just have to take what pleasure he could from her while he could and then move on.

CHAPTER 6

"Look who I found in the elevator!" Janice popped into the office Rachel shared with two other women, dragging Gabe in behind her. He was wearing another three-piece suit, charcoal-gray this time, and his shoulders seemed to fill the doorway. The cashmere blend stretched tautly across his powerful thighs when he moved, and Rachel couldn't help but remember how hard and strong that thigh had been wedged between her legs the night on the car.

Janice had her fingers twined through Gabe's, and something slippery rolled over in Rachel's gut. Janice was happily married and didn't mean anything by touching Gabe so casually. And she thought Gabe was just a friend of Rachel's fiancé. Her fake fiancé. Not the man Rachel was maybe dating.

Christ, this was getting confusing.

Rachel stood and patted her hair, trying to remember if she still had a pencil sticking out of her bun. "Hi, Gabe. You're early for dinner."

"Traffic was a breeze." Gabe held out his hand to her two coworkers, and Rachel made the introductions. Turning to face her, he slid his hands in his pockets, and rocked onto the balls of his feet. "Am I too early? I can wander around the building until you're ready. There was a cute elf by the tree downstairs. I wouldn't mind spending some time with her." He winked at Janice.

Oh, he was good. Making it look like they were nothing more than friends. The lie rolled off his tongue as smooth as molasses. At least, it'd better be a lie. Even though this was casual, Rachel still didn't want to hear from her date that he wanted to hit on another woman.

Her coworker, Rhonda, picked up some poster board. "We're just putting our latest story to bed." She turned to Rachel. "I'll take this down to Graphics."

Her other office mate, Beth, stepped out from behind her desk. "And I want to talk to Editorial about the spread we just sent them." She stepped behind Gabe and pointed at his back. "*Holy shit,*" she mouthed, shaking her hand like she'd been burned. Gabe was serious eye candy for this mainly XX-chromosome office.

Janice frowned, and dragged Beth to the door. Her boss might not approve of Rachel drooling over any man not her fiancé, but Beth was happy to encourage non-Trevor-related dirty thoughts. Beth didn't like the idea of a fiancé who never showed himself, and had never met Rachel's friends. She'd told Rachel a man like that wasn't to be trusted.

She and Beth had become close, close enough for Rachel to lose sleep over lying to her about Trevor. But she didn't want to put her friend in the position where she'd have to cover for her if Rachel told her the truth.

Guilt gnawed at her stomach. Rachel was the one who couldn't be trusted. She shoved the feeling away. Once she got the promotion, she'd get rid of the fiancé and come clean with her friend.

"Let me just close up shop." Turning to her computer, she started shutting it down. "I'll be ready in a couple of minutes."

"We'll see you tomorrow, Rachel." Nodding her head at Gabe, Beth said, "Have fun tonight."

Janice blew out a breath, and dragged Beth from the office after Rhonda. Beth snaked her hand out and closed the door behind them.

Gabe raised an eyebrow.

"Beth doesn't like Trevor."

"He doesn't exist. She's never met him." Gabe prowled around her office, examining the framed magazine covers hanging on the walls.

"That's the problem." Rachel stood and slid an arm into her coat. "She thinks any man who's serious enough about a woman to propose should meet her friends."

"She has a point."

The second jacket sleeve resisted her attempts to insert her arm. "I thought you weren't judging me on my fake fiancé."

Stepping behind her, Gabe laid a hand on her shoulder, stopping her twisting. He shook her coat and held the sleeve out for her arm. "I'm not judging the idea. Maybe just the execution of it."

"Riiight." Gabe left his hands on her shoulders, and she didn't step away. The solid weight felt too good, made her feel grounded.

He turned her to face him, and stepped in even closer, the lapels of his jacket brushing her breasts. "No, I admire a woman with ambition. Your drive is very . . ."

Admirable, commendable, inspiring. Any one of those adjectives would help Rachel feel better about her deceit.

". . . sexy." Gabe curled his lips up, the smile of a predator looking at a tasty morsel.

Rachel's core clenched. Okay, not where her mind was going, but that word worked for her, too. She stared at his lips, and swallowed. Those lips had proven very talented.

Gabe threaded his fingers into her hair. One by one, her bobby pins hit the carpet.

"I like your buttoned-up librarian look," Gabe said, the tips of his fingers kneading the back of her head, "but I really like it when you go naughty librarian."

Rachel closed her eyes. His touch was better than the head massage she got from her hair-dresser. His warm breath caressed her lips, making them tingle. But this was stupid. Her coworkers were on the other side of a flimsy door. This was—

She moaned, and the sound caught in Gabe's mouth. He nibbled on her bottom lip, traced the seam of her lips with his tongue. Damn, he was good at this. If his skill at kissing was any indication of his other skills . . .

Skimming his hands down her back, he gripped her ass through her A-line skirt. In one quick move, Gabe lifted and plopped her up on her desk, knocking over a jar of pens. Stepping into the space between her legs, he pressed her thighs wider.

Rachel hummed, her nipples growing tight, her breasts heavy. It had been too long since she'd felt like this. If ever. None of her previous lovers had half the skill in their entire bodies that Gabe had just in his tongue.

Putting her palms on his chest, she rubbed the hard muscle beneath the suit. Not good enough. She needed to feel him, skin to skin, heat to heat. Her fingers tangled in his vest's buttons. Impatient, she was a second away from ripping the damn thing open when Gabe covered her hands with his own.

Resting his forehead against her temple, he breathed heavily against her cheek. "As much as I'd love to take you on this desk, the door isn't locked." He sucked in a deep gulp of air, and took a small step back. "I don't want to be the reason you don't get your promotion."

Right. She straightened her skirt. Right. Her promotion. At least one of them was thinking straight. He was like a drug, eroding all of her common sense with the need to touch him. Reaching into her pocket, she tugged on her gloves, hoping the additional barrier would help her to keep her hands off of him. At least until they were somewhere safe.

She flicked a glance at Gabe out of the corner of her eye. It was nice he'd actually thought of her before his dick. He adjusted the large bulge in his pants, and Rachel licked her bottom lip. Very nice.

"You need a minute, or are you ready to go?" Rachel slid off the desk.

Gabe twisted his lips. "I'm fine. I'll just walk behind you."

Rachel bit back a laugh. Sliding her purse over her shoulder, she strode to the door and pulled it open. Janice and Beth glanced up from a nearby desk.

"Leaving so soon?" Beth asked. Rachel could just imagine the internal head shake happening in her friend's mind. A wasted opportunity with a beautiful man in a closed office.

"Yeah. There's a lot of St. Louis I want to show Gabe."

Janice settled a hip against the desk. "Oh? What are you guys going to see tonight?"

Gabe and Rachel looked at each other. His shoulders lifted minutely, his lips tipping up. He was leaving this lie in her court.

"Since Gabe's expressed an interest in all things Christmas"—*there'd better not be a hot elf by the tree downstairs*—"I thought I'd show him the lights in Tilles Park, or go see the tree in front of the Arch. Maybe go ice-skating."

"That sounds like fun," Janice said.

"And so romantic," Beth added.

Rachel glared at her, but her friend ignored it, too busy examining her from head to toe. "Do something different with your hair?" Beth raised an eyebrow.

"I let it down. I was getting a headache," Rachel muttered.

Hands shoved into his front pockets, Gabe stepped forward. "Well, we'd best be off. I don't want to keep Rachel out too late tonight. She's waiting for a call from Trevor."

"Of course." Janice beamed. "And since you're new here, and you like Christmas so much, I wanted to personally invite you to our company holiday party. Rachel's promised us that we'll finally meet Trevor there. You should come with them."

Heat rose up Rachel's face. Damn. She had promised that, a month ago. Another excuse she'd have to make up. Trevor really was a crappy fake fiancé.

Putting his hand on her elbow, Gabe tugged her toward the elevators. "Love to. I'll just check my schedule. Nice to see you all again. Gotta go."

Rachel stumbled after him. "You can't come to my company Christmas party." A garland framing the elevator's doors escaped from its tape. She frowned, and tried to tuck the greenery back into place. "It would be too weird having another guy there when Trevor cancels again."

The doors slid open, and Gabe drew her into the empty cab. "You could always use another service." He punched the button for the lobby. "Hire an actor to play Trevor."

Rachel played with the zipper of her jacket. "An actor?" She hadn't thought of that. Sounded expensive.

Gabe leaned back against the wall and watched her under hooded eyelids. "Forget that idea. It won't work."

"It won't?" She leaned her shoulder against the wall next to him. They were the only two people in a large elevator, plenty of room to spread out. She inched closer. The subtle scent of his cologne teased her nose, and she inhaled deeply.

His eyes flared. "I don't want another man touching you, even if it is just acting." Leaning down, he paused, lips inches from hers, his breath skating across her skin.

The elevator doors dinged and slid open. Rachel

jumped back as a group of three businessmen got on. Gabe crossed his arms over his chest, his gaze never leaving her face.

She swallowed. All her ideas on where to take Gabe dissolved. There was only one thing she wanted to show him, and that was her bed. Or his. She wasn't picky. But the ache between her legs told her she needed to get horizontal with this man soon.

Pressing her thighs together, she watched the numbers tick down to the lobby. She grabbed his sleeve and threaded her way through the crowd of people getting off work, dragging Gabe behind her.

Charlie waved at them, his bell clanging in the busy night, but she was too impatient to stop. Tomorrow she'd leave an extra-big donation. Tonight, she just wanted to leave with Gabe.

Disappointment hit her when she didn't see his car sitting out front. "Where are you parked?"

"The garage. Near your car." He stepped behind her, pressed his body against hers. His breath warmed her ear. "But I have another idea for transportation. Something that will get us in the holiday spirit better than skating or any damn arch."

Grabbing her hand, he led her across the street and through the park to the other side of the square. A row of horse-drawn carriages waited at the curb, large plumes of steam billowing from the horses' mouths.

"A carriage ride?" Rachel eyed the conveyance as Gabe handed the driver some cash. It was all very romantic, but right now she wasn't looking for romance. And she didn't think the carriage would drop them by her apartment.

"Come on." Gabe gripped her hips and lifted her into the carriage. Sliding over, she unfolded the faux fur blanket and spread it over their knees after Gabe settled beside her. He wrapped an arm around her shoulders and pulled her close. "There's something very important I need to ask you, Rachel. And I need an honest answer."

The carriage jerked into motion, the steady clapping of the horse's hooves mixing with the evening traffic. She snuggled closer to Gabe. His throat was inches from her mouth, and she longed to bridge the distance, nibble on that firm column. "Okay." If he asked her whether she wanted to go home with him, that answer would be a resounding yes.

But he didn't ask her that. Instead, lowering his head, he whispered, "Can you be quiet?"

And cupped her through her flowing wool skirt.

Rachel sucked in a breath. His hand was buried beneath the blanket. He didn't move it against her, not yet. But his grip was firm, proprietary. Heat started at her core and licked up her body. She wanted to throw off the blanket, let the cold air soothe her flushed skin. But that would leave her and Gabe exposed. She nodded once instead.

"That's good." Inching up her skirt, he dragged his fingers up the crotch of her tights, the stretchy cotton a minor barrier. She hissed in a breath. "Real good. Because I don't want to wait to get you home. I need to touch you. Now."

Rachel stared at the back of the driver's head. She needed something to fix on. It had been a while since a man had touched her there, and she might just fly out of her skin if she didn't concentrate on something other than Gabe's thick fingers. If she focused—

Gabe snaked his hand down the front of her tights, pulling her panties down along with them. His fingers brushed across her clit, and she squeaked.

He pressed her face into his coat with his free hand.

"Sorry," she whispered. "Cold hands."

His chest rumbled with his laugh. "I'll have to rectify that situation." Sliding his fingers between her folds, he found her entrance, circled it once before plunging a finger deep. "That should warm it right up."

"Oh God."

The driver cocked his head, but didn't turn. "Cold back there? I can dig out another blanket from under your seat if you'd like."

"No," both she and Gabe said together.

Gabe added a second finger, the palm of his hand rubbing against her clit with each plunge. "That's all right. We'll keep each other warm."

The driver chuckled. "I hear you. Would you two like to learn a little about the history of St. Louis?"

Clearing her throat, Rachel prepared to say yes. If the man was talking, there would be less of a chance of him hearing anything.

Gabe disagreed. "We're fine. We just want to sit here and enjoy the beautiful night, if that's all right with you."

The man lifted his shoulders. "Same price either way. Too bad it's a cloudy night. No stars."

Gabe's lips curved against her temple. "I don't know," he murmured. "I think you'll be seeing stars soon enough." He turned his wrist, scraped his fingers along her inner wall.

Rachel's hips flew off the seat. This was crazy. Gabe was crazy. She wasn't an exhibitionist. She didn't do things like this. His palm ground into her mound, and she bit back a moan.

Why didn't she do things like this? It felt freaking amazing. She sank against Gabe, letting her legs fall open a bit more. They were probably violating a couple of different laws, but Rachel didn't worry about getting caught. Something about Gabe made her feel safe. Probably his confidence.

He grabbed the back of her knee and lifted her leg across his, spreading her wide. He positioned her like her body was his to command.

Cocky, she amended, not confident. Gabe was all cocky swagger.

He pistoned his fingers faster, adding a twist. Her heart pounded painfully against her chest. His cockiness was well-deserved. Her muscles clenched, winding tighter and tighter. She dug her fingers into his coat.

"Breathe," he whispered.

Rachel shook her head. She couldn't breathe. If she opened her mouth she would scream. Her hips rocked against his hand, out of her control. A vise squeezed her lungs. Just when she thought she couldn't take it anymore, Gabe thumbed her clit, pressing hard, and she was gone.

Biting his sleeve, she rode out the orgasm until she was gasping for air.

Gabe withdrew his hand, and tucked her other leg over his lap so they both dangled over his knees. Gathering her close, he kissed her behind her ear. His lips curved against her skin. "Any stars?"

Well, she couldn't let that smugness go unchecked. As soon as she caught her breath, she said, "No stars."

He snorted.

"Okay, the light show was decent," she admitted. "But I think *I* might owe *you* a coat now. I might have bitten a hole through yours."

"No worries. My triceps took the brunt of the attack."

She lifted her head and caught his grin. She wanted to be annoyed, but her sated body wouldn't allow it. She settled for a harrumph.

Her pulse settled into the steady pace of the horse's clopping hooves. The tips of Gabe's ears were dark, and she pulled the edges of his scarf up high around his neck. Her body temperature had yet to cool, but he must be freezing.

She sighed. He was giving, he was funny, and he was smoking hot. This holiday fling might be going a little too well. A man like Gabe could become as addictive as her grandmother's spiced apple cake.

But Gabe also didn't seem to be looking for anything long-term. He was busy with his work, too. He'd keep the fling on track. His indifference would remind her to stay focused on her career. But while the fling lasted, she had a feeling it was going to burn hotter than any supernova.

She placed a hand on his thigh. "I live about two miles away. What do you say we take this indoors?"

His muscles jumped under her palm. He tapped the driver on the shoulder. "Time to head back." Taking her hand under the blanket, he placed it on his groin. He was hard and thick, and Rachel's core fluttered in anticipation. Just like that, she was hungry again. "I've got somewhere I need to be."

CHAPTER 7

Gabe took the stairs two at a time, eyes focused on the luscious ass swaying a couple of steps above him. Damn, Rachel had curves in all the right places. And he was just minutes away from sinking inside this sweet woman.

It was quite the Christmas gift. He'd never taken for granted his past women. Even though he didn't stick around long, he tried to be a respectful lover. But something about tonight was different, and Gabe couldn't put his finger on why. With all his blood pooled low, it was no surprise he couldn't think. Didn't even want to bother trying.

Fumbling with her keys, Rachel tried to unlock her door one-handed. Her other hand was busy burrowing under his shirt. He pressed into her body, nudging his erection against her soft stomach. Taking her mouth, he explored its depths, curling his tongue under the roof of her mouth.

Rachel dropped the keys.

"I need to get those," she said, her voice breath-less.

He leaned in deeper. "Yes."

Her lips curved beneath his. "We need the keys to get in my apartment. Where there's a bed."

"Beds are overrated," he said, but reluctantly stepped back, looking for where the keys had landed.

Rachel spied them first. Turning, she bent over. Gabe groaned, his hands drawn to her hips like metal to a magnet. "I used to say this as a teenager, but now I mean it. If you change your mind, I think I might actually die."

Laughing, she straightened, wiggling her pert ass in his crotch. "I believe that even less now than I did when I was a stupid teenager."

Gabe slid his hand from her hip to the top of her mound, circled over just the right spot.

She sucked in a breath. "Right. Inside. Now." She threw open the door and dragged him into her apartment by the front of his pants.

Gabe kicked the door shut, his fingers already peeling up her sweater. Her head popped free from the top, and her hair slowly drifted to her shoulders, static electricity making it stand out like a halo. In her red lace bra, she made a very naughty angel.

His lips tipped up.

She paused, her hands at the side of her skirt. "What's funny?"

Brushing her hands aside, he finished the job of unzipping her. "Your hair just got really big. It's cute."

Her skirt pooled around her ankles, and she

stepped out of the fabric. She stood before him in her bra and black tights, a hint of red lace peeking out at her waist. Her skin was creamy against the red and black underwear, her chest heaving beneath the semi-sheer cups of her bra. Gabe stared, becoming fully aware of each of his heartbeats as they pounded blood through his body.

Running her fingers through her hair, she rolled her eyes. "Last month we ran an article on proper hair care for the winter months. Obviously, I didn't follow the advice."

Gabe's smile slowly faded. Right. Her magazine. The job she loved so much that she was using his company to get a promotion.

The company that he hadn't told her he owned.

He had just intended to get to know Rachel as part of the bet. Sleeping with her wasn't supposed to be on his agenda.

His chest clenched. Was he as big an asshole as his friend thought?

Her eyes never leaving his, Rachel stuck her fingers in the waist of her tights. Bending over, she slowly peeled them down her legs, giving him a fucking fantastic view of her tits.

Screw it. Rachel had made it clear her career didn't leave room for a boyfriend. She just wanted a fun fling. It didn't matter what his job was; a little lie or two wouldn't hurt. He ran a finger along the tops of her bra cups. As long as he treated her well—and he would treat her very well—she would leave this temporary relationship satisfied.

Trailing his fingers alongside her bra straps, he made his way over her shoulders and to the clasp at her back. She shivered beneath his touch, and his cock throbbed in response beneath his pants.

The bra joined her skirt on the floor, and she filled his hands. Her nipples were as pink as her lips, and Gabe couldn't resist bending down for a taste.

She dug her fingers into his skull. "That feels so good." Her head fell back on her shoulders, exposing the length of her neck. All she wore was a teeny scrap of lace, the rest of her body unprotected, ready for the taking. But that scrap of lace covered some of his most favorite bits, and it had to go. One quick tug at the thong, and she was completely exposed.

He let his fingers roam everywhere his eyes had. Light freckles dusted her arms and chest. A small scar over her ribs demanded his kiss. And the neatly trimmed thatch of hair at her vee begged for his attention. He already knew the feel of her, how eagerly she clutched at his fingers, but Gabe couldn't take his eyes off of her core as he eased two fingers in and out of her body.

Grabbing his shoulders, she wobbled on her feet.

Her apartment wasn't large. It wouldn't take more than a couple of glances to understand the layout, but he couldn't tear his eyes off of her. "Where's the bedroom?"

"Too far." She gestured vaguely behind her. "Couch."

It was long and green and looked like a thrift store reject. But it appeared sturdy enough. The back was at just the right height to bend Rachel over, take her like his body demanded, but that was usually more of a second fuck position.

Standing, he swept her up and tumbled her onto the couch. His hips settled between hers, his mouth finding the sweet spot on her neck. She tasted like strawberries and cream. Delicious. He wanted to taste her everywhere.

She unzipped his pants and grabbed him through his boxers.

His mind blanked. Later. He'd taste her everywhere later. Right now, he just needed in.

"Back pocket. Wallet. Condom." That was all the instruction he could give.

"Take off your clothes and I'll get it," she said.

Clothes? Who gave a shit about clothes? His important parts were already uncovered.

She paused, condom in hand, to tug at his shirt. "I want to feel you. Skin to skin."

Well, okay, that sounded good. Gabe pulled his shirt up and over his head, not caring that a button popped off. Tugging his pants and boxers down his hips, Rachel slowly rolled on the condom.

Jesus, Mary, and Joseph, she was going to kill him. Grabbing Rachel behind one knee, he brought her leg over his hip, and pressed his way into heaven.

The stretch was delicious. Rachel opened her legs wider, wanting him deep. He eased his way in until his hips rested flush against hers.

Rachel sighed in contentment. She was so full, felt so connected, that she didn't even want Gabe to move. She could just lie this way for a long time, with him thick and heavy inside her, his chest pressing her down into the cushions.

He brushed his lips over hers. With his fingers, he tucked a piece of hair around her ear. The tender action surprised Rachel, and she kissed the inside of his wrist.

As slowly as he'd sunk into her, Gabe eased back until just the crown of his cock remained notched at her entrance. He set the pace, languid, easy, until it became excruciating. The muscles of his ass flexed beneath her hands, and she tried to urge him faster.

Chuckling, he nipped at the tip of her breast, resisting her efforts.

"Gabe . . ."

"Patience." Bracing himself on straight arms, he looked down to where they were joined. "You have the prettiest pussy I've ever seen. I love watching my dick sink into you. I'm not going to rush it."

Rachel followed his gaze. It was entrancing, his cock, dusky beneath the condom, disappearing into her body. His hardness enveloped by her softness.

Whimpering, she dug her heels into his back. Whereas Gabe wanted to drag out the moment, the sight of him fucking her only enflamed Rachel to want more.

"Please. Faster. Now."

Leaning down, he bit her earlobe. "Are you asking or demanding?"

"Whatever gets the job done." As an added incentive, she fluttered her muscles, practicing every Kegel exercise she knew.

Gabe groaned. "Oh, fuck me."

"No." Rachel licked around the shell of his ear and whispered, "Fuck me."

One hand at her hip, Gabe slammed into her. "Anything you want, baby." He buried his head in the crook of her neck and pounded into her, again and again.

Rachel held on and took everything he gave her. She needed it rough and dirty. Sweet was for relationships, something Gabe wasn't offering. This, the sweating and moaning, the slapping of skin against skin, this was what he had to give.

Rachel arched her back, took him deeper. The fullness in her body would have to compensate for the tiny hole opening in her heart. The hole where dreams went to die and whispered pleas of *"what if"* went unheard. What they had right now was going to have to be good enough.

And, damn, but it was good. Her lungs squeezed, her air caught in her chest. Her internal muscles rippled, every thrust bringing her closer. Gabe was close too, his jaw tight, sweat rolling down his temple. At this point, Rachel would usually help herself out, add her fingers to the mix so she wasn't left behind. But her arms felt too heavy to move.

Gabe drove into her, his movements growing frantic. His hand tightened in her hair. "Rachel . . ." he growled.

The deep rumble of his voice did it. Throwing back her head, she exploded around him. *Gabe!* She wanted to scream his name, but she only thought it, too busy gasping for air. Her core clamped down on his cock, and Gabe groaned, giving in to his own release.

Their breathing was loud in the silence. Rachel glided her hand up and down his spine, her body still twitching around him. She loved this moment, when you were still connected but no longer driven by primal urges. A moment when she could pretend that this might be the start of something wonderful.

Gabe lifted his head. His eyes were heavy-lidded, satisfaction oozing from every pore. "I hope you weren't thinking of kicking me out. Because we're doing that again." Lowering his mouth to hers, he whispered across her lips, "And again."

CHAPTER 8

Gabe whistled as he shuffled through a stack of marketing proposals on his desk. He should have been tired. He'd been in Rachel's bed almost every night for the past two weeks, and very little sleeping had taken place. But he felt energized. Invigorated. Like he was able to take on the world.

His phone vibrated, and Gabe smiled at the text. Whereas Trevor's and Rachel's texts had returned to being generic, Gabe's and Rachel's texts were hot enough to steam a Christmas pudding. He raised his eyebrows. If she made good on only half the things she promised in her text, he was in for a very entertaining night. Damn, she was sexy. And sweet. He just couldn't get enough of her.

Ben paused in the open doorway of his office. "Are you whistling 'Jingle Bells'?" His voice was all horrified fascination, but Gabe was in too good of a mood to care.

"And if I was?" Gabe plucked a proposal from the top of the stack. "We should hire this company.

I think their ideas will break us into a whole new market."

Flopping down in a chair, Ben shrugged. "Whatever. That's your department." He narrowed his eyes, examining Gabe closely.

Gabe looked down at his suit. "What? Did I spill something?"

"I just talked to Joe." Ben waited, as if that should be enough information to go on.

Gabe swung his legs onto his desk. "And?"

"He said you let everyone off early today. Told them they could leave at three this afternoon?"

Gabe spun his phone around on his thigh. "Yeah. I thought they could use the time to shop for Christmas. It was, uh, good for morale."

"So it was a business decision?"

"Of course." Gabe shifted in his chair. "A happy worker is a productive worker."

Ben's eyebrows disappeared beneath his mop of hair. "Really?"

"Oh, shut up," Gabe said without heat. "I'm not the Scrooge you seem to think I am." His thigh buzzed, and he looked down. A smile flashed across his face before he shut it down. "Excuse me a second."

Promises, promises, he typed. *If you want me to bring cheesecake, I'll need an added incentive.*

He ignored Ben's grin while waiting for Rachel's response.

What do you want? For cheesecake I'll do just about anything.

I want a sexy pic. Something that will get me through the afternoon until I see you tonight. And I want it now.

"Are you texting client 2375F?" Ben stretched out his legs and crossed his ankles. "Isn't it time you officially admitted you lost that bet? Our clients are obviously not losers."

I'm in a meeting. Think of something else.

My heart's already set. Get creative. Gabe scowled at his friend. "Yes. I concede. I already spoke with Deb in Accounting about my bonus. Or my lack thereof, now." Funny, he wasn't as upset about losing the bet as he'd thought he'd be. His employees worked hard. It might take a little longer, but he was confident they'd still go public.

Creative?

I'm assuming you're sitting at a table. If you're wearing a skirt, I can think of a couple intriguing possibilities. Now, chop-chop.

"What's happened to you?" His friend shook his head. "It's like you've been a different person these past couple of weeks. Did you just need to get laid all this time?"

"Hey, watch it." His friend's question was G-rated compared to a lot of their conversations, but Gabe didn't want to hear it this time. Rachel deserved better than locker room talk. "Besides, I got laid plenty before."

"You're right, you did. So, what's changed now?"

Gabe opened his mouth, shut it. That stumped him. His musings were interrupted by an incoming text.

Okay. Got creative. Showing you the body part you most deserve.

Gabe threw his head back and laughed.

"What's so funny?" Ben asked.

Gabe showed him his phone.

A crease lined Ben's forehead. "Someone flips you off and you laugh?"

"Yep." *While I adore every inch of you, I don't think your finger qualifies as sexy.*

"Any plans for the weekend?" he asked his friend. "You should take off early, too. No use us working in an empty office. In fact, I'm thinking of taking a long lunch." A really long lunch if he could get Rachel to play hooky. A lunch that just might extend until dinner and beyond.

"I'm going to see that new sci-fi movie." Ben fiddled with the hem of his shirt. "With Juliette."

Looking up from his phone, Gabe cocked his head. "Juliette?"

His friend blushed. "Just a girl I'm seeing."

Gabe shook his head. "You don't turn red like that over just 'a girl you're seeing.' You'd only get that embarrassed if . . ." He brought his feet down to the carpet. "You have a girlfriend."

He turned even redder. Well, damn. Ben had a girlfriend. His nerdy friend dated, sure, but this was the first time Gabe could remember him getting flustered about it. "Congratulations. Am I ever going to meet this Juliette?"

"Maybe. If you can be nice to her."

Well, fuck. If that wasn't a donkey kick to the gut. "Do you really think I'd be a jerk to someone you care about?"

"Maybe not intentionally. But you might be critical of how we met." Ben looked him straight in the eye, his expression firm. "And I won't have you making her feel bad about herself."

"What does that mean?" His phone vibrated, but he ignored it.

Stretching to his feet, Ben tossed him a small smile. "Look, you're busy. And you will meet Juliette. In fact, she's coming by the office today so we can go to lunch together. I'll bring her around. Just be your usual charming self and we'll be okay." He turned for the door, and stopped at the threshold. "But not too charming. This one's mine." Pointing his finger at Gabe, he pulled an imaginary trigger, and was gone, leaving Gabe all kinds of confused. How Ben could ever think Gabe would hurt a woman he cared for was beyond him. What kind of jerk had he become?

He spun his phone on his desk. Well, whatever he'd become, it stopped right now. Ben's friendship was too important to lose. And Gabe did think they'd become closer these past couple of weeks. Ben had dropped by his office more. They'd shared some laughs. Keeping his door open probably helped. Gabe eyed the exposed rectangle. The noise from his employees didn't annoy Gabe half as much as he'd thought it would.

But he should make actual plans with Ben, even if that meant spending a night away from Rachel. Glancing at his phone, he read her text. *I don't know. A finger can be very sexy. Just imagine what all I could do to you with it.*

But it wouldn't be this night. Shooting to his feet, Gabe responded while making his way to the elevators. *I don't want to wait until tonight to see you. I'll meet you in your cafeteria for lunch. 1 pm okay?*

See you then.

Gabe started whistling, caught the look from the other man in the elevator, and broke off with a cough. Oh, fuck it. He serenaded the poor dude with his squeaky rendition of "Joy to the World." Because the world looked pretty damn good right now. His friend was happy, and things were getting better between them. Business was good. And he was off to find cheesecake for tonight before having lunch with the most beautiful woman he knew.

Yep, life was good. Now, if only he could find a way to keep it that way.

Hooking the toe of her suede pump under Gabe's pants leg, Rachel rubbed his calf. Discreetly. None of her coworkers were in the cafeteria as far as she could see, but she wasn't about to get caught feeling up Gabe. She couldn't even hold his hand.

A bit of mayonnaise rested in the corner of his mouth, and she swiped it with her thumb, sighing. It had been fun sneaking around with Gabe the first week or so. Now she wished they could be open about their relationship. She cursed her fictional Trevor, and kicked herself for ever thinking him up.

Gabe took a sip of his coffee. "Problem? You look like you have the weight of the world resting on your shoulders."

"No problems." She picked at her Cobb salad. "What time can you get off tonight? Off *work*, I mean," she added when he smirked.

"Early. In fact"—he nudged her with his knee— "if you want to call in sick for the rest of the day, I'll make it worth your while."

"Can't. I have a four o'clock meeting."

"Another one? Too many business meetings start to eat away at work efficiency. It can be an indicator of poor management." Gabe broke his peanut butter cookie in half and gave her one side. The side with the majority of candy bits, Rachel noticed. She smiled.

"Mmm." Cracking open one eye, she swallowed her bite of buttery goodness. "What would a computer programmer know about office management? Did you get a promotion I don't know about?"

"Uh, no." He darted his eyes around the cafeteria. "Hey, look." Standing, he waved at someone near the salad bar. "It's my friend, Ben." He shifted his weight, and glanced down at her. "On second thought, I might just go over there and—"

"Too late." Rachel watched as the man standing beside a willowy brunette headed their way. "He's already on his way over. Who's that with him? His girlfriend?"

"Juliette, I assume." Gabe clapped his friend on the shoulder when he arrived. "Hey. I thought you were going out to lunch. Is this the Juliette you've been hiding from me?"

His friend blushed adorably, and wrapped an arm around the woman's waist. "Yeah. Juliette, I'd like you to meet Gabe. Gabe, Juliette."

They shook hands. "And this is Rachel. A friend of mine."

Friend. Right. Her stomach sank as she rose to meet them. "Hi. You work in the building, Ben?"

He looked anywhere but at her eyes. Rachel bit back a smile. Gabe's friend was as shy as Gabe was self-assured. A yin-and-yang friendship.

"Yeah." His voice trailed up, making it sound like a question. "Maybe we should get—"

"So, how'd you two meet?" Crossing his arms over his chest, Gabe stood with his feet wide apart. "Don't tell me it was at one of those gaming conventions you go to. Juliette is much too attractive to be interested in that."

Ben scowled. "First, offensive much? A lot of nice

woman go to those conventions, some of whom are very, well, at least, semi-pretty. Second—"

Juliette laid a hand on Ben's forearm. "Second, it was a compliment. To me, at least." She turned to Gabe, a smile on her lips. "But, no. Believe it or not, we met through Build-A-Boyfriend. When Ben began leaving me voice mails, I couldn't help but start to answer his calls. He was so cute and funny. And, well"—she lifted her shoulders—"one thing led to another."

Gabe's jaw dropped, and Ben looked at him and shrugged.

"You use Build-A-Boyfriend?" Rachel lowered her voice and glanced around to make sure no one was listening. "I use that service, too. What are the odds of that?"

Juliette cocked her head. "Well, considering the company we keep, not astronomical." She squeezed closer to Ben. "But I don't use the service anymore. Not since Ben."

"What do you mean?"

Scooping all their trash onto his tray, Gabe picked it up with one hand, put his other at Rachel's back. "She means that she doesn't have to use the service anymore since she's dating Ben now."

Rachel rolled her eyes. Well, obviously. That wasn't the part of Juliette's statement that needed clarification.

"We've got to get going," Gabe said. "Rachel has a meeting—"

"Not for another two hours."

"—and I have to get back to work. Lots to do." He herded her toward a trash can. "It was nice meeting you, Juliette."

Tucking her hand under Ben's arm, Juliette followed. "We'll go up with you. Ben wants to show me your offices."

Rachel stumbled to a stop. "You work here?"

Checking his watch, Gabe blew out a breath. "Our company has an office here and one a couple of buildings over. I usually work in the other building. Speaking of which, I really have to get going." He darted a look over her head toward his friend.

Ben cleared his throat. "Yeah, um, right. I want to get a brownie before I go up." He turned Juliette toward the bakery counter. "So, we'll just see you guys later. Right?"

Gabe waved over his shoulder and herded Rachel to the elevator. Pressing the Up button, he leaned down and kissed her cheek. "I'll see you later tonight. Thanks for lunch." And in a waft of expensive cologne, he was gone.

Leaving Rachel staring at her reflection in the elevator doors, a confused vee creasing her forehead. That was odd. First he asked to spend the afternoon with her, then he couldn't rush away fast enough?

She joined the crowd in the elevator and shuttled up to her office. And why hadn't he ever mentioned that his company had a branch in her building? She'd think that would be information that would have popped up in conversation. Because he didn't want to tell his temporary fling any more personal information about himself than he had to give?

Gabe had to be scared that when they broke things off, she'd be clingy. Rachel smacked open the door to her office, giving her office mates a tight smile in apology. She plopped down in her chair. What kind of woman did Gabe think she was? She wasn't clingy. She wouldn't stalk the man once their relationship went belly-up. And it was a little insulting that he'd think she would.

She stared at her computer screen and tried to focus on editing an article. Her mind didn't cooperate. She pulled out her phone and tapped off a quick text to Gabe. *Want to talk. Give me a call when you get a chance.* That sounded forbidding. Cold. She was irritated with Gabe, but he might have a good explanation for his behavior. *I miss you like crazy. Can't wait till tonight,* she added.

"Who're you texting?" Beth asked. Winding up a roll of lilac gauze, she looked away from her Easter egg construction long enough to glance at Rachel.

"Trevor, of course."

Beth rose, and rested her hands on her lower back, kneading. "Any good sexting? I could use some entertainment right about now. I've been swimming in insipid pastels for our spring issue." She sidestepped out from behind her desk.

Thumbs flying, Rachel changed the recipient address to Trevor's and hit Send. "No sexting." She showed her phone to her friend. "Just telling him I miss him. Sorry."

Beth sniffed. "Well, that's boring. But at least he's back in town. Will he be here for the office party?"

"Maybe." Rachel looked down from her friend's critical eye. "Probably. He has a life, too." Great. Now she was defensive over an imaginary man. But not all of her men were fake. She brought up the text, copied it, and sent it to Gabe. Putting her phone down, she turned to her coworkers. "Where are we on the March edition?"

The women huddled over their concept boards, putting in a solid hour of work before Rachel's phone vibrated with an incoming text. She kept working, but her gaze drifted toward her desk.

Rhonda sighed. "Do you want to check that?"

"No, let's keep working." Rachel chewed on her thumbnail. The story ideas in front of her faded out of focus.

Beth cocked a hip against her desk. "I have to say, I think I've been wrong about you and Trevor."

"You have?" That was a shock, coming from her friend who never said Trevor's name without grumbling.

"Yeah. These past couple of weeks you've seemed a lot happier. Work doesn't seem like it's the only thing in your life anymore." Beth twirled a pen between her fingers. "If Trevor makes you smile that much when you just look at his texts, I can't imagine what he does to you in person. I'm happy for you."

"Thanks." That was really sweet. Sweet enough to almost make Rachel forget that she was a lying ball of scum for deceiving her friends. But work was still important to her. She straightened her shoulders. It was her main focus. If she didn't get that promotion, she'd, well, she'd be . . .

In the same position she was now. Happy. In love. She blew out a breath. What was happening to her? When had her work stopped defining who she was?

She glanced over at her phone.

"Oh, just go look at it." Rhonda shuffled another foam idea board to the front of the stack. "You're not going to be useful here until you do."

Rachel skipped over to her desk and plucked up her phone. She slumped her shoulders. It was just from "Trevor." *Can't wait to see you tonight, too. I've got the cheesecake. I can't wait to eat it off your naked body.*

"Well?" Beth asked.

"Just that he misses . . ." Rachel brought the phone closer to her face and read the text again. Then read the sender's information. That didn't make sense. Yes, the Build-A-Boyfriend's texts had been getting a bit racier, but that didn't explain the cheesecake comment. That was something only she and Gabe knew about.

Sinking into her chair, Rachel's mind pinged between possible explanations. Her heart pounded, and a slight buzz took up residence in her ears.

The *"company we keep,"* Ben's girlfriend had said. Slowly, Rachel pulled up the Internet browser on her computer. Made a search for *Gabe Harris* and *Build-A-Boyfriend.*

"Rachel?" Beth asked. "You okay?"

She nodded dully. Row after row of search results for a Gabe Harrison taunted her. One of the article headings even showed a picture of a smiling Gabe, shoulder to shoulder with his "best friend and cofounder of Build-A-Boyfriend, Ben Givens."

She sat back, and swiveled to look out the window. Snow was softly falling in the afternoon's muted light. She stared out into the city she loved, but no answers came.

"I don't get it."

"Don't get what?" Rhonda came around the desk and laid a hand on her shoulder. "You didn't get dumped, did you?"

Rachel stared at her. That question didn't even compute. It just didn't make sense that Gabe owned the company that she used for her fake-boyfriend service. That he would be texting her under Trevor's name. What the hell was going on?

"I'm going to find out." Pushing to her feet, Rachel grabbed her phone. She didn't need her coat or her purse. She wasn't leaving the building.

Her friends exchanged baffled looks. "Find out what?"

"What's going on with my boyfriend." She strode out the door.

"We have a meeting soon," Beth called from the office doorway.

Rachel jabbed the elevator's Up button. Hit it again. "I might miss this one." Yeah, she might be in jail for assault if the answers Gabe gave her didn't add up. The doors slid shut on her friend's open-jawed amazement.

Assistant editors vying to become associate editors didn't miss staff meetings. Rachel didn't care. The building directory told her every morning as she waited for the elevator that Build-A-Boyfriend was on the top floor, so that's where she was going. Some things were just more important than her promotion. Finding out why Gabe had lied to her was one of them. She rubbed her sweaty palms over her hips. He had to have a good reason.

The elevator dinged, and the doors slid open onto a deserted office. Huh. She knew Build-A-Boyfriend was mostly automated, but still, she'd expected someone to be manning the desks. Maybe they didn't work on Fridays.

Except Ben was in the office building today. And Rachel was willing to bet Gabe was working, as well.

She headed down a hall, made a U around the west end of the office. Low voices down the next corridor made her steps falter. She clenched and unclenched her fists. She wanted answers. But her heart wanted only the right answers.

Sucking in a deep breath, she forced herself forward. She wouldn't be scared to face Gabe. To face the truth, whatever that might be.

His warm chuckle floated through the air. She stood outside the door to his office—yep, his name was right there on the placard, the lying bastard—and waited for her nerves to settle. Then froze as his next words sliced through her.

"Well, I'm not going to tell Rachel she was a bet. I can't see how that would end well for me."

"A bet you lost." Ben snickered. "I can't wait to tell the guys that you're sleeping with one of our 'loser clients.'" His voice dropped on the last phrase, right along with Rachel's stomach. She swallowed, her mouth dry, and struggled to keep her food down.

Leaning back against the wall, she missed what they said next, her blood pounding too loudly in her ears. Dizziness crept over her body, and she fought against it. She was a bet. She was a goddamn bet, and a laughingstock to boot.

Digging deep, she pulled up her pride and held on to it with both hands. If she was going to be sick, at least she'd get some use out of it. She'd go be sick right on the bastard's desk.

She knocked on the open door. "One 'loser client' here to see you," she announced.

Their horrified expressions gave her some shred of comfort.

Gabe jumped to his feet, his chair shooting back and striking the wall. "Rachel! It's not what you think."

She laughed, the sound twisted and bitter. "How disappointing. That's the phrase of liars and cheaters everywhere. I gave you credit for being more creative than that."

"Rachel . . ." He circled his desk, but she held up a hand, and he stopped.

Turning to Ben, she asked, "Do you want to let me in on your little bet? One of your 'loser clients' wants to know."

His shoulders curled over his chest. "It really isn't what you think. I mean, one of our clients is my girlfriend."

She took a step back. Her hands trembled. She pressed them to her sides, hoping they wouldn't notice. "I see. This is a game for you two. You use your own company as a picking ground for booty calls. That's sick. Both of you are sick."

"If you'd just listen to me." Gabe reached for her, but she jumped back out of range.

"Don't touch me. Not one damn finger."

Gabe closed his eyes for a moment, muttered something under his breath. When he opened them, they were resigned. As mournful as a hound dog's.

Rachel wasn't buying it.

"How did you even find out?" he asked, his voice low.

"You got mixed up." She held up her phone. "You texted me from Trevor's account as Gabe. Better luck next time."

"You texted the same thing to both accounts. I didn't pay close enough attention." Running a hand through his hair, he shook his head. "Rachel, please."

"Whatever you're asking for, I've got no more left to give." She backed into the hall. "Consider my subscription to your service cancelled."

Spinning on her heel, she walked on shaky legs down the corridor. As she made her way to the elevator, she thought of every foul thing she could say to him. Of every insult she could hurl. Of the palm-hand to the nose her father had taught her before she left for college. If Gabe chased after her, she was torn between which tactic she'd use. Maybe a combination of all three.

She needn't have bothered. He didn't follow.

CHAPTER 9

With the tip of his pencil, Gabe poked at the tiny Christmas tree on his desk. Sandra in IT had decided the office needed some sprucing up, and he'd found this plant in a coffee mug on his desk that morning. Its jaunty star and jolly red ornaments mocked him.

This Christmas was turning out to be anything but merry. It had been four days since Rachel had stormed out of his office. Four days of unanswered calls and texts. Four days of pounding on her door until the super kicked him out of her building. He couldn't go to her office, not without risking exposing her deception to her coworkers.

He prodded the bush again. The gold bell wrapped around its base tinkled. The cheerful noise was like nails on a chalkboard. Scowling, Gabe dropped the decoration into the wastebasket.

"Don't let Sandra see that." Ben leaned against the doorjamb, arms crossed over his chest. "She doesn't like feeling unappreciated."

"Who does?" Avoiding his friend's searching gaze, Gabe swung his chair and stared out the window. The afternoon sky was the same shade as Rachel's favorite nightgown.

The door snicked shut behind him. The visitor's chair slid against the carpet, and the cushion hissed as Ben settled onto it. "Since when have you felt unappreciated? Your whole life you've been the best at everything you tried. Your mom still keeps a room full of your high school trophies."

Gabe tried to force his shoulders to unclench. "That's not what I meant."

"Then what?"

"Rachel let me go really easily." Gabe waited a beat or two. "It's not a good feeling."

"She found out you'd been lying to her. Thinks we have some sick game going on." Ben made a sound of disgust. "How did you think she'd react?"

"She won't even let me explain." Gabe clenched his fist. He needed to go to the gym, pound out some of his frustration. Staring at his phone all day had left him feeling powerless. "It's like our relationship meant nothing to her."

Ben snorted. "She wouldn't have been so pissed off if that were true."

Gabe pondered that. She had been ticked off. And hurt. The anger couldn't hide the pain in her eyes. She looked like a kid who had just been told that Santa Claus didn't exist. He rubbed at the ache in his chest. He'd put that look there. He was responsible for hurting her.

If he could pound on himself, he would. Anyone who hurt Rachel deserved an ass-kicking.

"You said you were having some fun. A casual thing. It was going to end sometime." A chair creaked. Ben must have sat forward. "Are you upset because she ended it before you did? That you weren't the one who got to break it off?"

"No, damn it." Gabe spun around. "You really think I'm that fucking shallow?"

Ben widened his eyes. "You care about her. A lot."

Gabe pushed to his feet and paced across the office. He didn't want to have this conversation. He wasn't the type of man to talk about his feelings and all that bullshit. Didn't commiserate with other men unless there was a death in the family, or a Rams loss. Never whined about a broken heart, or feeling depressed.

He paused, midstride. He'd never felt anything about a woman that was worth talking about.

Until now.

Facing Ben, he blew out a large breath. "I love her. I need to get her back."

Striding to the trash can, he pulled the tree out, put it on his desk, and resumed pacing. "I need a plan."

"Okay." Ben smiled tentatively, his grin building with each second. "You're good at plans."

Gabe glared. "Oh, shut up."

"What?" He lifted a hand, his lips twitching. "What did I say?"

"You didn't have to say it." Gabe stepped behind his desk, pressed his palms to the surface. "You thought it. '*Gabe's in love. I never thought I'd see the day.*'" He gave his voice a high falsetto.

"Well, I didn't." Ben leaned back, lacing his fingers together and resting his hands behind his head. "And my voice doesn't sound like that."

Gabe rolled his eyes.

"So, what are you going to do?"

"I'm going to make her listen," Gabe said. "She won't pick up her phone, so I'll track her down." He narrowed his eyes. "I'll trap her in the elevator. Stop it. She'll have to listen."

"Uh, or she'll call the cops." The smile dropped from his friend's face. "I think that borders on stalking, dude. Come up with another plan."

"Fine." Gabe flopped into his chair, his brain spinning. Picking up a pencil, he poked at the tree again. Fa-la-la-la-fricking Christmas. He sat up straight. Christmas. A slow smile spread across his face.

Ben cleared his throat. "What's that look?"

Leaning back in his chair, Gabe kicked his feet up onto his desk. "Nothing. I just realized I know where Rachel's going to be tomorrow night." He smiled at his friend. "I have a plan."

Sighing, Ben shook his head. "Of course you do. Just no trapping. Or kidnapping. I don't want to bail you out tomorrow. I've got a date with Juliette." He pushed to his feet. "Christmas bonuses go out today. You want to walk around with me, hand out the cards?"

"Sure. What about our customers?"

Ben paused by the door. "What about them?"

"Do we have any sort of customer appreciation lined up for them?"

"Uh, we've never done that before. What did you have in mind?"

Gabe twirled his pencil. "I don't know. A free month?"

Ben's jaw dropped. "Are you kidding me? Don't be stupid. We have to make a profit."

Gabe grinned.

His friend twisted his lips. "Oh. You were kidding. Asshole."

"But it's nice to know you have a head for business, too." Gabe rose. "But maybe we could do something for our long-term clients. A free upgrade for a month or something."

"Holy shit, it must be love." Walking into the main office, Ben tossed over his shoulder, "Our Scrooge has gone soft."

Gabe caught up and punched him in the shoulder. "Shut up. Besides, it could be considered good marketing."

"Uh-huh. Whatever you say."

Gabe thought about hitting him again, but let his hand fall. He was feeling too good to let a little ribbing get to him.

Rachel didn't know it, but their separation was coming to an end. Because he had a plan. And damn it, his plans always worked. This one had to. He wouldn't accept anything less.

CHAPTER 10

Rachel's cheeks hurt from the forced smile that had been on her face all night. Standing in the corner of her office with a plastic glass of champagne in her hand, she avoided eye contact with her coworkers and waited for the clock to hit nine. She could leave the Christmas party at nine and not raise any eyebrows.

An editor and her husband came over and congratulated Rachel on her promotion. She tried to lace excitement into her voice, but knew she fell flat. Her first thought after being called into her boss's office that morning for the good news had been to call Gabe. Share it with him.

Instead, she'd thanked her boss while holding back tears. There was no one she wanted to celebrate with. The good things in life didn't amount to much if she didn't have someone to mark them with. She'd just wanted to go back home and cry.

And her depression had been threaded through with a lick of shame. Her boss had given her the promotion knowing she wasn't engaged. After finding out about Gabe, she couldn't use Build-A-Boyfriend anymore. She didn't have the heart to continue with the fake fiancé. So she'd told her coworkers the wedding was off, not caring if her single status stopped her from landing the promotion.

So when her boss had given her the news, she'd known she'd misjudged her coworkers. They hadn't cared that she wasn't going to be married; they just cared about her job performance.

Either that, or she'd been promoted out of pity. More than a few women had rubbed her shoulders consolingly, told her not to give up hope. The right man was still out there.

Rachel snorted, and covered up the sound with a cough. Excusing herself to refill her drink, she wended her way to the bar. So many happy people, excited for the holidays, full of good cheer. And cheap liquor.

Tipping up her glass, Rachel chugged the sweet champagne. If she couldn't join in their happiness, she could at least join in the drunkenness. Forget that the one man who'd lit her up like the tree at Rockefeller Center had seduced her as a bet. The alcohol turned to acid in her stomach.

Beth danced up to her in time to the music. Putting an arm around Rachel's waist, she hip-bumped her. "Girl, you're looking entirely too de-preshed for someone who just made associate editor."

"'Depreshed'?" Rachel took in her friend's glassy eyes. Shaking her head, she smiled wryly. "And you're looking entirely too happy for a girl about to hop on a plane to Tucson tomorrow. Christmas in the desert is just wrong."

"Holidays are where the home is." A furrow appeared in Beth's forehead. "Wait. Christmas is where the family is? What the hell am I trying to say?"

Rachel sighed. "That you're going to have a nice Christmas at home with your parents and brothers and sisters."

"You could still come." Beth reached across her to the bar, grabbing a handful of peanuts.

"Thanks, but I have my own family to go home to."

"Yeah, but they'll ask questions about why you and Trevor broke up, and mine won't." She bumped her hip into Rachel's again. "We'll have fun."

No, her family wouldn't ask questions. At least Rachel had never told that lie to them. Even with that saving grace, she still dreaded going home. Her parents' house would be decked out in an explosion of red and green. Her dad still plotted out new outdoor light designs each year to try to win the neighborhood decoration contest. All that holiday spirit would just depress her further. Why should everyone else get to be happy when her life was so miserable?

"Thanks, but my parents are expecting me." Rachel sipped the champagne and looked at the clock. Eight fifteen. She was getting closer.

Beth brushed her fingers against her green velvet skirt, wiping salt off. "Listen, the food here is crap. What say we go grab us some dinner? Maybe that Greek place you like so much?"

Rachel swallowed. "Last time I was there I was with Gabe. Let's go somewhere else."

Beth placed her empty glass on the bar, and ran her hands up and down Rachel's arms. "Honey, sometimes it sounds like you're going to miss Gabe more than you will Trevor. I know he's Trevor's friend, but you two were close, too. You should give him a call. I bet he doesn't want to take sides."

Biting back a hysterical laugh, Rachel shook her head. It was on the tip of her tongue to blurt out the truth to her friend, but she held back. She'd made the decision to wait until after Christmas to confess all her sins. Her heart was breaking as it was. She needed a little time to recover before she laid herself bare to Beth.

"I think it's safe to say that whatever Gabe and I had ended when Trevor and I did." Her coworker Sylvia climbed up onto a table and started to dance, the rest of the magazine staff cheering. Rachel's throat squeezed, and she had to fight for air. She couldn't be here anymore. She needed to be alone.

"I'm going to go to the bathroom and then head out." Rachel kissed Beth's cheek. "Have fun with your family. Tell them all Merry Christmas for me."

Her friend sighed. "If that's what you want. Be careful coming out of the bathroom. I put some mistletoe up at the entrance to that corridor."

Rachel wrinkled her nose. "Why?"

"What better place? If you see a man you like, you watch until he goes to the bathroom and wait for him when he comes out. It's foolproof."

Rachel chuckled, the first bit of genuine amusement she'd felt in days. "That's crazy, and a little gross."

"It's smart." Beth tapped a manicured finger to her forehead. "I've also hung them at the elevators and at the main window. 'Hi, cutie. Let's go look at the Arch. Oh, and what's that above our heads? Well, if we have to, we have to.' "

"Good-bye, Beth." Shaking her head, Rachel headed to the bathroom, darting under the sneaky mistletoe. When she came out, she looked for her coat and purse, remembered they were in her office.

Threading her way through the crowd, she almost didn't see him. He wasn't moving. Just standing in the entranceway. Watching her.

She stumbled, knocking into Janice. Wine splashed onto her boss's sweater. "I'm so sorry." Heart pounding, she looked over her shoulder at Gabe. Jaw set, he strode toward her.

Janice's husband handed her a handkerchief, and she dabbed at her stomach. "No worries. Luckily, it's white wine."

Twisting her neck, Rachel looked into Gabe's glacial eyes. Only about ten feet away now. She wanted to move. Needed to escape. But her feet were rooted to the floor.

"Rachel, are you okay?" Janice rested a hand on her arm. "You're really pale."

Gabe's body warmed her back, and she knew it was too late to run.

"Gabe!" Janice shifted on her heels. She shot a look at Rachel. "I wasn't expecting you, considering . . . Well, I'm glad you could make it."

His breath brushed across the back of her neck. "Considering?"

Heat raced through Rachel's veins. He came to her Christmas party and was going to act like nothing had changed? What the hell?

She spun, her nose almost hitting his collarbone. Stepping back, she glared up at him. "Con-

sidering I'm no longer engaged to your friend."
She leaned forward and hissed, "You have some
nerve showing up here."

"Right now all I have is nerve." His lips brushed
her ear. "I'm hoping to leave with more."

Rachel clenched her fist. She would not smack
the usual smugness off his face. Violence solved
nothing. Although, he wasn't looking smug. His
brows were drawn down low, his full lips pressed
into a flat line. He looked determined. Nervous.
Hopeful.

Stepping back, she took a deep breath. Whatever he had up his sleeve, she wasn't falling for it.
"Janice, great party, but I'm heading out. I'll see
you tomorrow."

Gabe wrapped his fingers around her wrist,
stopping her. "Rachel—"

"Let go of me." She kept her voice calm. Cold as
ice.

"What's going on?" her boss asked, lines creasing her forehead.

Gabe hesitated before releasing her hand. "What's
going on is Rachel lost a fiancé and I lost a friend.
I need to fix that." Looking into her eyes, he said,
"Please, Rachel. Give me a chance to explain. It
wasn't *all* what you think."

Narrowing her eyes, she considered him. She'd
noticed his modifier. He was admitting at least
some of what she thought was right. Somehow,
that made her want to hear the rest. It made him
sound sincere.

"You're Trevor's friend," Janice said. "Maybe
you shouldn't get involved."

Gabe spoke to her boss, but kept his eyes on
Rachel. "Trevor was an idiot. He didn't respect Ra-

chel. He wasn't honest. She deserves better. I'm going to give her better."

Rachel almost didn't hear Janice suck in her breath. Her pulse roared in her ears too loudly. Her boss's husband took Janice's elbow. "Why don't we give them some space?"

Janice used that elbow to jab her husband in the stomach. Her avid gaze flipped between Rachel and Gabe like they were opponents in a tennis match. She obviously wasn't going anywhere.

"Will you excuse us?" Rachel asked her boss. Without waiting for a response, she turned on her heel and searched for a quiet corner. Gabe followed at her heels. Some partygoers had invaded her office, so she stopped just to pick up her coat and purse and headed for the entry hall by the elevators. With the music down to a low background hum, she crossed her arms and faced Gabe. "Well?"

Blowing out a sigh, he ran a hand through his hair. "I don't know where to start. What you heard—"

"Why don't you start at the beginning? You knew I was a client, and you made a bet with your buddy that you could nail one of your pathetic losers."

"What? No. Well, part of that is yes, but most of it no." The elevator dinged, and a laughing couple emerged. Gabe grabbed her arm and led her into the corner of the hall. "Just to be clear, what you heard Ben say, he never meant. I was the one who thought our clients had to be losers. Ben always defended them. He was throwing my own words back at me."

Her heart clenched. He was confirming her worst fears.

She ground her jaw. "You're not helping your case."

"The guys in my company were disgusted with me." Gabe shook his head. "They bet me that if I met one of our clients, just to meet, mind you, I would find out that they were good people. If I changed my mind about our clients, I'd give up my bonus to my employees. If I won, I'd get some free hours of labor out of them." He searched her eyes. "I took that bet, knowing I'd win. Then I met you."

She stilled. Examined his words from all angles. He didn't have a motive to lie to her now, not one that she could see. If he had made a bet to sleep with her, he could be laughing about it with his friend right now. He didn't need to explain himself.

Unless he was worried about a lawsuit.

"I was an asshole," Gabe continued. "And way too wrapped up in my work. But when I met you, I found out I'd been missing out on life. There are a lot of things I still want for my business. But I want you more."

Rachel's fingers tingled. Licking her lips, she stared at Gabe. Her heart leapt like a demented rabbit in her chest. She wanted this. Wanted him. But trust was hard to come by.

"You hurt me," she whispered.

Tucking a piece of hair behind her ear, he smoothed her cheek with his thumb. "Yes. And I can't promise I won't again. But I'll always try to be honest from now on. And I'll do everything I can to make sure I never see you look at me again like you looked at me Friday night." He rested his forehead against hers, his breath soft on her lips. "That just about killed me."

She nodded her agreement. That night had just about killed her, too.

"Please, Rachel." His voice was low, pleading. "Give me another chance. I love you."

She squeaked. She couldn't help it. She had been wanting to hear him say that, but had given up all hope of it. Cheeks hot, she burrowed her fingers in his lapels and ducked her head against his tie.

His chest rumbled with a chuckle. "You weren't expecting that, were you? But it's true."

Trying to reclaim some dignity, Rachel wrapped her arms around his neck and raised an eyebrow. "I wasn't expecting you to sound so girly. I can't believe you said it first."

"Wait until we get home. I've got something for you to prove my man card." Hand on her lower back, he pressed their bodies close until she felt the hard bulge against her stomach. He paused, a flicker of uncertainty crossing his face. "That does mean you forgive me, right?"

She laughed, her whole body feeling as light and fizzy as her last glass of champagne. "Yes, I forgive you." Throwing herself at him, she wrapped her arms around his back and held on. She never wanted to let go. "Now, let's get out of here."

Hand in hand, they strolled to the elevator, Rachel's head resting on his shoulder.

"I knew you missed Gabe more." It was Beth's voice.

Rachel spun around and saw half the office peering at them with smiles on their faces. Heat stained her cheeks. Getting caught in a new relationship so soon after her fake engagement—

Oh, who cared? Being with Gabe was worth any awkwardness.

Beth stepped forward. "And you're going to have to apologize for making fun of me earlier."

Rachel raised her eyebrows. "Huh?"

Beth pointed, and Rachel and Gabe looked up at the sprig of mistletoe above their heads.

Gabe smiled down at her. He lifted his shoulders. "It's tradition. Can't mess with that."

"Well, if I have to suffer for tradition, I'm glad I'm suffering with you." The smile wouldn't leave her face, even after Gabe pressed his lips to hers. She faintly heard applause break out behind her, but she ignored it for the man wrapped around her.

The elevator doors slid open, and Gabe dragged her in, his mouth never leaving hers. Pressing her against the mirrored wall, he lifted his head, his chest heaving. He reached behind him and pressed the button for the lobby. The doors eased shut.

"I've been thinking about you in this elevator." Gabe nibbled his way down her throat.

"It is where we met." Staring at the ceiling, she sank into his embrace. She was in the arms of the man she loved. Santa had been very good to her this year.

"Well, yes, that too." Straightening, he looked down at her, eyes crinkling. "But my thoughts took a different turn." He stepped back. "You and me." Running his gaze up and down her body, he sucked his bottom lip into his mouth. "Alone." Gabe pressed the red Stop button, and the elevator slid to a halt. "Trapped and with nowhere to go."

She leaned back, the mirrors cool beneath her shoulder blades. She dropped her coat and purse at her feet. "And nothing to do?"

One hand loosening his tie, he stalked toward her. "I've got some ideas."

Grabbing his tie, she pulled him into her, and hooked a heel behind his calf.

"I thought you might."

And with eager fingers, she unwrapped her favorite present.

Don't miss Kate Angell's newest Barefoot William novel, *No Time to Explain*, available now!

Who says romance has gone to the dogs?

Richmond Rogues' left-fielder Joe "Zoo" Zooker has his own ritual for the start of spring training—a weekend of pure pleasure, including as many pretty faces and curvaceous bodies as he can charm into his bed. After that, he's all about baseball, especially with hungry minor leaguers eager for their own shot at the majors, just waiting for him to strike out. But when a beautiful woman with a smart mouth brushes off his flirting, he's determined to go to bat as often as it takes to win a smile aimed only at him.

Stevie may be new to the beach town of Barefoot William, but she's seen plenty of charmers like hot and hunky Zoo before. Managing her aunt's doggie daycare business, she's up to her ears in rowdy puppies—and she doesn't need a lifelong hound like Zoo breaking her heart. Still, there's no denying the attraction between them, and as spring training heats up, lust suddenly begins to look a lot like love . . .

Praise for Kate Angell and her novels

"Grab a beach chair, sunscreen, and a Kate Angell book for a great summer read!"
—Roxanne St. Claire, *New York Times* bestselling author

"Fast-paced. Fun characters."
—Lori Foster, *New York Times* bestselling author

CHAPTER I

'Here comes the bride'.

The wedding march echoed down the Barefoot William Boardwalk. The annual southwest Florida bridal event brought engaged and expectant women to the beach. It was a sea of sexy, sweet and everything in between. Joe 'Zoo' Zooker took it all in. Marriage made him sweat. It triggered his gag reflex. He could, however, admire the ladies planning their weddings, as long as they didn't involve him. He was a confirmed bachelor. For life.

"Does Crabby Abby's General Store sell condoms?" asked his Richmond Rogue teammate Jake Packer. Better known as Pax.

He and Pax presently leaned against the blue metallic railing that separated the boardwalk from the beach. Joe knew where the condoms were shelved. He'd stocked up earlier in the week. "They're back by the pharmacy, bottom shelf, next to douches and K-Y lubes."

"You need anything, bro?"

Joe shook his head. He had six Magnum XLs in his wallet to get him through the night.

"Be right back then." Pax pushed off the railing. He walked the short distance to purchase his protection. He planned to get lucky. So did Joe.

The team was in town for spring training, with a weekend to kill. Booze, babes, and sex would definitely come into play. Monday, and they'd turn serious. They'd live and breathe baseball. The entire team would assemble for workouts and scrimmages. Nine Roanoke Rebels would also hit the field. Affiliate Triple-A players, participating in preseason practices and an exhibition game. Showcasing their talent and hoping for the call to suit up in the majors.

Joe hated squad competition. Dean Jensen in particular got under his skin. The minor leaguer played left field. Joe's position. Joe had refused him, four years running. Under Rule 5 draft, Dean had one final year to either make the club's expanded forty-man roster or be passed over. The guy kept coming after Joe, harder and faster each season. He wouldn't let up. But then Joe wouldn't have either if the situation was reversed.

He rolled his shoulders now. Cracked his knuckles. It was too nice a day to dwell on the asshat. He turned and stared out over the Gulf. Clear skies. Turquoise water. White sugar sand. Sunbathers. Sand castles. Carnival rides, amusement arcade, and a long fishing pier stretched south. Paradise. He would retire here. Years from now. Following his last bat.

Joe waited patiently on Pax, for all of five minutes, before restlessness claimed him. He wasn't good at standing still. He was continuous motion. A few brave men mixed with the wedding-minded ladies. He tugged down the bill on his black baseball cap. His mirrored Maui Jim aviators allowed him to stare, and not be caught doing so. He stepped into the crowd. Pax would find him. Unless he found a hot babe first.

So many women. Blondes, brunettes, redheads. A chick with purple hair. The multicolored storefronts on the beachside shops were all open, welcoming the stirring breeze and aroma of salt air. The scent of freshly popped popcorn wafted, along with the aroma of chocolate fudge, cheesy nachos, cotton candy, and women's perfume.

Ladies came onto him. He was recognized by many. Flirted with by most. Inviting glances and promising smiles. His navy T-shirt scripted with *I've Broken All the Rules Today. So You'll Have to Make New Ones* drew whispered suggestions. Half naked women appealed. Kink tempted. He liked the attention. A lot.

Space was tight. Whether intentional or by accident, female bodies pressed him. Some snugged as close as skin. He didn't mind the touching. Although a few hands got downright personal. Arousal heightened his senses. He was looking for a weekend lover. No one fully caught his eye. So he kept walking with sex foremost on his mind.

Long decorated tables lined both sides of the boardwalk. Signs were visible. Bridal banners arced overhead. Women clustered, checking out the area's best photographers, florists, engraved invitations, caterers, bakers, wedding and reception venues, entertainment, hair stylists, makeup artists, prenuptial consultants, and other important services. Mannequins exhibited wedding gowns. Assorted accessories, from veils, crystal tiaras, rhinestone headbands, sashes, to jewelry came next. Along with the garters.

Garters. Worn on a bride's thigh. A total turn on. He scanned the ruffled, pearled, lacy, feathered, monogramed, broached, and rhinestoned collections. Foreplay. He might buy one for the pure pleasure of slipping it up his lady's leg, then slowly sliding it down. Sexy.

"Something blue," he heard a woman say, soft and wistful.

He glanced toward her voice. Stopped, and got an eyeful. A slender blonde stood in profile, alone at the end of the table, toying with a pale blue satin garter with a silver heart charm. He was a sucker for long hair. The sun had run its fingers through the strands, leaving them streaked and shiny. The ends touched her waist. He openly stared as she bent, her shoulders curving, her ass jutting out. Sweet cheeks outlined beneath her short skirt. Gently stretching the elastic, she worked the garter over a sandaled foot-her toenails painted silver-then up her calf, and onto her thigh. She had nice legs. Freckled knees. She straightened, admired the garter. She had yet to notice him. He appreciated her further.

Her smile came slowly, on a sigh. "Perfect, don't you think, Lori?"

He shifted his stance. Cast her in his shadow.

Then removed his aviators for a better look. Twirled them by an arm. He wasn't Lori, but that didn't stop him from saying, "Hot, sweetheart."

Look for more holiday cheer from Allison Charles this month in *The Christmas Wedding Swap*.

SOMETIMES YOU GET WHAT YOU NEED . . .

Allison Stuart has always been the odd-woman-out of her family. She wears her jeans a little too tight, colors her hair a little too blonde, and instead of going into medicine and law like her sisters, she runs a diner. She's also the only single sibling left. And while she won't change her style, and her meatloaf is to die for, thank you very much, she wouldn't mind her share of wedded bliss. So she makes an early New Year's resolution: No more meaningless flings.

Drop-dead sexy Luke Hamilton is everything Allison has sworn off. His only serious relationship has been with his five-star restaurant, Le Cygne Noir, in Chicago. When he's threatened by a lawsuit, Luke decides to hide out in Pineville, Michigan, until the statute of limitations runs out. The small town is filled with Christmas charm, but he can't imagine living there. Heating things up with the hottie who owns the local diner would make his exile bearable—*if* he can convince her to give up her ridiculous resolution . . .

CHAPTER I

Black Friday was a hopping day for her diner, The Pantry. Tired Pineville shoppers stopped by in droves, happily dumping their bags and getting off their feet, before diving back into the competitive sport of sales shopping. The bell on her register rang enough times to outfit heaven with an entire army of angels. Which was why Allison Stuart was more than a little surprised to find herself not in her bustling restaurant, where she belonged, but out with the mob of other Christmas shoppers, mired in consumerism and fifty percent off deals.

Even more shocking was the half-nelson she had wrapped around a middle-aged woman wearing a sweatshirt with a smirking gingerbread man. Emblazoned across the front in a bold, red font were the words "Bite Me." Allison seriously considered following the advice.

"Let go of me, you crazy b—*oosh*." The woman went limp in her arms as a teenage boy dressed like an elf tripped over her flailing legs and landed with a thud on her stomach, knocking the wind out of her.

Never one to miss an opportunity, Allison grabbed the Caty Cowgirl doll, the cardboard box only slightly dented when the rabid mother had torn it from her hands. She rolled out from under the woman, scuttling away like a crab, her prize clutched to her chest. Her niece, Molly, wanted this damn doll, and she, as the doting auntie she was, was damned well going to give it to her. It wasn't her fault it was the last one on the shelf, or that the other woman had been too short to grab it from its high perch. The woman shouldn't have walked down the aisle of Tinker Tots to look for something to stand on, not if she had been determined to land the prize. Nope, Allison had won the doll fair and square, and she was going to keep it.

The woman rolled to her hands and knees, gathering her breath. When she drew herself to her feet, Allison was quick to jump to hers, as well. She held the doll tighter, and searched for something to defend herself with. A basket full of wiffle-ball bats stood at the end of the aisle, and Allison inched toward it. The way her opponent was eyeing her, she was going to need a weapon. Gingerbread Woman might have been short, but she was fierce.

The elf rubbed his elbow. "I'm sure I can help you both find just the toys you're looking for. At Tinker Tots, we aim to make your shopping dreams come true." The sing-songy slogan of Pineville's premier toy store came out a little shaky as the teenager backed away.

Gingerbread Woman never took her eyes off Allison. "Do you have any more Caty Cowgirl dolls in the back?"

The elf tugged at his red-and-white striped turtleneck. "Uh, no. All our inventory for that item is on the shelf, but—"

"Then the only way my shopping dream is going to come true is if I get that doll." She leaped toward Allison, her fingers clawing the air inches from the box as Allison jumped back. "It was my doll, I saw it first!"

"You left it on the shelf. It's mine." Allison tucked the box under her arm like a football, and spun on her heel. The cash register was only an aisle away. She leapt over a pile of discarded toys and zig-zagged around an abandoned shopping cart. The small part of her brain that had managed to remain rational knew that her behavior had passed bat-shit crazy a while back. Christmas was supposed to be the season of peace, giving, and all those other sappy greeting card messages. And it was only a doll, after all.

But when Molly had looked up at her with those big brown eyes, her lips quivering as she explained how much she wanted the limited-edition toy, well, what was an aunt to do? Allison didn't have her own kids, and hadn't developed the immunity necessary to tell a little girl no.

And besides, once Gingerbread Woman had gotten physical, all bets were off. Allison had a competitive streak a mile wide, and no way was she going to lose now. She whipped around the end of an aisle and jumped over a child lying on the floor playing with a toy truck. Hah! All those years playing flag football with the neighborhood kids growing up weren't wasted. They were training, for this, for—

"Oof!" The breath hissed out of her as something hit her legs from behind and she went down. Caty Cowgirl rolled out of her hands, the box turning end over end for several feet before settling near the toe of a shiny black boot. . . .

Connect with

Visit us online at
KensingtonBooks.com
to read more from your favorite authors, see books
by series, view reading group guides, and more.

for sneak peeks, chances to win books and prize packs,
and to share your thoughts with other readers.

facebook.com/kensingtonpublishing
twitter.com/kensingtonbooks

Tell us what you think!

To share your thoughts, submit a review,
or sign up for our eNewsletters, please visit:
KensingtonBooks.com/TellUs.